Modern Critical Interpretations

Virginia Woolf's
Mrs. Dalloway

Modern Critical Interpretations

These and other titles in preparation

Virginia Woolf's
Mrs. Dalloway

Edited and with an introduction by
Harold Bloom
Sterling Professor of the Humanities
Yale University

Chelsea House Publishers ◊ *1988*
NEW YORK ◊ NEW HAVEN ◊ PHILADELPHIA

© 1988 by Chelsea House Publishers,
a division of Chelsea House Educational Communications, Inc.,
  95 Madison Avenue, New York, NY 10016
  345 Whitney Avenue, New Haven, CT 06511
  5068B West Chester Pike, Edgemont, PA 19028

Introduction © 1988 by Harold Bloom

Printed and bound in the United States of America

10 9 8 7 6 5 4 3 2 1

∞ The paper used in this publication meets the minimum
requirements of the American National Standard for Permanence
of Paper for Printed Library Materials, Z39.48-1984.

Library of Congress Cataloging-in-Publication Data

Virginia Woolf's Mrs. Dalloway / edited and with an introduction by
    Harold Bloom.
        P.   cm.—(Modern critical interpretations)
      Bibliography: p.
      Includes index.
        Contents: The symbolic keyboard / Allen McLaurin—Mrs. Dalloway
/ Hermione Lee—Mrs. Dalloway, Virginia Woolf's memento mori /
Maria DiBattista—"The common life" / Perry Meisel—Mrs.
Dalloway, repetition as the raising of the dead / J. Hillis Miller—
Narrative structure(s) and female development / Elizabeth Abel—
The unguarded moment/Lucio Ruotolo—Mrs. Dalloway and the social
system/Alex Zwerdling.

ISBN 1-555-46033-X (alk. paper): $24.50

    1. Woolf, Virginia, 1882-1941. Mrs. Dalloway. [1. Woolf,
Virginia, 1882-1941. Mrs. Dalloway. 2. English literature—History
and criticism.] I. Bloom, Harold. II. Series.

PR6045.072M738   1988

823'.912—dc19   87-15484

Contents

Editor's Note

This book brings together a representative selection of the best critical interpretations of Virginia Woolf's novel *Mrs. Dalloway*. The critical essays are arranged here in the chronological order of their original publication. I am grateful to Shawn Rosenheim for his aid in editing this volume.

My introduction centers upon the Paterian Impressionism of perception and sensation in *Mrs. Dalloway*. Allen McLaurin, arguing against Reuben Brower, demonstrates how the novel's recurrent images transcend mere decoration. In a detailed close reading, Hermione Lee emphasizes "narrative texture," which enables Woolf to link together Clarissa's past and present, and connect both to Septimus.

Maria DiBattista, in a feminist reading, relates Woolf's sense of her characters' identity to issues of history, state, religion, time, and power. Pater returns in Perry Meisel's analysis, which suggests that Clarissa survives, where Septimus cannot, because she has Pater's discipline of *ascesis,* and poor Septimus has not.

In J. Hillis Miller's deconstructive reading, *Mrs. Dalloway* is seen as being organized around various forms of recurrence, a "repetition of the past in memory." Elizabeth Abel, combining feminist and Freudian modes, argues that the novel foregrounds the domestic, romantic plot while burying the story of Clarissa's development as a woman.

Mrs. Dalloway's openness to life is the subject of Lucio Ruotolo, who affirms that she "transcends, however tentatively, the constraints of gender, class, and hierarchy." In this volume's concluding essay, Alex Zwerdling interprets the novel as a social text which both reflects a set class structure and also demonstrates a countervailing sensibility in several figures, most complexly in Clarissa Dalloway.

Introduction

In May 1940, less than a year before she drowned herself, Virginia Woolf read a paper to the Worker's Educational Association in Brighton. We know it as the essay entitled "The Leaning Tower," in which the Shelleyan emblem of the lonely tower takes on more of a social than an imaginative meaning. It is no longer the point of survey from which the poet Athanase gazes down in pity at the dark estate of mankind, and so is not an image of contemplative wisdom isolated from the mundane. Instead, it is "the tower of middle-class birth and expensive education," from which the poetic generation of W. II. Auden and Louis MacNeice stare sidelong at society. Woolf does not say so, but we can surmise that she preferred Shelley to Auden, while realizing that she herself dwelt in the leaning tower, unlike Yeats, to whom the lonely tower remained an inevitable metaphor for poetic stance.

It is proper that "The Leaning Tower," as a speculation upon the decline of a Romantic image into belatedness, should concern itself also with the peculiarities of poetic influence:

> Theories then are dangerous things. All the same we must risk making one this afternoon since we are going to discuss modern tendencies. Directly we speak of tendencies or movements we commit ourselves to the belief that there is some force, influence, outer pressure which is strong enough to stamp itself upon a whole group of different writers so that all their writing has a certain common likeness. We must then have a theory as to what this influence is. But let us always remember—influences are infinitely numerous; writers are infinitely sensitive; each writer has a different sensibility. That is why literature is always changing, like the

1

weather, like clouds in the sky. Read a page of Scott; then of Henry James; try to work out the influences that have transformed the one page into the other. It is beyond our skill. We can only hope therefore to single out the most obvious influences that have formed writers into groups. Yet there are groups. Books descend from books as families descend from families. Some descend from Jane Austen; others from Dickens. They resemble their parents, as human children resemble their parents; yet they differ as children differ, and revolt as children revolt. Perhaps it will be easier to understand living writers as we take a quick look at some of their forebears.

A critic of literary influence learns to be both enchanted and wary when such a passage is encountered. Sensibility is indeed the issue, since without "a different sensibility" no writer truly is a writer. Woolf's sensibility essentially is Paterian, as Perry Meisel accurately demonstrates. She is hardly unique among the great Modernist writers in owing much to Pater. That group includes Wilde, Yeats, Wallace Stevens, Hart Crane, as well as Pound and Eliot. Among the novelists, the Paterians, however involuntary, include Scott Fitzgerald, the early Joyce, and in strange ways both Conrad and Lawrence, as well as Woolf. Of all these, Woolf is most authentically Pater's child. Her central tropes, like his, are personality and death, and her ways of representing consciousness are very close to his. The literary ancestor of those curious twin sensibilities—Septimus Smith and Clarissa Dalloway—is Pater's Sebastian Van Storck, except that Woolf relents, and they do not go into Sebastian's "formless and nameless infinite world, quite evenly grey."

Mrs. Dalloway (1925), the fourth of Woolf's nine novels, is her first extraordinary achievement. Perhaps she should have called it *The Hours,* its original working title. To speak of measuring one's time by days or months, rather than years, has urgency, and this urgency increases when the fiction of duration embraces only hours, as *Mrs. Dalloway* does. The novel's peculiar virtue is the enigmatic doubling between Clarissa Dalloway and Septimus Smith, who do not know one another. We are persuaded that the book is not disjointed because Clarissa and Septimus uncannily share what seem a single consciousness, intense and vulnerable, each fearing to be consumed by a fire perpetually about to break forth. Woolf seems to cause Septimus to die instead of Clarissa, almost as though the novel is a single apotropaic gesture on its author's part. One thinks of the death died for Marius by Cornelius in Pater's *Marius the Epicurean,* but that is one friend atoning for another. However unified, does *Mrs. Dalloway* cogently link Clarissa and Septimus?

Clearly the book does, but only through its manipulation of Pater's evasions of the figure or trope of the self as the center of a flux of sensations. In a book review written when she was only twenty-five, Woolf made a rough statement of the stance towards the self she would take throughout her work-to-come, in the form of a Paterian rhetorical question: "Are we not each in truth the centre of innumerable rays which so strike upon one figure only, and is it not our business to flash them straight and completely back again, and never suffer a single shaft to blunt itself on the far side of us?" Here is Clarissa Dalloway, at the novel's crucial epiphany, not suffering the rays to blunt themselves on the far side of her:

> What business had the Bradshaws to talk of death at her party? A young man had killed himself. And they talked of it at her party—the Bradshaws talked of death. He had killed himself—but how? Always her body went through it first, when she was told, suddenly, of an accident; her dress flamed, her body burnt. He had thrown himself from a window. Up had flashed the ground; through him, blundering, bruising, went the rusty spikes. There he lay with a thud, thud, thud in his brain, and then a suffocation of blackness. So she saw it. But why had he done it? And the Bradshaws talked of it at her party!
>
> She had once thrown a shilling into the Serpentine, never anything more. But he had flung it away. They went on living (she would have to go back; the rooms were still crowded; people kept on coming). They (all day she had been thinking of Bourton, of Peter, of Sally), they would grow old. A thing there was that mattered; a thing, wreathed about with chatter, defaced, obscured in her own life, let drop every day in corruption, lies, chatter. This he had preserved. Death was defiance. Death was an attempt to communicate; people feeling the impossibility of reaching the centre which, mystically, evaded them; closeness drew apart; rapture faded, one was alone. There was an embrace in death.

The evasiveness of the center is defied by the act of suicide, which in Woolf is a communication and not, as it is in Freud, a murder. Earlier, Septimus had been terrified by a "gradual drawing together of everything to one centre before his eyes." The doubling of Clarissa and Septimus implies that there is only a difference in degree, not in kind, between Clarissa's sensibility and the naked consciousness or "madness" of Septimus. Neither needs the encouragement of "Fear no more the heat o' the sun," because each knows that consciousness is isolation and so untruth, and that the right worship of life is to defy that isolation by dying. J. Hillis Miller remarks that "a novel, for Woolf, is the place of death made visible." It seems to me difficult to defend *Mrs. Dalloway* from moral judgments that call Woolf's stance wholly nihilistic. But then, *Mrs. Dalloway*, remarkable as it is, is truly Woolf's starting-point as a strong writer, and not her conclusion.

The Symbolic Keyboard:
Mrs. Dalloway

Allen McLaurin

The title of this [essay] was inspired by Charles Mauron's introduction to Roger Fry's translations of Mallarmé. Virginia Woolf's sense of emptiness is similar to that of Mallarmé, and she attempts to create from it an art similar to that described by Mauron in his introduction to Fry's translation:

> The discovery of "something else" has altered everything, at least in appearance—for we know nothing of the psychological depths of the question. Something other than reality, however, in the last resort is—nothing. And the whole of literature (as Mallarmé, henceforth perfectly lucid, was to explain to the English public in a style at first sight incomprehensible) consists in the play of modulations between these two extremes.
>
> A capital discovery: for if one thinks at all about the conditions of what Roger Fry calls pure art, one cannot fail to see that the first of these conditions is the establishment of a keyboard. There can be no architecture without fixed points and subtle methods of passing from one to another: without the modal system, no Gregorian music: without "tempered" keyboard, no Bach: without depth and scale of luminous values, no true painting. And the great creators are those who not merely perform and construct, but in the

From *Virginia Woolf: The Echoes Enslaved.* © 1973 by Cambridge University Press.

first place cast their instrument to suit the kind of perform-
ance which is proper to them. Mallarmé from the very
first knew the two extremes of his own range—crude reality
and "grudging silence"; he suffered because he found himself rejected by each in turn. What he wanted was to write,
that is, to make free play from one extremity to the other. A
keyboard is nothing but a system of transitions.

The transitions between the recurrent images and symbols in *Mrs.
Dalloway* form a keyboard of this kind. In his excellent essay on *Mrs.
Dalloway*, Reuben Brower points out that the recurrent imagery in that
novel indicates an artistic integrity and an underlying consistent vision.
He stresses the use of repetitive devices:

> The unity of her design depends on the building up of
> symbolic metaphors through an exquisite management of
> verbal devices: through exact repetitions, reminiscent varia-
> tions, the use of related eye and ear imagery, and the recur-
> rence of similar phrase and sentence rhythms.

The integrity which Brower sees in the imagery of *Mrs. Dalloway* is
also evident in Virginia Woolf's works as a whole. Bernard Blackstone
points out that her work is a whole, in that each scene and image is
related to other scenes and images throughout all the novels. An image
of this type is the spider's web—the idea of people being attached to
each other by an invisible thread constantly recurs throughout her
works. In *Mrs. Dalloway*, this example is typical:

> And they went further and further from her, being attached
> to her by a thin thread (since they had lunched with her)
> which would stretch and stretch, get thinner and thinner as
> they walked across London; as if one's friends were attached
> to one's body, after lunching with them, by a thin thread.

Similarly, Virginia Woolf's novels are linked to each other by various
strands of imagery. (Another of these characteristic recurrent images,
that of the parrot, also occurs in *Mrs. Dalloway*.) Limiting himself to
the complexity of the imagery within *Mrs. Dalloway* itself, Brower
brings out the significance of certain key words such as "plunge" and
"party." He examines the use of the word "solemn" and finds that its
full significance is built up by repetition in different contexts. He sees a
two-fold sense of life in the novel, the enjoyment of being included

and the fear of exclusion: "But the sense of being absorbed in the process is inseparable from a fear of being excluded, from the dread that the process may be interrupted." This poise between inclusion and exclusion is in some ways a better expression of the "double nature of repetition" which I have been speaking of. The dual value of the "moment" can indeed be seen from the point of view of inclusion and exclusion from life, but if we persist in our investigation of repetition, I think that it is possible to see certain aspects of *Mrs. Dalloway* in a more favourable light than does Brower; it is possible to see a greater coherence in the keyboard of its images and symbols.

Our starting point in this analysis of the novel is a full recognition of Virginia Woolf's self-consciousness in her use of symbols and images. This involves an investigation into the nature of language and repetition, and not simply a description of her employment of recurrent images and symbols as rhetorical devices or decoration. This is a different emphasis from that of Brower, for he claims to detect in *Mrs. Dalloway* a certain amount of apparently irrelevant adornment. He argues that on occasion Virginia Woolf "elaborates the metaphor out of all proportion to its expressive value" and he instances "the interlude of the 'solitary traveller.' " If we bear in mind Virginia Woolf's introspective interest in language, then this apparent irrelevance becomes part of the complex meaning of the novel. As we saw [elsewhere], language does not repeat a given reality. This solitary traveller interlude is part of Virginia Woolf's investigation of the nature of image and metaphor. Brower's second objection is directly related to this theme: "Perhaps the most obvious examples of metaphorical elaboration for its own sake are the super-literary, pseudo-Homeric similes which adorn various pages of *Mrs. Dalloway*." If we look at the novel with an approach similar to that of Mauron's to Mallarmé's poetry, then these two "irrelevances" which Brower notes can be seen as bound up with each other as part of that "integrity" which he finds in the rest of the novel. What we have in *Mrs. Dalloway* is the establishment of a keyboard, a "system of transitions" which moves from the complete fusion to the complete separation of the human and the natural. If we take as our starting point the question "in what way are the image and symbol connected with each other and with external reality?" then the apparently irrelevant imagery becomes directly relevant.

Our symbolic keyboard is made up of images which range from the subterranean (the fish, physical sensation) to the aerial (the aeroplane, science); the third term in the triad is the terrestrial (the tree, myth and metaphor). Within this overall keyboard, Virginia Woolf constructs various scales. We saw [elsewhere] the scale which runs from the "scraping" images to those of "cutting." We can understand this process better, perhaps, if we concentrate on the three key symbols mentioned, the fish, the tree and the aeroplane. But it must be borne in mind that this is only one of the tunes played in the novel. This scale is one ranging from the complete fusion of internal and external reality in the scraping of the fish, to the complete separation of the human and the natural in the latest scientific marvel, the aeroplane. The old woman singing marks a transition from pre-linguistic sensation to the beginning of language, our first step out of the water into an amphibious region:

> A sound interrupted him; a frail quivering sound, a voice bubbling up without direction, vigour, beginning or end, running weakly and shrilly and with an absence of all human meaning into
>
> > ee um fah um so
> > foo swee too eem oo—
>
> the voice of no age or sex, the voice of an ancient spring spouting from the earth; which issued, just opposite Regent's Park Tube Station, from a tall quivering shape, like a funnel, like a rusty pump, like a windbeaten tree for ever barren of leaves which lets the wind run up and down its branches singing
>
> > ee um fah um so
> > foo swee too eem oo,
>
> and rocks and creaks and moans in the eternal breeze.

We have here again the evolutionary idea which itself involves the notion of a scale with "transitions" from one species to another—a very Butlerian theme:

> Through all ages—when the pavement was grass, when it was swamp, through the age of tusk and mammoth, through the age of silent sunrise—the battered woman—for she wore a skirt—with her right hand exposed, her left clutching at her side, stood singing of love—love which has lasted a million years.

This earthly creature is, on our scale, one note down from "mother nature" who appears in that "interlude of the solitary traveller" which Brower objected to as being irrelevant. In the passage to which he refers, the human and the non-human are beginning to separate:

> she seemed like the champion of the rights of sleepers, like one of those spectral presences which rise in twilight in woods made of sky and branches. The solitary traveller, haunter of lanes, disturber of ferns, and devastator of great hemlock plants, looking up suddenly, sees the giant figure at the end of the ride.

The human being has become a mere visitor on the earth and has to consciously project a human face onto the external world:

> Such are the visions which ceaselessly float up, pace beside, put their faces in front of, the actual thing; often overpowering the solitary traveller and taking away from him the sense of the earth, the wish to return, and giving him for substitute a general peace, as if (so he thinks as he advances down the forest ride) all this fever of living were simplicity itself.

Elizabeth, being further removed from "nature" in her concern with religious myth, rather than the myth of "mother nature," strongly objects to being compared to a tree, or having her beauty compared with the beauty of nature: "People were beginning to compare her to poplar trees, early dawn, hyacinths, fawns, running water, and garden lilies; and it made her life a burden to her." The next transition is from the use of cliché, in which nature is merely coinage, to the scientific attitude, in which nature is seen as "data." Between the two comes Septimus, who is "connected" with the trees, but in a way which, like the rest of his madness, is a pseudo-scientific relationship of apparent cause and effect: "But they beckoned; leaves were alive; trees were alive. And the leaves being connected by millions of fibres with his own body, there on the seat, fanned it up and down; when the branch stretched he, too, made that statement." This is also clearly part of the "thread" imagery which was mentioned earlier. On the blinds of the official car, the tree has been converted into a sign, it is simply a pattern "like a tree." But it triggers some hidden war-horror in Septimus' memory, it is "as if some horror had come almost to the surface and was about to burst into flames. . . . The world wavered and quivered and threatened to burst into flames." The same complex of tree, "grey" and fire is evoked later by the image of an artificial tree created by an indoor firework, a harmless employment of the gunpowder which had given Septimus shellshock: "as if he had set light to a grey pellet on a plate and there had risen a lovely tree in the brisk sea-salted air of their intimacy."

In *Mrs. Dalloway* Virginia Woolf examines some of the meanings of "symbol." The symbolic vision and the establishment of a keyboard run counter to the science of Bradshaw and Holmes. For them, symbolism is evidence of disease, as their diagnosis of Septimus indicates: "He was attaching meanings to words of a symbolical kind. A serious symptom to be noted on the card." In the novel, the aeroplane is the symbol of symbols. For Mr Bentley it is a triumph of scientific achievement:

> Away and away the aeroplane shot, till it was nothing but a bright spark; an aspiration; a concentration; a symbol (so it seemed to Mr Bentley, vigorously rolling his strip of turf at Greenwich) of man's soul; of his determination, thought Mr Bentley, sweeping round the cedar tree, to get outside his body, beyond his house, by means of thought, Einstein, speculation, mathematics, the Mendelian theory— away the aeroplane shot.

For the scientific man, Nature has become a strip of turf to be vigorously rolled, just as Septimus, according to Bradshaw, must be crushed into submission, and for Miss Kilman, human nature must be religiously "converted." Mr Bentley sees Man's achievements as mathematical and scientific, and so his interpretation of what is meant by a symbol is scientific. For different characters the aeroplane has various meanings. This symbol of man's soul, as Bentley calls it, is used for the trivial purpose of advertising some product or other (and people differ in their interpretation of what the plane is writing in the sky). It is not a straightforward symbol, simply standing for something else in an allegorical way. We must not go to the other extreme, as some critics are in danger of doing, of seeing it as completely meaningless, as simply a technical device which enables the writer to relate spatially separated characters and to jump from one mind to another. It is neither an allegory nor a technical device, but a symbol in a wider sense. It is related to religious symbolism:

> Then, while a seedy-looking nondescript man carrying a leather bag stood on the steps of St Paul's Cathedral, and

hesitated, for within was what balm, how great a welcome, how many tombs with banners waving over them, tokens of victories not over armies, but over, he thought, that plaguy spirit of truth seeking which leaves me at present without a situation, and more than that, the cathedral offers company, he thought, invites you to membership of a society; great men belong to it; martyrs have died for it; why not enter in, he thought, put his leather bag stuffed with pamphlets before an altar, a cross, the symbol of something which has soared beyond seeking and questing and knocking of words together and has become all spirit, disembodied, ghostly—why not enter in? he thought, and while he hesitated out flew the aeroplane over Ludgate Circus.

The religious, scientific and martial attitudes form a mutual criticism here; the three faiths are undercut and we are left with a trivial advertisement, and even that is ineffective:

It was strange; it was still. Not a sound was to be heard above the traffic. Unguided it seemed; sped of its own free will. And now, curving up and up, straight up, like something mounting in ecstasy, in pure delight, out from behind poured white smoke looping, writing a T, and O, an F.

We have seen how the solitary traveller episode fits into the rest of the novel, but there remains Brower's other objection, to the "pseudo-Homeric similes." Clearly, these are part of our keyboard, part of the transition between simile, metaphor and symbol which we have been tracing, and so a passage like the following has its place:

As a person who had dropped some grain of pearl or diamond into the grass and parts the tall blades very carefully, this way and that, and searches here and there vainly, and at last spies it there at the roots, so she went through one thing and another.

The dislocation here, the separation between vehicle and tenor, is clearly deliberate. Further, the similes are not "pseudo-Homeric" they are mock-heroic, for they fit into their own pattern of allusion and display the disjunction between the traditional martial values and the actual squalor and waste of the First World War, which is personified in Septimus. Brower has failed to sense the ironic tone of much of the novel, a tone and attitude close to Eliot's *Waste Land* which the Hogarth press had published four years earlier. So, Clarissa Dalloway shores against her ruin the song from *Cymbeline*:

> Fear no more the heat o' the sun
> Nor the furious winter's rages.

Brower's objection, then, to the Homeric similes and to the so-called interlude of the solitary traveller, on the grounds that they are irrelevant, is not tenable, for they are both aspects of that web of allusion which binds the novel together.

On the scale which we have established, the following passage marks the transition from myth to metaphor. This is the world of Ceres and Mother Nature, of Sirens and Mermaids:

> Such are the visions which proffer great cornucopias full of fruit to the solitary traveller, or murmur in his ear like sirens lolloping away on the green sea waves, or are dashed in his face like bunches of roses, or rise to the surface like pale faces which fishermen flounder through floods to embrace.

The mock-epic element in *Mrs. Dalloway* has often been compared with Joyce's use of epic in *Ulysses*. It is evident how much more general are Virginia Woolf's allusions. Her framework is not a particular epic, but, as I have tried to establish, a keyboard of symbols. She is much more concerned with the general type of simile or theme in epic poetry, and particularly with the glorification of war which led to the sickening waste of the First World War. This waste and degradation is conveyed in the irony of the allusion to Ceres in the following passage:

> Something was up, Mr Brewer knew; Mr Brewer, managing clerk at Sibley's and Arrowsmith's, auctioneers, valuers, land and estate agents; something was up, he thought, and, being paternal with his young men, and thinking very highly of Smith's abilities, and prophesying that he would, in ten or fifteen years, succeed to the leather arm-chair in the inner room under the skylight with the deed-boxes around him, "if he keeps his health," said Mr Brewer, and that was the danger—he looked weakly; advised football, invited him to supper and was seeing his way to consider recommending a rise of salary, when something happened which threw out many of Mr Brewer's calculations, took away his ablest young fellows, and eventually, so prying and insidious were

the fingers of the European War, smashed the plaster cast of Ceres, ploughed a hole in the geranium beds, and utterly ruined the cook's nerves at Mr Brewer's establishment at Muswell Hill.

The gods and heroes of the novel are made of plaster. Hugh Whitbread is not "the stout-hearted," he is "the admirable," and his role is simply that of a sycophant at court. "By Jove" is simply a mild expression of surprise: "How they loved dressing up in gold lace and doing homage! There! That must be—by Jove it was—Hugh Whitbread, snuffing round the precincts of the great, grown rather fatter, rather whiter, the admirable Hugh!" The threefold repetition of a name a little earlier establishes the mock-heroic undertone of these pages:

> But alas, Wilkins; Wilkins wanted her; Wilkins was emitting in a voice of commanding authority, as if the whole company must be admonished and the hostess reclaimed from frivolity, one name:
> "The Prime Minister," said Peter Walsh.

The military aspect of the epic is never forgotten. For example, Clarissa's parasol is seen as the sacred weapon of a goddess and Richard Dalloway comes "bearing his flowers like a weapon." The general ironic light of the novel plays over the symbols of public life:

> As for Buckingham Palace (like an old prima donna facing the audience all in white) you can't deny it a certain dignity, he considered, nor despise what does, after all, stand to millions of people (a little crowd was waiting at the gate to see the King drive out) for a symbol, absurd though it is; a child with a box of bricks could have done better, he thought; looking at the memorial to Queen Victoria (whom he could remember in her horn spectacles driving through Kensington), its white mound, its billowing motherliness; but he liked being ruled by the descendant of Horsa; he liked continuity; and the sense of handing on the traditions of the past.

Scientific, religious, and heroic faiths have been smashed by the First World War. The cross, the aeroplane, the monument of Queen Victoria are no longer acceptable whole-heartedly, for they no longer bring human beings together. All that Clarissa Dalloway can do is literally bring them together at a party, so that for one moment they feel their common humanity. This is itself only a symbolic gesture, a greeting to other beings across the emptiness which she sees at the heart of life. Septimus is there only in spirit, and represents all that has been lost in the War. The news of his death puts Clarissa's party into a Classical setting, with the theme of "Et in Arcadia Ego," and in an undertone is the Anglican Service for the Burial of the Dead:

> Oh! thought Clarissa, in the middle of my party, here's death, she thought.

Mrs. Dalloway

Hermione Lee

Jacob's biographer was hampered by an inhibition which Clarissa Dalloway also feels:

> She would not say of anyone in the world now that they were this or were that.

In *Jacob's Room*, the first novel to concentrate on the impossibility of pinning down the identity, there is, to some extent, a failure where Virginia Woolf expected it: "My doubt is how far it will enclose the human heart." *Jacob's Room* cannot begin to be a novel about the personality in action, engaged in relationships or recollection, because the emphasis is all on how it can be *known*. The only relationship of any real vitality in the novel is onesided—it is that between the biographer and her subject. But the struggle for knowledge, an end in itself in *Jacob's Room*, provides the groundwork for the consideration, in *Mrs. Dalloway*, of personalities at work. While we retain our sense of the inscrutability of the self, we are now taken from the narrator's efforts at penetration of those to the characters. We move inside "the human heart."

The background to this achievement was, as for *Jacob's Room*, a series of short stories, the first of which, "Mrs. Dalloway in Bond Street," soon "ushers in a host of others." On October 14, 1922, she recorded [in *A Writer's Diary*, ed. Leonard Woolf] that "Mrs. Dalloway

---

From *The Novels of Virginia Woolf*. © 1977 by Hermione Lee. Methuen & Co., 1977.

has branched into a book," but it was some time before she could find the necessary balance between "design and substance":

> Am I writing *The Hours* [its working title] from deep emotion? . . . Have I the power of conveying the true reality? Or do I write essays about myself? . . . This is going to be the devil of a struggle. The design is so queer and so masterful, I'm always having to wrench my substance to fit it.

Her ability to master the difficulties seems to come upon her quite suddenly, as when she realized how to write *Jacob's Room*:

> My discovery: how I dig out beautiful caves behind my characters: I think that gives exactly what I want; humanity, humour, depth. The idea is that the caves shall connect and each comes to daylight at the present moment.

The discovery of the "tunnelling process" enabled her to forge ahead, and the book was written in a year, gaining as it developed, a "more analytical and human . . . less lyrical" quality. These phrases suggest how different its concentration on the personality made it from *Jacob's Room*; but she wanted it to retain at the same time the haziness of the earlier novel, so that in spite of its carefully controlled design she would "keep the quality of a sketch in a finished and composed work." The terms, of course, are taken from painting, an analogy which was more extensively used in a correspondence she had with the painter Jacques Raverat towards the end of the writing of *Mrs. Dalloway*. They discussed fictional form. The problem about writing, Raverat said, is that it is "essentially linear"; it is almost impossible, in a sequential narrative, to express the way one's mind responds to an idea, a word or an experience, where, like a pebble being thrown into a pond, "splashes in the outer air" are accompanied "under the surface" by "waves that follow one another into dark and forgotten corners." Virginia Woolf replied that it is "precisely the task of the writer to go beyond the 'formal railway line of sentence' and to show how people 'feel or think or dream . . . all over the place.' " The concept of tunnelling into "caves" behind characters enfranchised her from the unwanted linear structure in which an omniscient narrator moves from points A to B. She arrived instead at a form which could "use up everything I've ever thought," giving the impression of simultaneous connections between the inner and the outer world, the past and the present, speech and silence: a form patterned like waves in a pond rather than a railway line. Many of the ingredients of the form had been tried out in *Jacob's Room:* the pronoun "one" allowing a fluid transference of recurrent images from one character to another, the connective "for" making a leap in thought seem like a progression, the use of "nothing but present particles" to evoke the simultaneity of thought and action, are recognizable techniques. But they are now more unobtrusively used for a style which is really very different from that of *Jacob's Room* in its fusion of streams of thought into a homogeneous third-person, past-tense narrative.

The maturing of techniques since *Jacob's Room* accompanied the maturing of characters. But, although *Mrs. Dalloway* was the first of the novels to concentrate on middle age, its social milieu, in part, returned Virginia Woolf (as the reappearance of characters from *The Voyage Out* suggests) to experiences of her adolescence. The Dalloways in *The Voyage Out* are considerably different from the later Dalloways. Richard is a sententious, prosing chauvinist who considers England to be demeaned by her bohemians and suffragettes. Clarissa, worshipping her husband, and sharing all his grandiloquent beliefs ("Think of the light burning over the House, Dick!") is presented as a creature of frills, charms and affectations. The satire in the later book is more complex and less obvious. But the social arena of the Dalloways, in both novels, reflects Virginia Woolf's fascinated dislike of the world of society hostesses, eminent politicians, distinguished doctors and lawyers, and grand old dowager ladies, in which powerful men talk a great deal of nonsense and the woman's place is decorative, entertaining and subservient. As the marriageable Miss Stephen, she had been miserably dragged round this world by her cousin George Duckworth and later by a family friend, Kitty Maxse, the original of Clarissa. Virginia Stephen found Kitty brittle and superficial and felt that her qualities might have over-influenced the portrayal of Clarissa: was she not "too stiff, too glittering and tinsely [sic]?"

> I remember the night . . . when I decided to give it up, because I found Clarissa in some way tinselly. Then I invented her memories. But I think some distaste for her persisted. Yet, again, that was true to my feeling for Kitty, and one must dislike people in art without its mattering, unless indeed it is true that certain characters detract from the importance of what happens to them.

Other adolescent feelings were recalled in the book; like Clarissa,

Virginia Woolf was tunnelling back into her past when she described
Sally Seton, who was based on her cousin, Madge Symonds. When
she was fifteen she was in love with Madge, who was, Quentin Bell
says, "very much a girl of the nineties." He describes how "Virginia
. . . gripping the handle of the water-jug in the top room at Hyde Park
Gate . . . exclaimed to herself: 'Madge is here; at this moment she is
actually under this roof.' " But present acquaintances were also used.
Lydia Lopokova, the dancer (and future wife of Maynard Keynes), was
"observed" "as a type of Rezia," and Lady Bruton was probably based
on Virginia Woolf's knowledge of the forthright Lady Colefax. Her
hostility to high society was not all drawn from memory:

> I want to bring in the despicableness of people like Ott
> [Ottoline Morrell]. I want to give the slipperiness of the
> soul. I have been too tolerant often. The truth is people
> scarcely care for each other.
>
> (A Writer's Diary)

Clarissa's world is, then, familiar to Virginia Woolf, as Septimus's is
not. But her personal experience was used in the characterization of
Septimus at a more profound level than that of social identity: "I
adumbrate here a study of insanity and suicide; the world seen by the
sane and the insane side by side." For the first time since the account of
Rachel Vinrace's fever, she was drawing on her own intermittent states
of madness, which had led, in 1895 and in 1915, to suicide attempts. In
The Voyage Out, Mrs. Dalloway and the characterization of Rhoda in
The Waves, we are given vivid accounts of these mental states, which
were evidently painful studies for her to make: "Of course the mad
part tries me so much, makes my mind squirt so badly that I can
hardly face spending the next weeks at it." In September 1923, while
writing about Septimus, she had a "mental tremor" fleetingly reminis-
cent of her periods of insanity: she was evoking them too intensely.

That the madness of Septimus was close to her own experience is
clear from the accounts given by Leonard Woolf and Quentin Bell.
Both make only tentative diagnoses. Quentin Bell follows Woolf in
saying that "her symptoms were of a manic depressive character,"
usually contenting himself with formulations such as "all that summer
she was mad," or with a jocular reference to Virginia Woolf at her
worst as a "raving lunatic." Leonard Woolf also refers to his wife's
illness as "manic depressive insanity," though "the doctors called it
neurasthenia . . . a name which covered a multitude of sins, symp-

toms, and miseries." His painfully clinical accounts of these symptoms—the progression from exhaustion and insomnia to states of excitement, violence and delusions alternating with comatose melancholia, depression, guilt and disgust at food—have points of resemblance to Septimus's. Virginia Woolf's hostility to her doctors, particularly to Sir George Savage (the model for Sir William Bradshaw), whom Leonard himself distrusted, is one such parallel. Both Leonard Woolf and Quentin Bell remark on the thin dividing line between her normal psychology and her insanity. Woolf comments on the rational quality of her delusions: the most fearful aspect of her disease was that, during its course, she was "terribly sane in three-quarters of her mind." Though such information adds nothing to a literary estimation of *Mrs. Dalloway,* it is inevitably of interest to know how much the "mad part" owes to her recollections of being mad herself—listening to the birds singing in Greek and imagining that King Edward VII lurked in the azaleas using the foulest possible language.

That Virginia Woolf should be combining, as materials for *Mrs. Dalloway,* her social acquaintances and her madness, suggests how carefully the different areas of the book have to be welded together.

> In this book I have almost too many ideas. I want to give
> life and death, sanity and insanity; I want to criticize the
> social system, and to show it at work, at its most intense.

This is written while the book is still being called *The Hours.* The change of title (uncharacteristic in that it rejects the abstract concept in favour of the individual name) points to the way in which she was having to manipulate the centres of interest. She decides that the emphasis is to fall on Clarissa in the title; but in the careful structure of the novel she tries to prevent any one of the book's "many ideas" from dominating the others. This is immediately apparent if one summarizes the "story" of *Mrs. Dalloway.*

At 10 A.M. on a warm, breezy Wednesday early in June 1923, Clarissa Dalloway, aged fifty-two, the wife of a Conservative MP, goes to Bond Street to buy some flowers for a party she is giving that evening at her house in Dean's Yard. She meets an old friend, Hugh Whitbread, on the way through Green Park. While she is buying the flowers, a VIP's car—the Queen's? the Prime Minister's?—goes past; it also passes a young couple, Septimus and Lucrezia Warren Smith, he an estate agent's clerk and shell-shocked veteran of the war, she an Italian girl who used to make hats in Milan. Septimus's madness has necessitated the calling in of doctors, first Dr Holmes, the GP, and now Sir William Bradshaw, the famous nerve specialist, with whom they have an appointment at 12:00. The Smiths walk up to Regent's Park, Clarissa walks home; both see an aeroplane advertising "Toffo" in the sky. When Clarissa gets home she finds a message to say that her husband is going out to lunch with Lady Bruton. She is disturbed at not having been invited. She starts to mend her dress for the party and is interrupted by an unexpected visit from Peter Walsh, the man she used to love in her youth, at her family house at Bourton, and from whom she parted, with great pain, after she met Richard Dalloway. They have seen each other occasionally in the last thirty years. Peter went to India, married, was widowed, and is now in love with Daisy, a young married woman with two children. His conversation with Clarissa, in which he bursts into tears as he tells her this, is interrupted by the entrance of Clarissa's seventeen-year-old daughter Elizabeth. Peter leaves Dean's Yard and walks up to Regent's Park, pursuing an attractive girl for part of his way. At a quarter to twelve he glimpses the Warren Smiths in the Park, who leave at 12:00 for their appointment with Sir William. The interview lasts precisely three-quarters of an hour and results in Sir William's arranging for Septimus (whom he can see to be a very serious case) to go into one of his homes.

At half past one Richard Dalloway and Hugh Whitbread meet for lunch at Lady Bruton's, where they help her to write a letter to *The Times*. Richard, hearing that Peter is in London, thinks of his own love for Clarissa and decides to go and see her after lunch. He buys her some flowers and goes home at three, to find her annoyed, because she has had to invite an unwanted guest to her party, and because Elizabeth is closeted in her room with her odious history teacher, Miss Kilman. After Richard has gone Elizabeth and Miss Kilman—whom Clarissa feels to be her enemy—leave for tea.

Elizabeth, though full of respect for Miss Kilman, is made uneasy by her emotional, possessive, greedy manner. She leaves her in the Army and Navy Stores and catches a bus up the Strand, while Doris Kilman, in despair, goes to pray in Westminster Abbey. At about five, when Elizabeth is going home from her bus ride, Septimus, lying in his room, experiences a momentary freedom from insanity, much to Rezia's relief. But this is interrupted by the intrusion of Dr Holmes, and Septimus, hearing the sounds of pursuit, jumps out of the window. The clock strikes six.

Peter Walsh, going back to his hotel, is passed by the ambulance carrying Septimus's body. He goes in to change, finds a note from Clarissa, has dinner, and, as evening falls, goes out again to walk to her party. At the party, Sally Seton, an old friend of Peter and Clarissa, of whom both have been thinking during the day, arrives uninvited. The Prime Minister, Lady Bruton, Hugh Whitbread, Ellie Henderson (Clarissa's unwanted guest)—all characters who have in some way been important during the day—are there. The Bradshaws come and Clarissa learns through them of Septimus's death, with which she feels a strong connection. Peter Walsh, who has spent much of the day criticizing Clarissa, is forced yet again into a moment of intense emotion for her—"for there she was."

Two things are apparent from this résumé of the plot. The first is that all the activity is carefully held together by a specific use of time and place. The second is that the meat of the book does not lie in the sequence of events: they are its bare bones. It would be difficult to discover from the summary how the book could be about the relationship of the past to the present, or how there could be any possible link between Clarissa and Septimus. This is because a plot summary, apart from mentioning the time at which things happen, leaves out the narrative texture, in which images, descriptive passages, leitmotifs and internal thought processes create the "substance" of the book.

For Clarissa does not, of course, simply walk through Green Park and up Bond Street and back again during the first thirty pages of the novel. She also perceives, thinks, remembers and generalizes, and in doing so she suffuses her present experience with the feelings and experiences of thirty years ago. What she remembers becomes a part of what she sees now, and these in turn contribute to what she thinks; her attitude to "life: London: this moment in June." No sooner have we read the first sentence of the novel, which looks deceptively like the start of a conventional "story," than we are plunged ("What a plunge!") into Clarissa's past. The delight of plunging into the London morning reminds her of similar feelings experienced as a girl at Bourton, and makes her think of Peter Walsh, which brings into her mind the fact that he is soon due to return from India. (Already we are made aware that the past is not in contrast with the present, but involved with it. Clarissa feels the same now as she did at Bourton; Peter, we shall find, is still making remarks about vegetables and playing with his pocket knife, which, like Hugh Whitbread's silver fountain pen and Rezia's delicate hats, is a symbol of his personality.) As she thinks how odd it is that only a few things about Peter stick in her mind—"his eyes, his pocket-knife, his smile, his grumpiness"—she is watched, while she waits to cross the road, by a neighbour, Scrope Purvis, who thinks how charming she is, and compares her to a bird, a "jay, blue green, light, vivacious," and notices how white she has grown since her illness. Already we hold in balance an external view of her—ageing, pale, elegant, charming—with the emotional life of which we are learning.

With this exception, we remain inside Clarissa's mind all the way to the flower shop. Her love of life, her admiration of fortitude, her pleasure in what she sees; the mixture of fondness and satire in her thoughts of Hugh; her memory of how she quarrelled with Peter about Hugh; their arguments, their parting; her ignorance, her intuitiveness, her feeling that in spite of death she might survive in "the ebb and flow of things" . . . so it continues, and, by the time she has reached the flower shop and Miss Pym, the flower lady, has noticed how much older she looks this year, we can recognize and analyse the method, and already have a sense of Clarissa's existence taking place on several levels.

The external level, at which Scrope Purvis and Miss Pym can approach her, is the social level: Clarissa as the society hostess, the ageing MP's wife. We are warned against judging people at such a level by the nature of the book—Peter Walsh assuming the Warren Smiths to be an ordinary young couple quarrelling emphasizes the danger of saying "of anyone in the world . . . that they were this or were that." Yet, though the external level may be a mockery of the inner self, it is, at the same time, a part of the self. All the judgements made about Clarissa, whether satirical or sympathetic, have a certain kind of truth in them. Scrope Purvis and Miss Pym hardly know her. But both bring to our notice the fact that she has been ill and looks older, thereby giving her love of life and vitality an air of pathos. At the same time, Scrope Purvis and Miss Pym both praise her; the former for her charm and elegant uprightness, the latter for her kindness.

Lady Bruton cannot see the sense in "cutting people up, as Clarissa Dalloway did." Richard reflects that "she wanted support"; Elizabeth notices that "her mother liked old women because they were Duchesses." At the party there are numerous "external" views of Clarissa. Ellie Henderson guesses that Clarissa "had not meant to ask her this year," Sir Harry, the Academician, likes her "in spite of her damnable, difficult, upper-class refinement, which made it impossible to ask Clarissa Dalloway to sit on his knee." Jim Hutton, the young intellectual, thinks her "a prig. But how charming to look at!"

There is, then, a recognizable external self, with characteristics which are appreciated or criticized in different ways by different people; up to a point, it is possible to say of someone that "they were this or were that." By this method of showing us external views of Clarissa, Virginia Woolf lets us "see" her without making any impersonal comment. Hence she emphasizes the "streaked, involved, inextricably confused" nature of existence, since any one person's view of anyone else is determined and qualified by their own limitations.

Clarissa, too, thinks of herself as a "character" and sums herself up rather as other people do. She looks in the mirror and sees herself, "pointed; dart-like; definite." She knows that this face is the result of drawing the parts together, and that the parts are infinitely different and incompatible. But it is this "definite" self, seen also by others, which has permanent, distinct characteristics; it is this self which "could not think, write, even play the piano . . . muddled Armenians and Turks," which admires old dowagers like Lady Bexborough, and which stiffens with pride when the Queen may be going past. It is this public, definite self, this "being Mrs Richard Dalloway," which stands at the top of the stairs being the perfect hostess, and wanting "that people should look pleased as she came in."

Below this lies her deeper self, made up partly of her feelings about experience—her love for Sally Seton and for Peter Walsh—and partly of her present emotions—for Elizabeth, Richard, Miss Kilman, her party, life itself. In this self there is a continual interplay between her sense of reaching out to others and withdrawing from them; between her sense of failure, loss and coldness, and her involvement with the vivid, energetic pulse of life. The party is the central image for the outgoing self:

> But to go deeper. . . . what did it meant to her, this thing she called life? Oh, it was very queer. Here was So-and-so in South Kensington; someone up in Bayswater; and somebody else, say, in Mayfair. And she felt quite continuously a sense of their existence; and she felt what a waste; and she felt what a pity; and she felt if only they could be brought together; so she did it. And it was an offering; to combine; to create; but to whom?

In contrast with her desire to bring people together, the image of the old lady moving from room to room in the house opposite sums up

Clarissa's fierce resistance to emotional possession, "love and religion," which attempt to force the soul and own people. Clarissa respects "the privacy of the soul," which is signified for her by the idea that "here was one room; there another." On the one hand, the party—the drawing together and harmonizing of people—expresses Clarissa's love of participation, as she felt it in her emotions for Sally and Peter. She still retains such strong, passionate feelings in moments of sympathy, sometimes for another woman, when she may have the "illumination; a match burning in a crocus," an emotional experience which is described as a sexual orgasm. She still has a strong passion of hatred for Miss Kilman, who is trying to steal Elizabeth from her, and in hating whom there is an energy and a life; "It was enemies one wanted, not friends." But in contrast with such involvement is her withdrawal. Clarissa going indoors like "a nun who has left the world," going upstairs to her narrow bed like "a child exploring a tower," virginal, failing Richard sexually, unable to abandon herself, feeling her slice of life dwindling away because Lady Bruton has not asked her to lunch, is possessed of a cold, ageing world, in contrast with the warm passionate experiences of her youth, to which Peter's visit recalls her. The contrast is expressed in a strange and brilliant image, unexpectedly but arrestingly appropriate:

> It was all over for her. The sheet was stretched and the bed narrow. She had gone up into the tower alone and left them blackberrying in the sun.

There is a deeper and more remote level of existence in Clarissa which has nothing to do with failure or success and is not susceptible of satire. At this level, furthest removed from her "external," social self, Clarissa feels the possibility (one already found in *Jacob's Room*) of going beyond the exigencies of time and place to participate in the ebb and flow of existence. This elusive, intangible self awaits death as a release, a way into communication with the general life of things:

> Or did it not become consoling to believe that death ended absolutely? but that somehow in the streets of London, on the ebb and flow of things, here, there, she survived, Peter survived, lived in each other, she being part, she was positive, of the trees at home . . . part of people she had never met; being laid out like a mist between the people she knew best . . . but it spread ever so far, her life, herself.

On this plane she experiences a sense of identity with Septimus, feeling that his death redeems the hollowness, the "corruption, lies, chatter" of her life. The connection cannot be known at any more external level, being, in fact, in sharp contrast to the world of the party in which it takes place.

The method by which layer upon layer of Clarissa's character is revealed holds good for all the other figures in the novel. Peter Walsh, for example, is, on a public level, jobless, in love, aged fifty-three, and just back from India. Deeper down, he dwells on his past and present feeling for Clarissa; and, beyond that, he is dimly aware of some kind of universal, shared life-force, suggested by the old woman singing outside Regent's Park tube. On that plane, he becomes the "solitary traveller" of his dreams. Rezia is summed up at an external level by comfortable, endearing images: she makes a noise like "a kettle on a hob" or "a contented tap left running"; she tries to keep out Holmes "like a little hen, with her wings spread." But this simple, sympathetic character is in possession of one of the most fluid and ambiguous trains of thought in the novel. There is no such thing as simplicity of character: all minds work, deep down, in the immensely complex manner used to describe the aftermath of Rezia's words in Regent's Park "You should see the Milan gardens." The words, spoken to no one, fade like "the sparks of a rocket" into the darkness. In the darkness, invisible houses give out "trouble and suspense" until the relief of daylight. Rezia's loneliness is like the darkness seen by the Romans in their first visit to the country. Then, in the middle of her thoughts, "as if a shelf were shot forth and she stood on it," she remembers that she is Septimus's wife; but then, like a shelf falling, she thinks for a moment that he has gone away to kill himself. This cumbersome, elongated, disconnected image portrays the leaps and bounds of the mind, as well as incorporating the plot—the Romans landing in England being a reminder that Rezia has come from Italy. In some characters the penetration into their underworld may be so brief as to have the quality of a vignette; in this way, for a page or so, we drift into Lady Bruton's childhood, or slip into an experience of Maisie Johnson's which will "jangle again among her memories" fifty years hence, or share, briefly, the daydreams of Clarissa's maid Lucy as she sets out the silverware, and anticipates her mistress's triumph at the party: "Of all, her mistress was loveliest—mistress of silver, of linen, of china." The language makes Clarissa seem slightly ridiculous, and is characteristic of a mock-heroic diction used to impress on us the worthlessness of her social existence. Thus, Lucy, "taking Mrs Dalloway's parasol, handled it like a sacred weapon which a goddess, having acquitted herself honourably in the field of battle, sheds, and places it in the umbrella stand." Thus, Clarissa's objects of veneration—Royalty, the Empire, the Government—are made to look silly, as in the description of the VIP's car, for which Clarissa, thinking "It is probably the Queen," wears "a look of extreme dignity":

> Greatness was passing, hidden, down Bond Street, removed only by a hand's-breadth from ordinary people who might now, for the first time and last, be within speaking distance of the majesty of England, of the enduring symbol of the state.

Similarly satirical tones are used of Hugh Whitbread, whom Clarissa likes:

> He had been afloat on the cream of English society for fifty-five years. He had known Prime Ministers. His affections were understood to be deep.

Clarissa's feeling of rejection at having been excluded from Lady Bruton's lunch party is put in proportion when the lunch party itself is described:

> With a wave of the hand, the traffic ceases, and there rises instead this profound illusion . . . about the food—how it is not paid for; and then that the table spreads itself voluntarily with glass and silver, little mats, saucers of red fruit; . . . and with the coffee (not paid for) rise jocund visions before musing eyes.

Lady Bruton herself, one of several grand old dowagers whom Clarissa admires and respects, is, like Hugh, an object of explicit satire:

> Debarred by her sex, and some truancy, too, of the logical faculty (she found it impossible to write a letter to the *Times*), she had the thought of Empire always at hand, and had acquired from her association with that armoured goddess her ramrod bearing, her robustness of demeanour.

Clarissa is indicted with her society. Peter Walsh has no patience with her in her role as a "perfect hostess":

Here she's been sitting all the time I've been in India; mending her dress; playing about; going to parties.

He attacks her assimilation of Richard Dalloway's standards:

The public-spirited, British Empire, tariff-reform, governing-class spirit. . . . With twice his wits, she had to see things through his eyes.

He attacks her worldliness, her coldness, her "timid; hard; arrogant; prudish" manner, her conventionality, her party air, "effusive, insincere." Though our view of the characters is entirely opposed, Peter Walsh's attacks on Clarissa's social self have something in common with Doris Kilman's. Miss Kilman attacks Clarissa from hatred and jealousy, not, like Peter, from love and admiration; but the grounds of the attack—Clarissa's useless, luxurious existence, her "delicate body, her air of freshness and fashion"—are similar. Their criticisms are borne out by the trivial elements in Clarissa's inner thoughts; it is not only from the outside that she is satirized. When Clarissa considers with admiration "Mrs Foxcroft at the Embassy last night eating her heart out because that nice boy was killed and now the old Manor House must go to a cousin," or when she includes in her vision of "life: London: this moment in June," "the mothers of Pimlico" giving "suck to their young"; when she muses over the artistry of her dressmaker, now retired in Ealing, and says of her dresses that "You could wear them at Hatfield; at Buckingham Palace. She had worn them at Hatfield; at Buckingham Palace"; when she considers that by loving her roses she is helping "the Albanians, or was it the Armenians?" (whose concerns she leaves to Richard): at these points we are invited to direct against her the kind of hostility felt by Doris Kilman, or, at least, the kind of satire expressed by Peter Walsh.

At the party the various methods of satire used throughout the book cohere; Clarissa's feeling of identity with Septimus is set as sharply as possible against the "corruption, lies, chatter" of her life. The party emphasizes the ironic dichotomy between youthful aspirations and middle-aged resignation, most startlingly in the actual appearance of Sally Seton: no wild young thing (as we have continually imagined her) but a complacent Mancunian housewife. Sally and Peter compare past hopes with present achievements: " 'Have you written?' she asked him. . . . 'Not a word!' " Lady Bruton observes that Richard has lost his chance of the Cabinet. Those who are failures are thriving on a system of which Septimus Smith has been the victim. Hugh Whitbread eating cake with Duchesses, the Prime Minister ("You might have stood him behind a counter and bought biscuits"), Lady Bradshaw "a sea lion at the edge of its tank, barking for invitations"—all are ridiculous, even when, like Sir Harry or Professor Brierly, they are harmless. They are seen mostly through the eyes of Peter Walsh who has throughout been the most ruthless critic of Clarissa's society. But his criticisms are not the only means of undercutting Clarissa's "triumph": the way the party starts in the servants' quarters, and moves up the stairs, sets it in its full triviality against the world of the "lower classes" which Virginia Woolf (though never very realistically) likes to use as a contrast to the world of the "gentry." And Ellie Henderson, neglected and overawed, whom Clarissa despises, is, more endearingly than Doris Kilman, a critic of the society in that she is excluded by it.

Thus Clarissa's "offering," her "triumph," her attempt to "kindle and illuminate," on which the book converges, is seen as hollow, trivial and corrupt, providing satisfaction for the least satisfactory part of her character. It is not at this level, but at the deepest one, that her real triumph takes place, in her response to the death of Septimus, of which she hears from the Bradshaws.

Sir William Bradshaw is the most repulsive character in the book. His presentation is even stronger than that which turns Miss Kilman, through emphasis on her ugliness, her mackintosh, her greed and her lust for possession, into nothing more than a great hand opening and closing on the table. For Sir William, the mock-heroic language is used at full strength.

> Proportion, divine proportion, Sir William's goddess, was acquired by Sir William walking hospitals, catching salmon, begetting one son in Harley Street by Lady Bradshaw, who caught salmon herself and took photographs scarcely to be distinguished from the work of professionals. Worshipping proportion, Sir William not only prospered himself but made England prosper, secluded her lunatics, forbade childbirth, penalized despair, made it impossible for the unfit to propagate their views until they, too, shared his sense of proportion.

Sir William "forces the soul"; and he is the representative of a way of life, supported by Clarissa's Prime Minister, in which individuals are made to tow the line, or are put away. Septimus sees Sir William (and

Dr Holmes) as human nature, "the repulsive brute, with the blood-red nostrils" which wants to attack and pin him down. Clarissa recognizes that Sir William would "force the soul," and responds as Septimus does to the goddesses of Proportion and Conversion. As an alternative to the lust for domination which Sir William calls Proportion and Miss Kilman calls "love and religion," Clarissa recognizes an underlying unity of all things which can coexist with the privacy and integrity of the individual. In this she is against Sir William, against the social world of which she is a part, and on the side of Septimus.

Virginia Woolf's main concern about *Mrs. Dalloway* was that "the reviewers will say that it is disjointed because of the mad scenes not connecting with the Dalloway scenes." Certainly the plot does not connect Clarissa and Septimus, apart from the arbitrary link provided by Sir William, and the situational resemblance of their both having witnessed the death of someone close to them. But the connection between them at an experiential level is intimate and vital, and in it consists the novel's most remarkable achievement. The similarity in the way they respond to life leads the reader to feel that madness is an intensification or distortion of the method of perception that Virginia Woolf feels to be normal. Their response to experience is always given in physical terms, often remarkably similar ones:

> It rasped her, though, to have stirring about in her this brutal monster! to hear twigs cracking and feel hooves planted down in the depths of that leaf-encumbered forest, the soul; never to be content quite, or quite secure, for at any moment the brute would be stirring, this hatred, which, especially since her illness, had power to make her feel scraped, hurt in her spine.

> Septimus heard her say "Kay Arr" close to his ear, deeply, softly, like a mellow organ, but with a roughness in her voice like a grasshopper's, which rasped his spine deliciously and sent running up into his brain waves of sound which, concussing, broke.

> This gradual drawing together of everything to one centre before his eyes, as if some horror had come almost to the surface and was about to burst into flames, terrified him. The world wavered and quivered and threatened to burst into flames.

> Why, after all, did she do these things? Why seek pin-

nacles and stand drenched in fire? Might it consume her
anyhow! Burn her to cinders! Better anything, better bran-
dish one's torch and hurl it to earth than taper and dwindle
away.

In these two pairs of quotations, both Septimus and Clarissa translate
their emotions into physical metaphors, which are indistinguishable
from the emotion itself. The climax to this method of perception is
Clarissa's response to Septimus's death: "her body went through it."

The difference between Clarissa and Septimus—between sanity
and madness—is that Clarissa does not lose her awareness of the
outside world as something external to herself even while she responds
to it at a physical level. The physical response does not, in her case,
become so overwhelming that it subsumes the reality which induced
it. She hears Big Ben, and her thoughts about it are translated into a
physical response: she "feels" the sound as leaden circles dissolving, or
as a bar of gold flat on the sea, or as a finger falling into "the midst of
ordinary things." But Clarissa does not, hearing the sound, appropriate
and respond to its qualities without understanding what the sound
means, nor does she think Big Ben is speaking to her. She retains her
awareness of reality while she responds to it. Septimus, by contrast, is
not always able to distinguish between his personal response and the
indifferent, universal nature of external reality. He struggles to do so:
in Regent's Park he keeps trying to remind himself that the "shocks of
sound" which assault him come from "a motor horn down the street"
or "an old man playing a penny whistle," and he is capable of sane,
indeed satirical comments on reality: "The upkeep of that motor car
alone must cost him quite a lot," he says of Sir William. But, in his
madness, he feels that if the birds sing they must be speaking to him; if
the aeroplane writes in the sky it must be signalling to him. The
distinction between self and external reality is as blurred, in his mind,
as the distinction between different forms of physical response; sight,
sound, touch. In an attempt to sort this out as it happens to him,
Septimus, the victim of Science and Proportion, tries to be "scientific";
but the universe he inhabits, in which the usual categories are merged
beyond recognition, defies analysis:

Leaves were alive; trees were alive. And the leaves being
connected by millions of fibres with his own body, there on
the seat, fanned it up and down; when the branch stretched
he, too, made that statement. The sparrows fluttering, ris-

ing, and falling in jagged fountains were part of the pattern; the white and blue, barred with black branches. Sounds made harmonies with premeditation; the spaces between them were as significant as the sounds.

This impressionist picture is very like the picture Virginia Woolf creates in a sketch such as "Kew Gardens." Septimus's perceptions are those of a normal sensibility taken to its illogical conclusion.

Clarissa and Septimus are linked by a mutual leitmotif, the quotation from *Cymbeline* ("Fear no more the heat o' the sun"), which Clarissa reads in Hatchard's shop window in the morning, and which comes into Septimus's mind as he lies in his room:

His hand lay there on the back of the sofa, as he had seen his hand lie . . . on the top of the waves, while far away on shore he heard dogs barking and barking far away. Fear no more, says the heart in the body; fear no more.

His experience is like a re-enactment of Clarissa's while she is sewing her dress. For both it is a moment of tranquillity, an escape from the body, and possibly an anticipation of death. The quotation from *Cymbeline* is appropriate, not only to their mutual sense of death as a triumphant escape, but also to their situations. The lines are spoken over one who only appears to be dead, by those who don't know themselves to be her brothers. So, Clarissa is unaware of her kinship with Septimus; so, neither of them can be thoroughly known and understood by those who look at and speak to them. The lament is spoken for Imogen, an outcast from her society, and an innocent victim of cruelty and lies: and isolation from society is experienced both by Septimus and Clarissa. "Fear no more the heat o' the sun" casts an air of serenity over the encounter with death to which the whole book leads up. For the major connection between Clarissa and Septimus is, of course, that his death enables her to encounter hers.

Septimus thinks of himself as a scapegoat for society, as a "drowned sailor, on the shore of the world," who has died and come back, a risen God from the dead, in order to communicate the true meaning of life. When he asks himself "to whom" he should speak (as Clarissa asks herself "to whom" the offering of a party should be made), the reply comes (rather as in Clarissa's case)—"the Prime Minister." This suggests that Septimus's sense of the true meaning of life is no more compatible with the superficial social fabric epitomized by the Prime

Minister than is Clarissa's inner self. His message is given, indeed, not to the world at large, but to Clarissa. Like

> Lazarus, come back from the dead,
> Come back to tell you all, I shall tell you all
> (T. S. Eliot, "Love Song of J. Alfred Prufrock")

he speaks to Clarissa after his death, showing her that "Death was defiance. Death was an attempt to communicate. . . . There was an embrace in death." At this impressive climax, where the "too many ideas" cohere, the book's strongly moral nature, as well as its structural unity, can be thoroughly perceived.

Clarissa and Septimus connect at an intense moment of consciousness which is ironically contrasted with the moments measured out by the striking clock. Their communication defies "real" time, since it is made after, and in spite of, the hour of Septimus's death, and takes place outside the room where the "strained time-ridden faces" (T. S. Eliot, "Burnt Norton") of the partygoers bears evidence to the domination of "clock time." Within the party, the effort to vanquish "clock time" fails: the youthful idyll of life at Bourton, which has been painfully and pleasurably recollected throughout the novel, is time lost, not time regained. Though its protagonists are all reassembled at the party, they are ageing, unsuccessful, disillusioned; the victims of real time.

The party is the climax to the tension between the two kinds of time in the novel. The strictly limited "clock time," covering just over twelve hours, and impressed on the reader (as we saw in the plot summary) at regular intervals, is combined with a continuous flowing of various consciousnesses (reflected by the fluid sentence structures) in which past, present and future are merged. "Consciousness time" is frequently associated with the image of a vista. During her conversation with Peter, Clarissa has an image of herself as

> a child throwing bread to the ducks, between her parents,
> and at the same time a grown woman coming to her parents
> who stood by the lake, holding her life in her arms which,
> as she neared them, grew larger and larger in her arms, until
> it became a whole life, a complete life, which she put down
> by them and said, "This is what I have made of it! This!"

Clarissa's approach to her parents down a vista of time is rather like the vision of the "solitary traveller," who may or may not be Peter

Walsh. As he falls asleep in the park, the figure of the nurse knitting at the end of the bench becomes transformed into a giant female figure seen at the end of a forest ride by the traveller, which leads him on, "taking away from him the sense of the earth, the wish to return, and giving him for substitute a general peace." Our feeling that this is meant as Peter Walsh's dream comes from the fact that elsewhere he uses two images related to this passage—the nurse waving at the window, and Clarissa like a "lolloping mermaid" with her Prime Minister. But the image is purposely generalized into a universal idea of death as peace. Looking down the vista of time, the traveller sees his own end in sight. It is an alarming, but at the same time a consolatory vision.

The future seen at the end of a vista is used again to show the characters struggling to approach each other through the barriers of generation, separation and death. Septimus sees Evans coming towards him through the trees. Richard watches Elizabeth through a press of people at the party and, for a moment, does not recognize her. At the end, Clarissa is framed in the doorway and Peter apprehends her reality in a moment which transcends time; "for there she was."

The most complex example of the "vista" used as an image for "consciousness time" is the passage in which Peter, taking off his boots in the hotel, considers whether or not he should marry Daisy. At one point in present time in his hotel room, he remembers one point in past time when Daisy ran to meet him, crying that she would give him everything. At the same moment he imagines a hypothetical future time when he might "go to Oxford and poke about in the Bodleian":

> Vainly the dark, adorably pretty girl ran to the end of the terrace; vainly waved her hand; vainly cried she didn't care a straw what people said. There he was, the man she thought the world of . . . padding about a room in a hotel in Bloomsbury, shaving, washing, continuing, as he took up cans, put down razors, to poke about in the Bodleian, and get at the truth about one or two little matters that interested him.

The actual past moment, the actual present moment and the hypothetical future moment are here merged in one.

The clocks in *Mrs. Dalloway* recall people from such inner fluidity to the burden of real time and place, and in this sense the leaden circles are the enemy, the spokesmen of Proportion, like Sir William:

> Shredding and slicing, dividing and subdividing, the clocks
> of Harley Street nibbled at the June day, counselled submis-
> sion, upheld authority, and pointed out in chorus the su-
> preme advantages of a sense of proportion.

Against them is set an infinity which goes beyond all limits, even that
of the personal consciousness, as in the song of the old woman outside
Regent's Park tube:

> Through all ages—when the pavement was grass, when it
> was swamp, through the age of tusk and mammoth, through
> the age of silent sunrise—the battered woman—for she wore
> a skirt . . . stood singing of love—love which has lasted a
> million years . . . love which prevails, and millions of years
> ago her lover, who had been dead these centuries, had
> walked, she crooned, with her in May . . . and when at last
> she laid her hoary and immensely aged head on the earth,
> now become a mere cinder of ice . . . then the pageant of
> the universe would be over.

This impersonal infinity is felt, too, in the music Elizabeth hears in
Fleet Street:

> This voice, pouring endlessly, year in, year out, would
> take whatever it might be; this vow; this van; this life;
> this procession; would wrap them all about and carry
> them on, as in the rough stream of a glacier the ice holds
> a splinter of bone, a blue petal, some oak trees, and rolls
> them on.

As in *Jacob's Room,* that natural infinity is in contrast with the time by
which history is measured and wars are made, leaving a world (in
which manners and customs, as Peter notes, are greatly changed)
where the people who pick up life as it was, who open bazaars and go
shopping and give parties and write letters to *The Times,* are ironically
contrasted with the victims of the war, the poor, the shell-shocked,
and the dead:

> Really it was a miracle thinking of the war, and thousands
> of poor chaps, with all their lives before them, shovelled
> together, already half forgotten; it was a miracle. Here he
> was walking across London to say to Clarissa in so many
> words that he loved her.

But it is an over-simplification to say that "consciousness time" is always in conflict with "clock time." The leaden circles dissolving in the air may be reminders of death, but they are also, for Clarissa, the pulse of life itself. Big Ben and St. Margaret's often usher in the moments of intense feeling, those still points of concentration like a "falling drop," in which all life seems to be contained. The notes strike like warnings but, as they dissolve, they seem to sum up and become part of the activity of life. Big Ben's first stroke in the book is followed by Clarissa's response: "Heaven only knows why one loves it so"—"it," as so often, being life itself. Later, the different sounds of the clocks suggest the different sides to her life:

> But here the other clock, the clock which always struck two minutes after Big Ben, came shuffling in with its lap full of odds and ends, which it dumped down as if Big Ben were all very well with his majesty laying down the law . . . but she must remember all sorts of little things besides—Mrs Marsham, Ellie Henderson, glasses for ices.

Peter Walsh thinks of the bell of St. Margaret's ("like a hostess") as being Clarissa herself; the sound suggests to him both her life ("as if this bell had come into the room years ago") and her death ("Clarissa falling where she stood, in the drawing-room").

The bells, which are fluid symbols of life and death, and which act at the same time as structural connections, are the precursors of a similarly used motif, the lighthouse, in Virginia Woolf's next, and greatest, novel.

Mrs. Dalloway:
Virginia Woolf's Memento Mori

Maria DiBattista

THE EMPTY CENTER

The emergence of Woolf's distinctive literary identity can be dated, as Woolf herself dated it, to her fortieth year, just after the completion of *Jacob's Room:*

> There's no doubt in my mind that I have found out how to begin (at 40) to say something in my own voice; and that interests me so that I feel I can go ahead without praise.
>
> (*A Writer's Diary*)

Woolf's diary entries for 1922 and 1923 speak exultantly of her newfound freedom of expression, her "excitement" in discovering new narrative methods to provide her novels with the encompassing unity they had previously lacked. But three more authentic signs of Woolf's coming of age confirm her claim to literary ascendancy: her decreasing reliance on the motive of praise in her writing, essential to her project of forging an autonomous, yet nonegotistical voice; her whetted sense of competition with her contemporaries; the growing ambition of her narrative designs. The example of Joyce, also forty in 1922, looms large in her consciousness. While writing *Jacob's Room,* Woolf was justifiably anxious that "what I'm doing is probably being better done by Mr. Joyce," but by the time of *Mrs. Dalloway,* she was bold and confident enough to engage *Ulysses,* answering Joyce's patriarchal

From *Virginia Woolf's Major Novels: The Fables of Anon.* © 1980 by Yale University. Yale University Press, 1980.

fiction with her own critique of history, memory, law, and the art of life.

It is in reflecting on her rivalry and friendship with Katherine Mansfield, recently dead, that Woolf makes a more balanced assessment of her powers as a writer and her feelings about the novel that will become *Mrs. Dalloway:*

> Have I the power of conveying the true reality? Or do I write essays about myself? Answer these questions as I may, in the uncomplimentary sense, and still there remains this excitement. To get to the bones, now I'm writing fiction again I feel my force glow straight from me at its fullest. After a dose of criticism I feel that I'm writing sideways, using only an angle of my mind. This is justification; for free use of the faculties means happiness. I'm better company, more of a human being. Nevertheless, I think it is important in this book to go for the central things. Even though they don't submit, as they should, however, to beautification in language.

To be free, to be happy, to be more completely human, to go for the central things—these are the imperatives and the perquisites that justify and motivate the writing "I." Yet the central things, life and death, the objects of her imaginative desire, remain stubbornly resistant to the penetrating force of her mind. It is not so much that Woolf's center will not hold; it is that the imaginative center, where truth and beauty, life and death coexist as terms in the transparent equation of reality, eludes, as *Mrs. Dalloway* will dramatize, the spirit's grasp.

Mrs. Dalloway is a novel about "people feeling the impossibility of reaching the centre which, mystically, evaded them." Reaching that center is the human categorical imperative because there is housed "the thing that mattered"—the privacy of the soul, the sanctuary of the sovereign "I." The feeling of impossibility, which contributes to the novel's vague but universal sense of malaise, of spiritual incapacity, of frustrated expectations, originates in the intuition that the passage to the center is blocked by real and phantom presences. For Miss Kilman, "It is the flesh"; for Septimus Smith and Clarissa Dalloway, the obscurely evil power of the "Other," personified in the alienist Bradshaw, to commit with impunity the "indescribable outrage—forcing your soul." Or "the overwhelming incapacity" may have its origin in the terror, the awful fear before life itself, "this life, to be lived to the end, to be walked with serenely."

The pervasive, middle-aged dysphoria of *Mrs. Dalloway* contrasts to the original euphoria of *Jacob's Room*, a novel that centered itself in "the obstinate irrepressible conviction" of youth—"I am what I am and I intend to be it." But the hero's freedom to form and realize an absolute individuality—the I am what I am—proves illusory. "We start out transparent," reflects the narrator, "and then the cloud thickens. All history backs our pane of glass. To escape is vain." The sense of futility that infects the moral and psychological atmosphere of *Mrs. Dalloway* may be a symptom of the malady of history itself, devitalizing and encroaching on the unique privacy of the soul. "When a child begins to read history one marvels, sorrowfully, to hear him spell out in his new voice the ancient words," observes the narrator [in *Jacob's Room*]. History not only reveals but repeats itself in Jacob, the eternal repetition that constitutes the "mother's sorrow."

Mrs. Dalloway incorporates the elegiac motifs of *Jacob's Room*, but it examines more closely and more fruitfully the limits of personal freedom, the use and abuse of history in the determination of the "modern" self, and the meaning as well as the source of human happiness. The June day on which the novel centers justifies its claims to importance by being the day during which Mrs. Dalloway realizes and recovers from the "illness" afflicting her heart. The therapeutic agency of the novel is what Nietzsche calls [in *The Use and Abuse of History*] the "plastic power" of the creative individual, community, or culture, "the power of specifically growing out of one's self, of making the past and the strange one body with the near and the present, of healing wounds, replacing what is lost, repairing broken molds." The novel's specific project is to unite in one body the memories of the past, symbolized by Bourton, the scene of Clarissa's youth and the legacy of a familial and national heritage, with the present and near, symbolized by the city of London, which incarnates "this moment in June."

The novel begins with a gaiety and an inconsequence that both belie and confirm the "momentousness" of the events that follow. Clarissa Dalloway sets out on her morning errands in a state of exhilaration: "What a lark! What a plunge!" This carefree plunge into the present moment "fresh as if issued to children on a beach" suggests the possibility of an unhistorical happiness, a happiness measured, as Nietzsche says, by the ability to "go into" the present "like a number, without leaving any curious remainder." Experiencing such pleasure initiates an impulsive forward motion in consciousness and life that subsequent events, like some curious remainders, will check or qualify. Intimations of the counter-motion immediately appear when Clarissa, recovering the image of the past at Bourton, suddenly feels her light-hearted gaiety shadowed by the solemnity of darker historical reflections:

> How fresh, how calm, stiller than this of course, the air was in the early morning; like the flap of a wave; the kiss of a wave; chill and sharp and yet (for a girl of eighteen as she then was) solemn, feeling as she did, standing there at the open window, that something awful was about to happen.

In a curious conflation of historical "times," the past eclipses the present with its premonitions of a disastrous future. This tension between the unhistorical happiness in plunging spontaneously into the present and the anxiety such spontaneity produces determines the emotional rhythm or contratempo of the novel.

This dialectic between unhistorical happiness and historical memories and intuitions, related through the primary metaphor of an expanding and contracting spirit, is the source of the novel's exquisite suspense and excitement. These "pulsations" produce the "excitement of . . . rising and falling," an excitement associated with but not confined to Clarissa's heart. To expand and contract is to rise and to fall, build up and come down, like the "waves of that divine vitality which Clarissa loved." These verticalities describe the peaks and the depths of the novel's image of life as wavelike motion: "So on a summer's day waves collect, overbalance, and fall; collect and fall." Each moment, like Yeats's "one throb of the artery," is an occasion for creation and decreation, an affirmation that generates its own negation. This metaphor has its base in a physiological reality. A permanently dilated heart, like a permanently contracted heart, is a sign or portent of death. Whatever is alive is throbbing; the pulse *is* the one "vital" sign of life.

The cumulative effect of these discrete moments of rising and falling, however, constitutes a constructive action. Waves collect as they rise. In the expansive moments of the "heart," such as Mrs. Dalloway's delight in the morning, her walk through London, her sewing ("building it up, first one thing, then another"), and her giving a party, life is collected, generating the illusion that life is a movement forwards as well as upwards. The contractive moments, most obviously symbolized in the suspenseful pauses that precede the tollings of Big Ben, solidify the seriousness of the narrative. Rising and falling as vertical motions have their counterparts in anticipation and retrospection as horizontal movements. These vertical and horizontal narrative lines intersect to form the temporal axis around which the novel revolves. They are the coordinates, however, of a structure whose center is hollow. "There is an emptiness about the heart of life," observes the narrator, just as Clarissa, on hearing of Septimus's suicide, exclaims, "Oh, in the *middle* of my party, here's death" (emphasis mine). To reach the center is to find, like Rezia, "sheltering under the thin hollow of a leaf," or, like Septimus, to see in the pattern of rising and falling the image of a "hollow wave." In the middle, at the center, is emptiness, stasis, death.

The empty center that paradoxically manages to coordinate a structure of temporal relations also governs the nexus of personal relationships. The central relationship of the novel is between Clarissa and Septimus Smith, a relationship that only exists in terms of the novel's thematic and metaphoric texture. In orchestrating Clarissa Dalloway's spiritual recovery with the suicide of Septimus Smith, Virginia Woolf saw that her original intention in writing the novel—to depict "the world seen by the sane and insane side by side"—would only be justified if she could bring the two visions into conjunction. She solved the narrative problem by splitting the traditionally indivisible atom of narrative climax into its constituent parts—the catastrophe (or suicide) and the belated anagnorisis that reveals its meaning. Through this purely formal device, Woolf could dramatize the proximity of the mad and sane vision of the world without obscuring or blurring the distinction that makes madness and sanity adjacent, *never identical,* aspects of the same reality. Thus Clarissa can, through Septimus's suicide, reach the mystical center, the fatality buried in the heart of the novel, but because she is sane, avoid succumbing to it herself.

As the novel's initiatory and recurrent desire to plunge modulates into the climactic action of Septimus Smith's fatal "fall," the narrative discloses the mythic origin of its image of fatality. Septimus Smith, "lately taken from life to death, the Lord who had come to renew society," identifies the ever receding, ever approaching "center" as "the meadow of life beyond a river where the dead walk." The mythos of voyage and solitary travelling that informs the novel's metaphoric surfaces is organized and revolves around the epic motif of the descent into the underworld, conventionally the realm wherein the secrets of history and human destiny are revealed. Such descent myths operate powerfully, if subliminally, on "the public-spirited, British

Empire, tariff-reform, governing-class spirit," the "Dalloway" spirit, adding a special poignancy, perhaps illegitimate, to England's sense of national mission. Clarissa's social faith, which Peter Walsh attempts both to criticize and explain, rests on the metaphoric foundation that conceives of the British body politic as an imperilled, foundering ship of State: "As we are a doomed race, chained to a sinking ship (her favourite reading as a girl was Huxley and Tyndall, and they were fond of these nautical metaphors), as the whole thing is a bad joke, let us, at any rate do our part."

The interpolation of this mythos also implies a more complicated relationship between *Mrs. Dalloway* and *Ulysses,* whose resemblances have been examined by many commentators, a relationship not based exclusively on Woolf's revisionist impulse to "re-do" the Viceregal cavalcade in *Ulysses* or to compete with the patriarchal fiction of Joyce's one-day narrative with a feminine fiction of her own. Woolf's admiration for the "Hades" episode in *Ulysses* suggests that *Mrs. Dalloway* continues as well as reinterprets the modernist preoccupation with Ulyssean narratives and Wasteland myths. There are, for example, close symbolic analogues between "Hades" and *Mrs. Dalloway,* particularly in their shared system of double and warring images of heart—the "organ" of "Hades" as it is of *Mrs. Dalloway*—and ghosts, the spectres of the past, both personal and impersonal, haunting the consciousness of characters who have "been through it all." Both narratives deal with the profoundest memories of human loss that test, criticize, and often mock "the atheist's religion" of their central characters: the memory of Clarissa's sister, Sylvia, felled in the prime of life resembling Bloom's recollections of his dead son, Rudy. Both struggle with the knowledge, unprotected by myth, that history and injustice are one.

Where Woolf departs from Joyce is in her thorough skepticism about the structures (Joyce's micro- and macrocosms) Western culture has constructed on the "void incertitude" and in her radical inquiry into the grounds and legitimacy of the authority commanded by the phantom powers of history, society, and religion over life itself. Because the center of life *is* empty, its territory is both haunted and humanly disputed. Contending for hegemony over the void incertitude are those "spectres which one battles in the night; . . . spectres who stand astride us and suck up half our life-blood, dominators and tyrants." The chief spectre for Clarissa in this passage is Miss Kilman, whose name is itself antithetical; there is the obvious pun on "killman," the vampire spirit that feasts on human vitality, but also "Doris," the gift of god, from the sea. This "double" name accounts for the doubleness of Clarissa's feeling about the "mixed" gifts of the gods and about Miss Kilman herself: "for no doubt with another throw of the dice, had the black been uppermost and not the white, she would have loved Miss Kilman. But not in this world. No." History, Miss Kilman's specialty, carries the authority of irrevocability; unlike a game of chance, its course is irreversible.

The most important spectre of domination, then, is the ubiquitous power of time itself. The working title of the novel, *The Hours*, mythologically the daughters of Themis, goddess of Order, and guardians of the gates of Heaven, conveyed the idea of an autonomous temporality that mediated between history and eternity. The impressive specificity of the finished novel's chronological sequence, its obsessive time-keeping, acknowledges the rein of the Hours, while systematically demystifying their authority. In a passage cancelled in the final revisions of the manuscript, Woolf had identified the "seat of time" in the island of Westminster:

> It might have been the seat of time itself, this island of Westminster, the forge where the hours were made, & sent out, in various tones and tempers, to glide into the lives of the foot passengers, of studious workmen[,] desultory women within doors, who coming to the window looked up at the sky as the clock struck, as if to say, What? or Why? They had their choice of answers.

The mythological project of fashioning the Hours devolves into the human order where time-keeping becomes an arbitrary, though necessary, convention. Westminster *might* have been the seat of time, had not the human congregation appealed to a higher authority to verify the meaning of this secular usurpation. The "choice of answers" available to the human subjects of time suggests Woolf's interest in decentralizing and displacing the power of time from its royal seat and distributing it among separate and multitudinous centers, all generating their own interpretations of time's meaning. Thus the comic dispute between St. Margaret's and Big Ben that "now, really & indeed, it was half past eleven." Thus the necessity to "think how not merely that time differed but that the tone of it was possessed of the strangest power; now militant and masculine; now curtly prosaic, & now in the voice of St. Margaret's flower in the mind." The demystification of the reign of time as an incontestible order explains why, of all the experiences of time, prescience is the most suspect. Peter Walsh's famous predictions that Clarissa would marry a Prime Minister and stand at the top of the stairs is emblematic of Woolf's Shakespearean sense of prophecy as equivocation. Time is both what is and is not, what speaks, but, like the witches in Macbeth, speaks imperfectly.

The indeterminacy of time explains the transposition of the passage quoted above into its final form. The narrator's quasi-allegorical fantasy of the Hours yields to the more emotional resonances of the "tone" in which time speaks to Clarissa:

> For having lived in Westminster—how many years now? over twenty,—one feels even in the midst of the traffic, or waking at night, Clarissa was positive, a particular hush, or solemnity; an indescribable pause; a suspense (but that might be her heart, affected, they said, by influenza) before Big Ben strikes. There! Out it boomed. First a warning, musical; then the hour, irrevocable. The leaden circles dissolved in the air. Such fools we are, she thought, crossing Victoria Street. For Heaven only knows why one loves it so, how one sees it so, making it up, building it round one, tumbling it, creating it every moment afresh.

In the midst of day or in the dead of night may come that indescribable pause intervening, perhaps blocking, the passage from one moment to the next. But the association between this disruptive pause in the continuous traffic of life and the portentous feeling that something awful is about to happen may be the feeling peculiar to the "affected" or diseased heart. Clarissa herself dismisses the idea of an "irrevocable" hour as her mind submits to the flux, the unstructured flow of moments that constitutes the vital and creative motion of life—"making it up, building it round one, tumbling it" every moment afresh. The shift from past tense to present participles, verb forms of continual or continuing motion, introduces a new feeling for time as a pure and fluid medium out of which the mind creates, destroys, and recreates its own subjective order. Time is Janus-faced, an image of freedom and an image of fate. As a series of occasions on which to make and build up one's moment, time guarantees the freedom to create life "each moment afresh." But that series is inscribed on "a dial cut in impassive stone," on whose graduated face Clarissa reads her irrevocable fate—"how it is certain we must die."

This is the complex patterning that determines the dual and decentralized structure of fate in *Mrs. Dalloway*. On the one hand, time mediates between experience and the experiencing self:

> There was a mystery about it. You were given a sharp, acute, uncomfortable grain—the actual meeting; horribly painful as often as not; yet in absence, in the most unlikely places, it would flower out, open, shed its scent, let you touch, taste, look about you, get the whole feel of it and understanding, after years of lying lost.

Such is the Woolfian version of "spots of time." The experience ("a sharp, acute, uncomfortable grain") flowers over time and permits the experiencing self to feel and to understand the meaning of its singular life. The recovery of experience echoes the theme of Clarissa's recuperation and suggests the way in which spiritual reparation is to be achieved. The continuity between past acts and present feelings insures that over time the self is continuous and stable. Time contributes to the stability of personality in its role as the preserver, the advocate of the individual self in the uniqueness of its experience. On the other hand, time is the destroyer, the agent of mutability and change, the threat to continuity and "this interminable life." Between the woof of time the preserver and the warp of time the destroyer is woven—the self.

THE SCENES OF INSPIRATION

Also subject to Woolf's decentralizing and discriminating intelligence is the category of homogeneous space. Time presents the occasion, space the scene for that continual dilation and contraction that constitutes the source of the novel's exquisite suspense and delight. The authority of space is disseminated and distributed among three controlling metaphors of place: the London streets; the house; and, within the house, the final interiorization of subjective space, the "attic" room. Each setting provides its own unique consolation to the irrevocable decrees of time—how it is certain we must die.

The public spaces of London's streets represent what pastoral landscapes represented to the Romantics—the inspiriting scene that provides the "plaguy spirit" with intimations of its own immortality. Clarissa's youthful "transcendental theory" of life evolves out of her experience of urban place. In an important reminiscence, Peter Walsh recalls the occasion and logic of her theory:

> Clarissa had a theory in those days—they had heaps of
> theories, always theories, as young people have. It was to
> explain the feeling they had of dissatisfaction; not knowing
> people; not being known. For how could they know each
> other? You met every day; then not for six months, or
> years. But she said, sitting on the bus going up Shaftesbury
> Avenue, she felt herself everywhere; not "here, here, here";
> and she tapped the back of the seat; but everywhere.

Here space, the indivisible space of the self, is, like time, unseated from
its confining locality of "here, here, here" and rendered, again like
time, ubiquitous. This theory modulates into a kind of comic urban
gothic in which Clarissa entertains the possibility that "the unseen part
of us, which spreads wide, the unseen might survive, be recovered
somehow attached to this person or that, or even haunting certain
places after death . . . perhaps—perhaps." "Street-haunting" is one of
Woolf's favorite metaphors for the "London adventure" of the inquisi-
tive spirit seeking in life the scene of its future haunts, projecting
beyond its own death the prospect of its eternal attachments to people
and places.

Clarissa Dalloway's own adventure in street-haunting confirms
and persuades that the spirit will survive in space:

> Did it matter then, she asked herself, walking towards Bond
> Street, did it matter that she must inevitably cease com-
> pletely? All this must go on without her; did she resent it, or
> did it not become consoling to believe that death ended
> absolutely? But that somehow in the streets of London, on
> the ebb and flow of things, here, there, she survived, Peter
> survived, lived in each other, she being part, she was posi-
> tive, of the trees at home; of the house there, ugly, rambling
> all to bits and pieces as it was; part of people she had never
> met; being laid out like a mist between the people she knew
> best, who lifted her on their branches as she had seen the
> trees lift the mist, but it spread ever so far, her life, herself.

Transcending the ruins of time (the house rambling all to bits and
pieces) and the imperfect knowledge that plagues all human relationships, is the power of the single life to disperse itself so far and so wide
beyond its physical or visible boundaries that no one death can completely annihilate it. Clarissa's faith in the ubiquity of the spirit con-

soles her that death ends the seen, but not the unseen, essential part of human existence. This extension and investment of the self into its human and physical surroundings answers to a deep need in Clarissa, her need, as Peter Walsh says, to be "like something alive which wants to confide itself, to disperse itself, to be, with a tremor of delight, at rest." To be at rest, with its attendant tremor of delight, echoes the "indescribable pause" that precedes the tolling of the irrevocable hour and reinforces the notion that death represents an attenuation rather than a termination of life. It is this sense of life as "something central which permeated" that lends peacefulness to the images of death as a laying or a stretching out. Death seems to complete rather than disrupt a life whose inner dynamic has been one of dispersing and projecting the self out of the body that houses but cannot contain it.

Self-dispersal is both the augury of immortality and the antidote for temporal anxiety. Yet the antidote may have averse as well as therapeutic effects on the diseased heart. The unforeseen consequence in "street-haunting" is to disperse and confide the self so widely that the seen and the unseen become radically disassociated. The crucial metaphor of invisibility, on which the whole structure of Clarissa's transcendental theory of being is based, is transposed into a metaphor for vacancy: "She had the oddest sense of being herself invisible, unseen; unknown; there being no more marrying, no more having of children now, but only this astonishing and rather solemn progress with the rest of them, up Bond Street, this being Mrs. Dalloway; not even Clarissa any more; this being Mrs. Richard Dalloway." The latent schizophrenia in Clarissa's divorce of body and spirit surfaces in the self-perception that she has become a public personage, appropriately labelled "Mrs. Richard Dalloway," that coexists but is not identical with the private person, Clarissa. Now the urban gothic is transformed into psychological gothic, the ghost haunting the mind is the insubstantial body itself: "this body, with all its capacities, seemed nothing—nothing at all." The body exists as a reminder of the prior claims Nature exerts over the spirit.

The chastising of the vagabond spirit is movingly represented in the "homecoming" scene when Clarissa returns from her morning excursion in street-haunting. She allows her "self" to be sheltered and enclosed within the protective confines of the house. The house provides a more humanized sense of space because, as Gaston Bachelard has remarked, "its councils of continuity are unceasing. Without it man would be a dispersed being" (*The Poetics of Space,* tr. Maria Jolas).

But at the heart of the house, with its intimations of personal, social, and historical continuities, there exists the attic room and *its* councils of ritual isolation. This explains why Clarissa's withdrawal from the world and her subsequent exploration of interior space is conceived as an ascetic rite of absolution and why her central confession consists in acknowledging "the buds of the tree of life" for "the flowers of darkness they are." It also explains why the ritual of self-confrontation occurs at midday, the *hora demonium* in which the human aspiration to penetrate the mystery of life is simultaneously a recognition of the vanity of such knowledge. Clarissa's spiritual ascent thus culminates in an equivocal epiphany: "There was the green linoleum and a tap dripping. There was an emptiness about the heart of life; an attic room. Women must put off their rich apparel. At midday they must disrobe." The use of "must" implies that such penetrations into the interior constitute the categorical imperative for the feminine consciousness, perhaps because men have abandoned—or delegated—responsibility for the house and its mysteries to women. Given Clarissa's undisputed hegemony over the "interior," it is surprising that the human lust for mastery does not assert itself. As the room's two resident symbols of bed and mirror suggest, the feminine space provides the scene, not of self-assertion, but self-abnegation (complicated by the ritual reluctance to disrobe) and self-contemplation. In bed, the soul is recumbent, allowing itself to be visited by the spectres of its own failures and the admonishing voice of Nature (who is invariably wise):

> So the room was an attic; the bed narrow; and lying there reading, for she slept badly, she could not dispel a virginity preserved through childbirth which clung to her like a sheet. Lovely in girlhood, suddenly there came a moment—for example on the river beneath the woods at Clieveden—when, through some contraction of this cold spirit, she had failed him. And then at Constantinople, and again and again. She could see what she lacked. It was not beauty; it was not mind. It was something central which permeated; something warm which broke up surfaces and rippled the cold contact of men and women. For *that* she could dimly perceive. She resented it, had a scruple picked up Heaven knows where, or as she felt, sent by Nature (who is invariably wise).

Here the memory of place—Clieveden and Constantinople—works to contain and localize the moments of failure that occur "through some contraction of this cold spirit." The bounding of failure in specific places is important, for it releases the idea of virginity from the bondage of general and universal malaise. As a symbol of *sexual* failure, virginity is confined to the marital bed, where it does indeed suggest the lack of "something warm which broke up surfaces and rippled the cold contact of men and women." But virginity is also an exclusively feminine symbol of freedom and integrity. Thus Clarissa's resentment of the scruples sent by Nature are later transposed and defended in the great scene with Peter Walsh when she involuntarily responds to his intrusive, if welcome, appearance by hiding the dress she had been mending, "like a virgin protecting chastity, respecting privacy." The encounter between Peter and Clarissa, he brandishing his pen-knife, she defending herself against his implicit criticisms, is a comic variation of what Northrop Frye calls [in *The Secular Scripture*] "the stock convention of virgin-baiting." Deep within this convention, Frye explains, "is a vision of human integrity imprisoned in a world it is in but not of, often forced by weakness into all kinds of ruses and stratagems, yet always managing to avoid the one fate which really is worse than death, the annihilation of one's identity."

It is this deep, alternative understanding of virginity as a symbol of spiritual inviolability that accounts for the complementary symbols of bed, where virginity is contemplated as an image of failure, and mirror, where virginity is contemplated as an image of integrity. Gazing into her mirror, Clarissa recovers a vision of intact identity in "seeing the delicate pink face of the woman who was that very night to give a party; of Clarissa Dalloway; of herself." Now the public personage, Mrs. Dalloway, coexists and is identical with the private person, Clarissa. In the complete transparency of this moment of integration, Clarissa can see her face, "with the same imperceptible contraction," in a more positive way:

That was her self—pointed; dartlike; definite. That was her self when some effort, some call on her to be her self drew the parts together, she alone knew how different, how incompatible and composed so for the world only into one centre, one diamond, one woman who sat in her drawing-room and made a meeting-point, a radiancy no doubt in some dull lives, a refuge for the lonely to come to, perhaps.

The virginal contraction of spirit collects and concentrates the self into a diamond shape that acknowledges its status as a necessary social fiction "composed so for the world only into one centre." The different, often incompatible facets of that "diamond," identity, converge in a unified center, a meeting-point that assembles and composes, without annihilating, its separate parts into a whole. Thus the title of the novel, *Mrs. Dalloway,* which emphasizes the social radiancy and centrality of its heroine, yields to and is absorbed by its transformative ending—"It is Clarissa, he said"—an ending that is both the meeting-point and the terminal point of Clarissa Dalloway's quest for social and spiritual integration.

Frye suggests that the emblem for the virgin's closely guarded secret of invulnerability and preserved integrity is a "diamond set in a black horn, with the motto attached 'yet still myself' that appears in Sidney's *Arcadia*." Certainly it is this radiant yet fragile clarity that is the source of the "integrity" of Clarissa's feeling for Sally Seton, a feeling that is not based so much on narcissistic identification as feminine allegiance, the "sense of being in league together, a presentiment of something that was bound to part them (they spoke of marriage always as a catastrophe)." Clarissa's presentiments prove true, and the "catastrophe" of division and separation is narratively rendered in their respective marriages. But beneath the romantic fable, grounded in the scruples sent by Nature, that virgins marry and live "happily" ever after, there persists a virginal integrity that remains the exclusive knowledge of the female and a powerful source of feminine bonding.

As Frye concludes, "the beleaguered virgin may be more than simply a representative of human integrity: she may also exert a certain redemptive quality by her innocence and goodness, or, in other contexts, by her astuteness in management and intrigue." Woolf's portrait of the female artist of life, while incorporating the qualities of innocence and goodness, does not invoke them unconditionally. Knowing that these virtues ironically serve to promote the myth of innate feminine altruism, Woolf also emphasizes the guile of her feminine heroines, the strategy often adopted by the helpless or physically weak. The victory of guile is a comic victory, as Frye remarks, and in many ways assures a more lasting victory than the heroics of tragedy. The tragic, while making "the greatest impression on us," nevertheless often concludes with the death of the hero and the perception that strength is, after all, not invulnerable. What is curious and innovative about Woolf's comic victory over violence, alienation, and the tragic recognition of the inhuman and absolute power of time, is that her heroine of life, Clarissa Dalloway, gradually absorbs the traditional emblems of tragic posturing into her own social bearing and demeanor. The various mock-epic similes of the novel (such as the mock-heroic return from "battle" in which Lucy "disarms" Clarissa of her umbrella) assume more serious meaning in the novel's final sequence—the party itself.

The scene is the drawing-room that mediates between the public streets and the private rooms where we exist "alone, alone, alone." During the party, the criticisms of Peter Walsh ("the perfect hostess he called her") and Miss Kilman (that her life "was a tissue of vanity and deceit") are silenced by Clarissa's ability to act on her feeling for life. The metaphor verifying the connection between Clarissa's vision of life and life itself is the indispensable metaphor of the heart: "Like the pulse of a perfect heart, life struck straight through the streets," comments the narrator. Clarissa's "triumph" is announced in similar terms: "walking down the room with him [the Prime Minister], with Sally there and Peter there and Richard very pleased, with all those people rather inclined, perhaps, to envy, she had felt that intoxication of the moment, that dilation of the nerves of the heart itself till it seemed to quiver, steeped, upright." Clarissa's exultant posture recalls the "perfectly upright and stoical bearing" bred into the English by "this late age of the world's experience" and is associated with "the woman she admired most," Lady Bexborough, who opened a bazaar with the telegram announcing the death of her favorite son in her hand. It is the bearing of women of a certain class, conscious inheritors and continuers of the tradition of public service, hostesses who, reluctant to inflict their individuality, bury their private grief.

THE MYTH OF SOCIAL HAPPINESS

But Clarissa's upright bearing in the company of the Prime Minister also discloses a connection with a more ambiguous authority, miming as it does the posture of political power. Peter Walsh's prediction, complete with ironical twists, that Clarissa would marry a Prime Minister and stand at the top of the stairs, implies a real, perhaps unconscious fascination with power that manifests itself in Clarissa's lapses into snobbery. The correspondences between the public and private exercises of the will are dramatized when Clarissa, observing the talismanic disc of authority flashed by the royal car, consciously equates the power of the State, a power held "by force of its own lustre" with her own power to kindle and illuminate: "She stiffened a little; so she would stand at the top of her stairs." The symbolic presence of the "State" in *Mrs. Dalloway* is so imposing because the state possesses a special kind of power and authority. The state enjoys perpetuity in time and omnipresence in space (symbolized by the Union Jack and other portable symbols of imperial dominion). Thus as the motorcade embodying "the voice of authority" passes through the heart of London, it exerts a formidable and emotional common appeal: "for in all the hat shops and tailors' shops strangers looked at each other and thought of the dead; of the flag; of Empire." Paradoxically, the imminence of Royalty that makes the gathering crowd think "of the heavenly life divinely bestowed upon Kings" derives its own authority through the most fugitive of communal voices; it exists virtually by the power of rumor.

As the congregations of loyal subjects gather at the gates of Buckingham Palace, they cannot even locate the seat of the power they revere and obey, bestowing their emotion vainly, as the narrator satirically observes, "upon commoners out for a drive." Nevertheless, the "phantom" power of the state is perceived as absolute, making the community "ready to attend their Sovereign, if need be, to the cannon's mouth, as their ancestors had done before them." The revived memory of past violence, the renewed readiness to attend their Sovereign to more violence, accounts for the horror that Septimus experiences as the motor car passes him. The necessary collective myth of national unity, once centered in an absolute icon of authority ("this gradual drawing together of everything to one centre before his eyes"), terrifies him:

> The world wavered and quivered and threatened to burst
> into flames. It is I who am blocking the way, he thought.
> Was he not being looked at and pointed at; was he not
> weighted there, rooted to the pavement, for a purpose? But
> for what purpose?

Septimus's presence in the novel is symbolically juxtaposed to the Prime Minister's to suggest that his "purpose" is to testify to the ambiguous status of social and political authority. The Prime Minister stands, with Clarissa, at the top of stairs, a visible symbol of the power of the ascendant classes, while Septimus occupies the threshold to that lower world where the myths of national destiny and identity originate. Like Forster's Leonard Bast in *Howards End,* Septimus embodies and characterizes the aspirations of the rising lower classes whose assimilation into the aristocratic upper order includes a radical reeducation in the established culture. As an English "type," Septimus, unlike the venerable Sir Hugh and the domineering Bradshaw, or even the aristocratic Lady Bruton, is drawn almost completely from the low-mimetic conventions of folktale and picaresque. He is a Dick Wittington figure who goes to London "leaving an absurd note behind him, such as great men have written, and the world has read later when the story of their struggles has become famous." The War, of course, provides the ironic culmination to Septimus's picaresque adventures. It is the European War that finally extinguishes his identity and exposes "the whole show"—friendship, helpless love for Isabel Pole, the England that consists almost entirely of Shakespeare's plays. And it is the war that transforms Septimus, the lower class upstart who failed in his effort to rise, into Septimus the scapegoat who assumes society's burden of guilt. The Prime Minister is a symbol of Empire without guilt, for all disgrace has been displaced onto Septimus, tormented by his sense of having committed "an appalling crime." Septimus thus obtains a double status in the novel, being both society's scapegoat and its "giant mourner." It is he who most radically challenges, by the fixity of his vision and the oppressive weight of his guilt, the myth of social happiness.

Woolf's vision of society and the State is grounded in an irresolvable ambivalence: she recognizes that the basis for personal and historical continuity resides in the illusion of community and social order, but is plagued by the knowledge, never completely redeemed, that the power of social illusion is closely allied to delusion. This is the meaning of the airplane sequence that concludes the morning adventures of the novel and reveals, through its horribly deflationary denouement, that the communal symbols of aspiration, of shared dreams, of the spiritual determination to transcend the limits of material existence, are themselves written in corrupt and corruptible words. Even the narrator shares Bond Street's fascination with the looping airplane "sped of its own free will" and ascending "straight up, like something mounting in ecstasy, in pure delight." But haunting this apparition of sublimity and absolute freedom is a deep fear, the deepest fear of Clarissa herself, that grubbing at the roots of her soul, of every soul, is the monster hatred, that "the whole panoply of content [was] nothing but self love!"

It is this panoply of content—"all pleasure in beauty, in friendship, in being well, in being loved"—that the myth of social happiness upholds and sustains. It is through grubbing at the roots of this myth that Woolf makes her most searching criticism of the social order, partially through the self-inquisitions of Clarissa confronting her own hatred, loving her enemy Miss Kilman, partly through the sublime and unbearable madness of Septimus Smith, the "border case" who is the happiest man in the world and the most miserable.

Hatred in *Mrs. Dalloway* is both satisfying and real, more satisfying, more real, and finally more lasting than love itself. The true poet, Goethe remarks, must learn to hate, and perhaps Septimus's failure as a poet to communicate the birth of a new religion and the cult of universal love originates in his inability to isolate and oppose the objects of his hatred. For him, it is human nature itself which is "the brute monster," personified in but not confined to the figures of Holmes and Bradshaw. He cannot disassociate, as Clarissa and the narrator can, monstrous ideas from the people who personify them, a telling and ultimately fatal confusion. Woolf's enlightened woman reserves her hatred "for ideas not people." Through such an act of discrimination, Clarissa registers her psychological victory over Miss Kilman. When Miss Kilman waits for Elizabeth at the top of the stairs, a usurping presence standing "with the power and taciturnity of some prehistoric monster armoured for primeval warfare," Clarissa allows the idea of Miss Kilman to diminish and watches her become "second by second merely Miss Kilman, in a mackintosh, whom Heaven knows Clarissa would have liked to help": "At this dwindling of the monster, Clarissa laughed."

Clarissa's laughter, sign of an internal triumph over hatred, triggers her defiant assault on the monster herself. "Remember the party," she cries out to her enemy, the triumphant cry of the soul that Kilman had wished to subdue. Clarissa's laughter is also thoughtful laughter, as her subsequent meditations on the idea of love and religion, now divorced from the "body" of the departed Miss Kilman, reveal. In the novel's most sustained inquiry into the motives and principles of human action, Clarissa rejects love and religion, the traditional foundations for social law and the favorite masks of the authoritarian will, as moral or ethical absolutes. It is not just that love and religion, like all "causes," make people callous, but that they destroy, through the sheer force of their will to universality, Woolf's only absolute—the privacy of the soul:

Why creeds and prayers and mackintoshes? when, thought
Clarissa, that's the miracle, that's the mystery; that old lady,
she meant, whom she could see going from chest of drawers
to dressing-table. She could still see her. And the supreme
mystery which Kilman might say she had solved, or Peter
might say he had solved, but Clarissa didn't believe either of
them had the ghost of an idea of solving, was simply this:
here was one room; there another. Did religion solve that,
or love?

The old lady, who throughout the novel represents an inviolable
individuality, symbolizes the mystery and the perplexity complicating
Clarissa's—and by extension Woolf's—effort to create a stable,
nonauthoritarian community of relations. No solution may be forthcoming, because of the contrary and conflicting claims of liberty, the
irreducible and inalienable right of the soul to its privacy, and community, which more often than not exists by virtue of an enforced or
passive conformity. The repeated references to Kilman's mackintosh
and to Septimus's shabby overcoat suggest the authentic nature of this
dilemma, echoing as they do John Stuart Mill's famous analogy in *On
Liberty*:

Human beings are not like sheep; and even sheep are not
undistinguishably alike. A man cannot get a coat or a
pair of boots to fit him unless they are either made to his
measure, or he has a whole warehouseful to choose from:
and is it easier to fit him with a life than with a coat,
or are human beings more like one another in their whole
physical and spiritual conformation than in the shape of
their feet?

Mrs. Dalloway is, of course, filled with characters who, like Clarissa,
refuse to be suitably fitted with the life prescribed for them, and even
those, like Septimus, who cannot find a coat made to his measure.
Only the thoroughly socialized, if "admirable" Sir Hugh, is blessed
with a "very well-covered, manly, extremely handsome, perfectly
upholstered body" that even Clarissa suspects is "almost too well
dressed." Love, religion, and the social faith that adorns the manners
and the breeding of the English character exercise a powerful but
dubious authority in the novel. They inspire both admiration (Peter,
despite his "horrible passion," is "adorable," Kilman possesses an

impressive historical mind, Hugh Whitbread is useful in drafting letters to the *Times*) and fear.

This fear is localized and personified in Bradshaw, who Rezia and Clarissa, besides the mad Septimus, both intuit to be obscurely evil. It is in the authoritarian figure of the benevolent thaumaturge that the individual and social lust to effect a tyrannical synthesis of physical and spiritual conformation is dramatized. Bradshaw administers and executes the law of social happiness. He insists that the mad regain their sense of proportion (for health is proportion), ordering bed rest, solitude, silence and rest "until a man who went in weighing seven stone six comes out weighing twelve." The long excursus on Bradshaw's twin goddesses, Proportion and Conversion, coming almost in the dead center of the novel and ironically reflecting on Clarissa's own *hora demonium* (Septimus's interview with Bradshaw occurs, like Clarissa's ritual disrobing, at midday) represents Woolf's most systematic and sustained attempt to demystify established structures of authority.

In his study of *Madness and Civilization,* Michel Foucault identifies these structures: "Family-Child relations, centered on the theme of parental authority; Transgression-Punishment relations, centered on the theme of immediate justice; Madness-Disorder relations, centered on the theme of social and moral order." Bradshaw is the resolute champion of all these orders, inspiring the respect of his colleagues, the fear of his subordinates, and the gratitude of his patients' families. But he is an even more resolute defender of the inherited prerogatives of class in propagating the self-serving myth that the unsocial impulses of the defenseless, exhausted, and friendless are "bred more than anything by the lack of good blood." Class pride, however, is itself a metaphor for the fanaticism of all true believers, the self-righteous elect confidently asserting that "this is madness, this sense." Bradshaw, and the prosperous England whose will he executes, is not hesitant, like Clarissa Dalloway and Woolf herself, to define reality for others. Hence the quasi-incestuous relationship between his goddesses, Proportion and her sister Conversion, twin divinities masquerading as universal love, duty and self-sacrifice, yet secretly in love with their own stern countenances. It is this self-love that grubs at the roots of England's panoply of content and that provokes Conversion's desire "to impress, to impose, adoring her own features stamped on the face of the populace." In the heat and sand of India, in the mud and swamp of Africa, in the purlieus of London, comments the narrator, the dissenting, the dissentient, the dissatisfied receive the impress of the English will, bow to the overriding lust of Conversion "to stamp indelibly in the sanctuaries of others the image of herself."

MADNESS AND THE WORK OF ART

To cleanse the sanctuary and to cast from the temple its false idols of Proportion and Conversion is the special mission of the novel. Woolf dramatizes several self-defensive strategies by which the soul attempts to protect and secure its right to privacy. One is fantasy, "the better part of life," as Peter Walsh notes as he follows a young woman across Trafalgar Square, "making oneself up; making her up; creating an exquisite amusement, and something more." The object of Peter's fantasy emits her own curious kind of "excitement," whispering as she does "his name, not Peter, but his private name which he called himself in his own thoughts." But private fantasy, harmless and disinterested as it is, refreshing the soul with its promise of reckless, romantic adventure, is only an exquisite amusement—and nothing more. As Peter realizes, such fantasies cannot be shared: "It smashed to atoms."

Besides fantasy, there are unconscious cosmic reveries, like Clarissa's "star-gazing" and its opposite, "musing among the vegetables." And there are actual dreams, like Peter Walsh's diseased dream proclaiming "the death of the soul." Staring out of that dream is the countenance of a more benevolent female deity "showering down from her magnificent hands compassion, comprehension, absolution." This giant figure of divinized womanhood is metamorphosed, through the curious dream-logic of Peter's midday visions, into the spectral figure of an "elderly woman who seems . . . to be the figure of the mother whose sons have been killed in the battles of the world." The wish content of Peter's dream, also latent in the novel itself, is to restore the privileged relationship between mothers and sons, fathers and daughters. Sally Seton's maternal pride in her five sons, Elizabeth's devotion to her father contribute to the emotional success of Clarissa's party. But the dream of restoring these familial bonds is threatened by solitary experiences and private fears: Clarissa, anxious about losing Elizabeth to Miss Kilman; Rezia separated from her family, and of course, the radical alienation of Septimus Smith. It is partially to escape his mother that Septimus leaves home.

The phantasmagoric visions of "the solitary traveller" find their most complete expression in the madness of Septimus Smith. Septimus is the eschatological figure in whom and through whom the novel's revolutionary millennialism is voiced. Disguised by his delirious and ecstatic prophecies of universal love and the end of the reign of Death is the authentically subversive content of his vision: the unsettling and dismantling of natural and social hierarchies, the levelling of the great chain of being in which dogs turn into men, the unmasking of human nature as a breed of "lustful animals, who have no lasting emotions, but only whims and vanities, eddying them now this way, now that." Septimus's creed of universal love is a deception of a deception, for illness, as Woolf remarked in her essay "On Being Ill," "often takes on the disguise of love, and plays the same odd tricks":

> It invests certain faces with divinity, sets us to wait, hour after hour, with pricked ears for the creaking of a stair, and wreathes the faces of the absent (plain enough in health, Heaven knows) with a new significance, while the mind concocts a thousand legends and romances about them for which it has neither time nor taste in health.

In the hallucinations of illness (like Clarissa's influenza), in the delirium of frustrated passion (like Peter Walsh's fearful premonition of "death that surprised in the midst of life, Clarissa falling where she stood"), and in the apocalyptic fantasies of the mad Septimus (the world threatening to burst into flames), the line of division between the real and the imaginary is erased, disclosing the void incertitude. The buried anxiety of the novel is that the lunatic, the lover, and the poet *are* of imagination all compact in bodying forth the forms of things unknown.

This anxious intuition that the work of art and the hallucinatory forms of madness interpenetrate and communicate with frightening familiarity suggests a disturbing relationship between the narrator and Septimus, the visionary poet. His innumerable scribblings and his poetic testament, an immortal ode to Time, reflect on the narrator's romantic treatment of time as a structure of symbolic correspondences. He, like the narrator, is the transcriber of voices issuing from the land of the living and the dead. He exercises an enviable freedom with words and symbols and those meaningless sounds through which the beauty of the world is communicated. Viewing the soaring airplane inscribing letters in the sky, he can interpret the beauty of the world which lies "beyond seeking and questing and knocking of words together":

> So, thought Septimus, looking up, they are signalling to me. Not indeed in actual words; that is, he could not read

the language yet; but it was plain enough, this beauty, this exquisite beauty, and tears filled his eyes as he looked at the smoke words languishing and melting in the sky and bestowing upon him in their inexhaustible charity and laughing goodness one shape after another of unimaginable beauty and signalling their intention to provide him, for nothing, for ever, for looking merely, with beauty, more beauty!

If, as Peter Walsh speculates, "Nothing exists outside us except a state of mind," it is just possible that the universal state of mind—the world itself—may be mad, that is, without a determinate meaning or language of its own. In the intemperate madness of Septimus, who questions, impiously, life itself, the world reveals its beauty, a beauty that words can't express nor reason explain. This is the special dispensation in being ill:

> Incomprehensibility has an enormous power over us in illness, more legitimately perhaps than the upright will allow. In health meaning has encroached upon sound. Our intelligence domineers over our sense. But in illness, with the police off duty, we creep beneath some obscure poem by Mallarmé or Donne, some phrase in Latin or Greek, and the words give out their scent and distil their flavour, and then, if at last we grasp the meaning, it is all the richer for having come to us sensually first, by way of the palate and the nostrils, like some queer odour.
>
> (Woolf, "On Being Ill")

In illness, sounds are released, legitimately perhaps, from the meaning that has encroached upon them in health. Through the queer power of synaesthesia enjoyed by the diseased imagination, Reason, the tyrant, is dethroned. Sound is set free, like the sound of St. Margaret's, to glide into the recesses of the heart and bury itself in ring after ring of sound. Is this ring of sound the origin of "poésie pure," as Woolf's reference to Mallarmé suggests? Does the creativity of the poet lie in "taking his pain in one hand and a lump of pure sound in the other," just as, Woolf theorizes [in "On Being Ill"], "perhaps the people of Babel did in the beginning" when the first words were formed? Or is the non-sense spoken by the mad no language at all, merely words languishing and dissolving into their constituent sounds—"ee um fah um so / foo swee too eem oo"—the sounds of the eternal, unreasonable world itself? Is the primal voice of the earth "a frail quivering sound, a voice bubbling up without direction, vigour, beginning or end, running weakly and shrilly and with an absence of all human meaning . . . the voice of no age or sex"?

These unanswerable, not rhetorical questions suggest that the language of madness and the language of art may be continuous or contiguous discourses through which the mind, burdened with its visions of beauty and truth, communicates with and about the world. This does not mean, as Michel Foucault observes [in *Madness and Civilization*], speaking of the peculiar status of madness in the "modern" art of Nietzsche, Van Gogh, and Artaud, "that madness is the only language common to the work of art and the modern world." What it does mean, he argues, is that

> through madness, a work that seems to drown in the world, to reveal there its non-sense, and to transfigure itself with the features of pathology alone, actually engages within itself the world's time, masters it, and leads it; by the madness which interrupts it, a work of art opens a void, a moment of silence, a question without answer, provokes a breach without reconciliation where the world is forced to question itself. What is necessarily a profanation in the work of art returns to that point, and, in the time of that work swamped in madness, the world is made aware of its guilt.

The suicide of Septimus Smith constitutes the necessary profanation in *Mrs. Dalloway,* its illegality, its impiety, through which the world of the novel, assembled at its meeting-point in Clarissa Dalloway, is made aware of its guilt: "Somehow it was her disaster—her disgrace." In the time in which Clarissa's body ("Always her body went through it first") and mind succumb to the profound darkness and experience the suffocation of blackness symbolized by Septimus's death, Clarissa begins to question herself:

> A thing there was that mattered; a thing, wreathed about with chatter, defaced, obscured in her own life, let drop every day in corruption, lies, chatter. This he had preserved. Death was defiance.

With the clock striking the hour, the words "Fear no more the heat of the sun" come back to her, words that earlier in the day had disclosed to her the real time of the world, sounds of that eternal spring sighing throughout the novel's summer's day:

So on a summer's day waves collect, overbalance, and fall; collect and fall; and the whole world seems to be saying "that is all" more and more ponderously, until even the heart in the body which lies in the sun on the beach says too, That is all. Fear no more, says the heart. Fear no more, says the heart, committing its burden to some sea, which sighs collectively for all sorrows, and renews, begins, collects, lets fall.

THE LAWGIVER

But Clarissa, unlike Septimus, does not drown in the world's time. The lines from Imogen's dirge in *Cymbeline* connecting the visionary madness of Septimus to Clarissa's diseased heart, a heart which wishes to commit its burden to the sea, only seems to be saying "that is all." For just as Imogen is not really dead, so Clarissa's desire to succumb, to let fall, is surmounted by the "waves of that divine vitality which Clarissa loved." The sequence of the world's time that "begins, collects, lets fall" is not a single action, but a series of actions that repeat and renew this pattern. Septimus is the "drowned sailor" desperately trying to return to the shores of life, but his fatal plunge is echoed and transfigured by Clarissa's plunge into dark seas:

> She entered, and felt often as she stood hesitating one moment on the threshold of her drawing-room, an exquisite suspense, such as might stay a diver before plunging while the sea darkens and brightens beneath him, and the waves which threaten to break, but only gently split their surface, roll and conceal and encrust as they just turn over the weeds with pearl.

Clarissa can dive into deep seas, but she can also rise to the surface. For her, the waves that threaten to break "just turn over." This "turn" of the waves absorbs and transforms the profoundly tragic rhythm of the world—the tragic rhythm of rising that always concludes with a "fall"—into a comic arc. Clarissa, like Imogen, only feigns death. In her plunge into dark seas she does not drown but undergoes a Shakespearean sea-change:

> For this is the truth about our soul . . . our self, who fish-like inhabits deep seas and plies among obscurities thread-

ing her way between the boles of giant weeds, over sun-
flickered spaces and on and on into gloom, cold, deep,
inscrutable; suddenly she shoots to the surface and sports on
the wind-wrinkled waves; that is, has a positive need to
brush, scrape, kindle herself, gossiping.

Clarissa's ability to dart to the surface and sport on the wind-wrinkled
waves like a "creature floating in her element" distinguishes her from
Septimus, who goes "on and on into gloom." She undergoes a sea-
change, metamorphosed into a mermaid "lalloping on the waves."
Septimus is the dying god, his "body . . . macerated until only the nerve
fibres were left. It was spread like a veil upon a rock."

Thus while Septimus apprehends and is sacrificed to the "ghastly
beauty" of the world, it is Clarissa who comprehends the soul's divine,
precious truth. Woolf can affirm Septimus's tragic posture, his ceremonial baring of the body on the sacrificial rock, only as an act of
expiation and atonement, not as the sublime rebellion of the apocalyptic imagination. Like Joyce, she resists the apocalyptic urge to uncover
and expose the bare rock of the world and its inhuman time and
grounds her supreme fiction of the earth on the comic myths of eternal
return, eternal renewal. Her art is the art of lying, the art that creates
those necessary fictions that conceal the void incertitude, the Conradian
art that finds its ultimate justification in the lie that saves. Only Miss
Kilman prides herself in her incapacity to tell lies, but her commitment
to "truth" is associated with her demythifying desire to unmask, to
demoralize, to master the "soul" of Clarissa and the life she, unlike
Miss Kilman, loves. The failure to comprehend the characteristically
modern forms of Woolf's romanticism, the romanticism of Joyce,
Lawrence, and Conrad, has led many critics to misrepresent Woolf's
illusionism. Philip Rahv's criticism of the novel is in many ways
representative:

> Septimus is the mysterious stranger, the marked man, the
> poet upon whom an outrage has been committed. . . . This
> apparition haunted Mrs. Woolf, but she always strove to
> escape from it. She felt more at home with Mrs. Dalloway.
> ("Mrs. Woolf and Mrs. Brown")

Woolf's achievement, as Forster appreciated [in *Two Cheers for
Democracy*], was in conveying the sublimity of Septimus's apocalyptic
visions, without sentimentalizing his madness. If she evaded the spec-

tral apparition, it was a conscious evasion effected by adhering to the sanative and prescriptive formulae of comic art. *Mrs. Dalloway* is not a work of madness, but a work of art, and as Foucault reminds us, "where there is a work of art, there is no madness."

The point at which the narrative disassociates even as it emerges from the mad imaginations of Septimus is in the interpretative appropriations of the dirge from *Cymbeline,* "Fear no more the heat of the sun / Nor the furious winter's rages." For Septimus, "the message hidden in the beauty of words" in Shakespearean art is loathing, hatred, despair: "The secret signal which one generation passes, under disguise, to the next is loathing, hatred, despair. Dante the same. Aeschylus (translated) the same." Of course, it is precisely through such a secret and covert transmission of signals on which the narrator relies to effect the climactic and transformative identification of Clarissa with Septimus: "She felt somehow very like him, the young man who killed himself." But the message Septimus meant to communicate—"how Shakespeare loathed humanity—the putting on of clothes, the getting of children, the sordidity of the mouth and the belly!"—is misinterpreted and transvalued by Clarissa: "He made her feel the beauty; made her feel the fun. But she must go back. She must assemble. She must find Sally and Peter." Septimus either cannot feel the fun of life, the crime for which he stands self-condemned, or he feels the beauty of life too much. His tears, the tears of the "giant mourner" shed for all the sorrows of the world, are emblems of that morbidity that "is fatal to art, fatal to friendship," as Peter Walsh notes. Clarissa's feelings about suffering are of a different order. She transmutes her feelings of pain and loss into the art of life. Having penetrated into the heart of human corruption, she revives, and, obeying the summons of recall, returns to Sally and Peter, her "companions in the art of living."

This is the "normal outcome" in the work of mourning, which consists, as Freud writes, not in defying, but in deferring to reality:

> In what, now, does the work which mourning performs
> consist? . . . Reality-testing has shown that the loved object
> no longer exists, and it proceeds to demand that all libido
> shall be withdrawn from its attachments to that object. This
> demand arouses understandable opposition—it is a matter of
> general observation that people never willingly abandon a
> libidinal position, not even, indeed, when a substitute is
> already beckoning to them. This opposition can be so in-

tense that a turning away from reality takes place and a clinging to the object through the medium of a hallucinatory wishful psychosis.

("Mourning and Melancholia")

The dirge, Woolf suggests in her interpolations from *Cymbeline,* may be the original form of human art, the imagination's first radical testing of reality, the first necessary dissimulation by which the mind compromises and transforms its grief. The dirge artfully mourns the dead; its art soothes and consoles by disguising, and thus mocking, the verdict of reality. Certainly the work of mourning is the primary labor performed by the feminine imagination. Feminine art always seeks to restore the oppressed and mournful to the reality of ordinary life with its chatter, its gossip, its fun.

Even Septimus appreciates the compassionate presence of this feminine power as he watches and listens to Rezia as she sits sewing flowers on Mrs. Peters's hat, building it up, first one thing, then another, the slow, painful process, as Freud describes mourning, of carrying out the command of reality:

> Mrs. Peters had a spiteful tongue. Mr. Peters was in Hull. Why then rage and prophesy? Why fly scourged and out-cast? Why be made to tremble and sob by the clouds? Why seek truths and deliver messages when Rezia sat sticking pins into the front of her dress, and Mr. Peters was in Hull? Miracles, revelations, agonies, loneliness, falling through the sea, down, down into the flames, all were burnt out, for he had a sense, as he watched Rezia trimming the straw hat for Mrs. Peters, of a coverlet of flowers.

The female art consumes and transforms the apocalyptic hallucinations of the grief-stricken mind, its sobs, its trembling revelations, into "a coverlet of flowers." Flowers are the primary materials of feminine art, the transient, evanescent flowers of life and of darkness. But they are also emblems of the figurative powers of the feminine imagination, the flowers of the female mind that blossom for Rezia after Septimus's death when, half dreaming, there comes to her the "whisperings, . . . the caress of the sea . . . murmuring to her laid on shore, strewn she felt, like flying flowers over some tomb." For Septimus, Rezia herself is the flowering tree of life through whose branches he glimpses the face of the lawgiver:

She was a flowering tree; and through her branches looked out the face of a lawgiver, who had reached a sanctuary where she feared no one; not Holmes; not Bradshaw; a miracle, a triumph, the last and greatest. Staggering he saw her mount the appalling staircase, laden with Holmes and Bradshaw, men who never weighed less than eleven stone six, who sent their wives to Court, men who made ten thousand a year and talked of proportion; who different in their verdicts (for Holmes said one thing, Bradshaw another), yet judges they were; who mixed the vision and the sideboard; saw nothing clear, yet ruled, yet inflicted. "Must" they said. Over them she triumphed.

The last and greatest triumph in *Mrs. Dalloway* is in inaugurating, in the time of the novel, the reign of the feminine lawgiver who has reached the sanctuary where she fears no one. The lawgiver may be Nature, who is invariably wise. She may be that "state of mind" that exists outside us that Peter Walsh endows with womanhood. She may be Maisie Johnson sardonically advising that "life had been no mere matter of roses," but who transmutes the matter of her life through the work of mourning, imploring pity, "Pity for the loss of roses." The most imposing avatar of this female lawgiver who, staggering, mounts the appalling staircase, is the nameless old lady who reappears intermittently throughout the novel, the last time in connection with Septimus's death. She remains nameless, perhaps because, like the hostess, she is reluctant to inflict individuality. She exists as a psychic projection, a metacharacter whose function is to embody the dignity of our solitude and to suggest the infinite mystery about ourselves as "alone, alone, alone." She is indisputably the antitype of Clarissa and Septimus, both "lost in the process of living" in different ways. She preserves throughout the narrative her fascination for Clarissa as the one who does not suffer the "death of the soul." The attic room in which she moves is the sanctuary whose light is glimpsed at the moment it is extinguished.

It is clearing and defining this sacred inner space before it is overcome by darkness, defaced in corruption, that makes *Mrs. Dalloway* such a healthy work of the imagination. Possessed of the sanctuary, the lawgiver dispenses of her law, the law of natural, mutual, and voluntary association. Happiness, as Clarissa intuits, cannot be legislated by acts of parliament. It must be created through "pleasure-making," the pleasure-making symbolized by Clarissa Dalloway's party:

> But to go deeper, beneath what people said (and these judgements, how superficial, how fragmentary they are!) in her own mind now, what did it mean to her, this thing she called life? Oh, it was very queer. Here was So-and-so in South Kensington; some one up in Bayswater; and somebody else, say, in Mayfair. And she felt quite continuously a sense of their existence; and she felt what a waste; and she felt what a pity; and she felt if only they could be brought together; so she did it. And it was an offering; to combine, to create; but to whom?
>
> An offering for the sake of offering, perhaps. Anyhow it was her gift.

The degenerate, despotic utopias of Holmes and Bradshaw can only exist by enforcing the law of compulsive physical and spiritual conformity. Such utopias represent totalitarian social forms in which no exit, no protest is possible; their moral closure never admits of an opening. Men must not weigh less than eleven stone six and must accept, without appeal, the partial judgment that "this is sense, this madness" as the final, irrevocable decree of the goddess Proportion. Clarissa's ideal comic society is fashioned by another kind of symmetry, the symmetry of beauty, not the crude beauty of the eye, as Peter Walsh puts it, but beauty anyhow:

> It was straightness and emptiness of course; the symmetry
> of a corridor; but it was also windows lit up, a piano, a
> gramophone sounding; a sense of pleasure-making hidden,
> but now and again emerging.

The symmetry of beauty, and the pleasure it arouses, is the symmetry, the unbroken straightness, of the will exercising its right to moral choice. It is this symmetry that discloses and encloses that empty but unobstructed corridor that leads to the privacy of the soul and its freedom. Clarissa's party preserves the principle of voluntary, unenforced participation by acknowledging the gratuitousness of its existence. She does not, like Holmes and Bradshaw, inflict her vision of life on the dissatisfied, the lonely, the weak. She offers for the sake of offering, refusing to force people to be free or to force them to be happy.

This crucial disassociation of the creative will from the corrupting impulse for mastery is the triumph of feminine art, of Clarissa's "exquisite sense of comedy." Even though she needs, as Peter Walsh realizes, "people, always people to bring it out," she never invades the sanctuary, never forces the soul. In giving her party to "kindle and illuminate," she never uses the imperative "must," but, in imitation of that original moment of creation, prefers the authoritative, yet self-absenting word, "let." All pleasure and all beauty can only be created and communicated through such gratuitous offerings, as Richard's gift of flowers suggests and as Septimus's death testifies. In taking his life, Septimus protests that

> It was their idea of tragedy, not his or Rezia's (for she was with him). Holmes and Bradshaw like that sort of thing. . . . He did not want to die. Life was good. The sun hot. Only human beings—what did *they* want? . . . Holmes was at the door. "I'll give it you!" he cried, and flung himself vigorously, violently down on to Mrs. Filmer's area railings.

Septimus's gift, the thing that human beings want, the thing that matters, is life itself, the mixed gift of life and death Nature gratuitously bestows. But Septimus's gift is forced from him. His offering is associated with the ritual sacrifices of tragedy and not the festive exchange of gifts by which comedy traditionally celebrates and cements its achieved social concord. Clarissa may be glad that Septimus had thrown it away, her guilt modulating into self-reproach as she remembers the shilling she had thrown into the Serpentine. But she is for the party.

For Woolf, the world is the theatre of "free play" in which beauty is scattered and tossed to the winds; and society is but a fortuitous, haphazard collection of So-and-so in Kensington, So-and-so in Mayfair. She feels, like Clarissa, that this dispersed spectacle of life can and should be collected and assembled and created into new, more human forms. Ultimately, the justification for art as mere gift derives its authority from the banal yet profound cliché that in giving, one receives. Clarissa's offering to life is the self-rewarding gift, the "extraordinary gift, that woman's gift, of making a world of her own wherever she happened to be." This power of making a world of her own is the power exercised by the narrator who, even more than nature or the old woman ascending the stairs, is the lawgiver of the novel. She is nameless, never inflicts her individuality, yet succeeds in combining and creating out of the diffuse matter of life a work of art. As the dreamer who dreams the world of the novel, the narrator is like her characters, engaged in reverie, imagining their memories, transcribing their dreams.

The difference between the dreamer and the dreamed ones of the novel consists in what Gaston Bachelard sees as "the radical difference" between the ordinary dream and the conscious reverie:

> While the dreamer of the nocturnal dream is a shadow who has lost his self (*moi*), the dreamer of reverie, if he is a bit philosophical, can formulate a *cogito* at the center of his dreaming self (*son moi rêveur*). Put another way, reverie is an oneiric activity in which a glimmer of consciousness subsists. The dreamer of reverie is present in his reverie. Even when the reverie gives the impression of a flight out of the real, out of time and place, the dreamer of reverie knows that it is he who is absenting himself—he, in flesh and blood, who is becoming a "spirit," a phantom of the past or of voyage.
>
> (*The Poetics of Reverie*, tr. David Russell)

In the presence of the omniscient, though insubstantial narrator of *Mrs. Dalloway*, Woolf was beginning to formulate and implement her philosophy of anonymity in which the creative mind consciously absents itself from the work it creates. Through this dissolution of the importunate, egotistical narrative "I," the narrative consciousness becomes pure spirit, a phantom of the past or of the voyage it imagines. Through this dissolution, then, the work of mourning and of dreaming in withdrawing, testing, and, in the normal outcome, returning to the real, become one and join forces against the madness which represents the *actual* flight of the mind out of time and place and the confines of the real. In the cooperative labor of mourning and dreaming, Woolf began to discover and recover the "center" that, mystically, had evaded her in her apprentice works. As *To the Lighthouse* demonstrates, Woolf would transform the work of mourning into an elegy for her lost parents, those lawgivers in whose countenances, beautiful and stern, she would see reflected her own face.

Virginia Woolf and Walter Pater: Selfhood and the Common Life

Perry Meisel

If we need to be convinced that selfhood is not a given in Woolf's work, let us turn to *Mrs. Dalloway* for as thorough a meditation on the nature of self and identity as there is in her fiction. Retiring to her bedroom after her morning errands, Clarissa's reveries reach a kind of conclusion when she gazes into the mirror to examine her face:

> She pursed her lips when she looked in the glass. It was to give her face point. That was her self—pointed; dartlike; definite. That was her self when some effort, some call on her to be her self, drew the parts together, she alone knew how different, how incompatible and composed so for the world only into one centre, one diamond, one woman who sat in her drawing-room and made a meeting-point, a radiancy.

The sense of selfhood here is one of achievement or accomplishment, the result of "some effort, some call on her to be her self." That Woolf chooses to punctuate "herself" with two words instead of the usual one suggests that the achievement of this "definite" quality of a self "composed . . . into one centre" is the result, not of a sure and natural process of development, but of a discipline and curtailment that makes the "parts" given to Clarissa in time past cohere and harmonize. Most important of all, of course, is that Clarissa draws "the parts together"

From *The Absent Father: Virginia Woolf and Water Pater.* © 1980 by Yale University. Yale University Press, 1980.

by means of beholding her image in the looking-glass. Without the mirror, Clarissa is "incompatible," "different" from herself. With the mirror, she gains in her reflection what she does not possess organically, a whole version of herself, although an identity, to be sure, that is still "different" from itself because the price of its wholeness is its constitution as the image of another.

Even apart from her mirror self, or as a reflection of it, Clarissa's identity is already constituted in different ways by the different tropes or images by which she is represented, and by which she has learned to represent herself. The two primary ones, of course, are "Clarissa" and "Mrs. Dalloway," with each proper name signifying a different cluster of the various and incompatible "parts" that constitute her "own" or "proper" self—under the rubric "Clarissa," for example, her memories of Bourton, her relationship with Peter Walsh, her sexual fascination with other women, and so on; under "Mrs. Dalloway," her marriage to Richard, her daughter Elizabeth, her role as hostess, and so on.

Even more, Clarissa's "definite" self is figured here under the name of a gem—a "diamond"—that sends us back to that Paterian definition of selfhood whereby personality fashions itself into a crystal. Clarissa's diamond, of course, is just such a crystal, and the "radiancy" of its momentary perfection before the glass—the product of the discipline Clarissa undergoes so as to "compose" this "one centre" or central self—is a "meeting-point" like the one that constitutes the "focus" of Paterian intensity, together with the sacrifices such a single focus ("only") requires. Thus, as "Mrs. Dalloway," she must forego much of what falls under the trope "Clarissa," just as her momentary returns throughout the day to the world of "Clarissa" require her to sacrifice the "thousand" other "sympathies" that fall under her identity as "Mrs. Dalloway." From this point of view, it is also her "self" that Clarissa sees when she gazes at the old woman in the window across from her bedroom late in the novel, an image of age, loneliness, and approaching death that she fashions into a (self-)portrait of dignity and repose.

What is lacking, or at least what is not given, is the "something central which permeated" that is Clarissa's most celebrated lament. Although she thinks such an absence is peculiar to her alone, it is, of course, a common absence built into Woolf's very notion of character as an image alienated from the self it defines, as a distinctive mark or graphic symbol (to take character at its letter) like the "I" itself.

At the start of her noontime meditation, of course, Clarissa feels her identity ebb, "feeling herself suddenly shrivelled, aged, breastless, the grinding, blowing, flowering of the day, out of doors, out of the window, out of her body and brain which now failed." The passing away of those "currents" of "influence" on whose "extended surface" one normally positions oneself makes Clarissa acutely aware of the "forces" of which her various selves are composed, the power they have to fill her becoming particularly apparent once they begin to pass out of and away from her to suggest the nothingness of death and the end of troping or illusion with which death is equivalent. It is, moreover, especially noteworthy that Woolf deploys the Paterian figure of the house to describe the ebb of Clarissa's sense of self ("out of doors, out of the window, out of her body and brain"), since it allows us to see how central the figure of the dwelling or manmade enclosure is to both writers' notion of selfhood as a fortified space of property. The stable "I," of course, is, if nothing else, a "capital" disposition of character, with its capital qualities suggesting a notion of selfhood as one, quite literally, of ownership or "property."

A sense of self-dissolution, however, is not unusual with Clarissa, and if it functions as an ebb or loss here, it also functions as a positive joy or advantage elsewhere in the novel. Indeed, the dissolution of her identity back into its component and nonidentical "parts" is what gives her faith in her ability to endure after death, at least if one is attentive to the shared or common nature of the circuits through which selfhood is composed:

> Somehow in the streets of London, on the ebb and flow of things, here, there, she survived, Peter survived, lived in each other, she being part, she was positive, of the trees at home; of the house there, ugly, rambling all to bits and pieces as it was; part of people she had never met; being laid out like a mist between the people she knew best, who lifted her on their branches as she had seen the trees lift the mist, but it spread ever so far, her life, herself.

With "the house" or self "rambling all to bits and pieces" here, the narrator foregrounds instead the common pathways by which its "parts" or "pieces" are orchestrated. The "branches," "trees," and "mist" are in fact only one set of images by which the narrator represents those currents of being that connect people throughout the novel, even people one "had never met."

Although the figures in this instance are organic ones, the novel also includes recurrent images like the binding "thread" that almost literally tie or unite characters, events, and places throughout the story, and that designate not so much a natural unity to life as they do a common life of tropes and conceptions shared by characters and narrators alike. From this point of view, the anonymous old woman who sings Strauss at the underground station almost at the center of the novel comes to represent the voice of the common life itself, with its anonymous murmurs trickling down from origins so remote that to fix them would be impossible. In many ways, too, the Tube woman is even a radical deidealization—a common-ing down—of a figure like Pater's Mona Lisa, with both figures representing the same force even if they are otherwise so different.

Indeed, Woolf's novel is itself designed to be such a vessel or container of the world's common languages. Although "no mathematical instrument . . . could register the vibration" of "common appeal" that the mystic car sends through the crowd early in the novel, Woolf's prose turns out to be just such a seismographic "machine" built to monitor such "vibration" as it echoes or resonates through the labyrinthine pathways of public and private association represented by the novel's figural apparatus, and which the novel also doubles as a set of resonant linguistic pathways in its own right.

These figures or, really, metalanguages, are often organic ones, and suggest a vision of life as a pattern of connections "drawn out" on "every leaf on the trees." Among these naturalizing figures may be included the patterned and patterning figures of "smoke," "mesh," "mist," "veins," "waves," "branches," "leaves," "leaf," "trees," "twig," "nerve fibres," "entrails"—all of them signifying the movement or "vibration" from "branch to branch" of these networks of networks.

The patterning power of Woolf's networks is to be seen even more clearly in those figures of manmade patterns that are woven through the narrative, too, particularly the figures of fabric and of houses, both of which represent system and display its operations at the same time. Hence the "pink gauze" that Sally Seton "seemed" to wear at Bourton not only represents the pathways of psychic association by which Clarissa's memory of her is put into operation, but also serves as the token of the memory itself. Similarly, the "transparent muslins" of the dancing and "laughing girls" in Clarissa's fantasy of courtly parties early in the novel not only double "the soft mesh" of the "morning air" in which the fantasy unfolds as Clarissa walks through the park, but also render it, in a cluster of puns, a "mesh" of threads which, "as the day wore on, would unwind."

The master tropes in this rhetorical thread of fabrics are the figures of "silk" and "folds" connected with Clarissa's "sewing," which as an activity doubles the narrator's own propensity for weaving and threading the world together, and which is doubled in turn by the way Septimus's wife Rezia "must stitch" her "sewing" in an attempt to repair her married life. Indeed, even "our soul," thinks Peter on his way to the Dalloways' party, is always "threading" its way through the pathways or "gauze" of memory and association, even though in this last instance the narrator mixes her metaphors by using the figure of fabric in tandem with a vision of watery depth ("our soul . . . fish-like inhabits deep seas and plies among obscurities threading her way"). Thus, too, Richard Dalloway feels his attachment to Lady Bruton sustain itself after lunch "as a single spider's thread . . . attaches itself to the point of a leaf." Here we should also include the "screen" that lies over the world for Septimus, as well as the "fine tissue" and "fine net" of "service" that "spread round" Lady Bruton and her house, and which also double "that fibre which was the ramrod" of Lady Bruton's "soul." Among the figure's permutations are to be included the figure of the "curtain," the "tissue" of life, and the "string" of attachment.

Under the figure of the house fall a series of figures for structure, too, among them the "innumerable bedrooms" of Buckingham Palace through whose corridors messages of all kinds can circulate, even those barroom insults that "echoed strangely across the way in the ears of girls buying white underlinen threaded with pure white ribbon for their weddings," with this last figure doubling and tripling within itself the threading operations it describes. The movement of Peter's mind is described in terms of a house, too, "as if inside his brain by another hand strings were pulled, shutters moved," while the "swing doors" in Lady Bruton's house signify the same movement of "service" as the "tissue" or "net" that also describes it and that represents the same space of social interaction as the "swing doors" of the florist or the unhinged spaces of the Dalloways' house where the party will take place.

The novel's most literal organizing figure as well as its most Joycean one is to be found in the streets of London themselves. In a phrase like "the traffic hummed in a circle," the synesthetic movement from the traffic's noise to the visual pattern of the "circle" which such sounds make here and elsewhere in the novel (especially in the "circles" of Big Ben's chimes) is also a movement from one representation of systematicity to another, with the rings of the "circle" simply a more fleeting cipher for the kind of networks more concretely embodied by the pattern of London streets that maps out common pathways throughout the novel. Characters, in fact, are often positioned at a moment of crossing as the narrator uses this rather literal metaphor of roads and junctions to suggest those points at which circuits of influence intersect to produce the puns and the transformations that designate the crossing of figural systems and the conjunction of characters by means of them.

All these figures taken together draw nothing less than a "map of the world," with the narrator's allusions to Greenwich grounding her figure much as the streets of London ground her notion of junctions and pathways in the network of the common life. The figure of the map and the territory it represents and organizes is a particularly resonant one given the way the novel's interest in political economy and imperialism underlies all the metaphors of exchange, psychical and commercial alike, of which life in *Mrs. Dalloway* is composed. In order to address the role of politics in the novel, however, we should look first at Septimus Warren Smith.

Septimus's difficulty, of course, is his inability, unlike Clarissa, to compose his "parts" into the "one centre" of a "self." To Septimus, "one centre" is a "horror." Without discipline—without *ascesis*—he admits into his world virtually all of the sympathies or currents of being that most of us filter, select, and harmonize through a blindness or a deferral necessary for the proper establishment of an ego. Thus Septimus is always in dissolution ("he was not Septimus now"), since he fails to position himself in the flux of influence that buffets him with its overdetermined abundance. He "was always stopping in the middle, changing his mind; wanting to add something; hearing something new." Despite his claim that "he could not feel," what troubles him is that he feels too much:

> He could not read the language yet; but it was plain enough,
> this beauty, this exquisite beauty, and tears filled his eyes
> as he looked at the smoke words languishing and melting
> in the sky and bestowing upon him in their inexhaustible
> charity and laughing goodness one shape after another

of unimaginable beauty and signalling their intention to provide him, for nothing, for ever, for looking merely, with beauty, more beauty! Tears ran down his cheeks.

Septimus, then, fails to sustain or perfect any particular reading of life and so remains a diffuse and hazy locus of the forces or languages that course and collide in a semantic field not proportioned into what custom calls a self. Indeed, Septimus's many possible self-conceptions are described in a litany akin to the one in "Street Haunting":

> The most exalted of mankind; the criminal who faced his judges; the victim exposed on the heights; the fugitive; the drowned sailor; the poet of the immortal ode; the Lord who had gone from life to death; to Septimus Warren Smith, who sat in the arm-chair under the skylight staring at a photograph of Lady Bradshaw in Court dress, muttering messages about beauty.

"Every power," says the narrator, "poured its treasures on his head," with "avalanche" the equivalent term from "A Sketch of the Past." These "treasures," of course, include the "diamond" of selfhood, but Septimus must let the gem that is Clarissa's prize elude his grasp.

Thus Clarissa is Septimus's "double," as Woolf puts it in the novel's preface, only insofar as she possesses what he lacks—a mirror image or "double" to provide him with a sense of self. To the extent that Septimus attempts any such identification at all, of course, it is with Evans, the officer blown to bits in the war, and an image not of wholeness but of fragmentation, of the body in pieces.

What the coercion of the doctors Holmes and Bradshaw adds to our notion of the selfhood Septimus cannot achieve is that the mapping or coordination of a self is also to be understood in political terms. For not only is the "capital" character of the "I" reflected in the notion of ownership or possession embodied in the bourgeois figure of the secure house; it is also reflected in the way the settlement and rule of a territorial ego is a manifestly imperialist activity to be located in the "tropic gale" in Clarissa's "breast" or in the company of the "assembly of powers" that marshal Peter the Indian Army officer's mature life.

Indeed, much as the "Captain self" is above all a "good citizen" in

"Street Haunting," Clarissa's youthful desire to "found a society to abolish private property" gives way in later years to her capital propensities as Mrs. Dalloway, wife of a Conservative member of Parliament and a hostess who takes pleasure in "being part" of imperial society, especially "since her people were courtiers once in the time of the Georges." Moreover, Septimus's job before the war was as clerk for "land and estate agents," "valuers," in short, of property. Now, of course, the very notion of property is foreign to him, and it is the job of the doctors Holmes and Bradshaw to reeducate him in the ways of capitalist territory.

The doctors, of course, are "dominators," with Bradshaw's identification with the maintenance of civil order and prosperity made explicit in the novel. Even his colonized wife is described as "wedged on a calm ocean, where only spice winds blow," a kind of prisoner on a British frigate cruising for the "spice" or "treasure" of the Indies. Here, too, we should recall that Lady Bruton's power over her friends is the power of a "spectral grenadier" who "had the thought of Empire always at hand," and that Peter's career imperialism only makes explicit those dominating aspects of his personality that caused Clarissa not to marry him. Of course, Clarissa's marriage to Richard makes her nonetheless dependent on the "deposit" of his affection, a figure that also points to the marital bank account and the wealth of the colonies which sustains its value, all brought together in a harmonic triad of meaning. Now even the "diamond" of Clarissa's self carries with it the additional meaning of South African riches.

Thus the "dominion" and "power" which Bradshaw possesses bespeaks the properties necessary to the rule of the capital "I." If Septimus will not colonize himself (as Doris Kilman has), then it will have to be done for him. Thus he becomes a fugitive in an imperialist landscape: "Holmes and Bradshaw are on you. They scour the desert. They fly screaming into the wilderness"; "their packs scour the desert." Much as the "bayonets" of London "pinioned" evening to the sky, so the doctors' imperial "powers" will pinion Septimus into a proper space of self whether he likes it or not.

Septimus, however, refuses the "knife" as the instrument of his suicide, and thereby refuses all the weaponry of imperialism, whether the "bayonet" or, indeed, the "blade" that Peter habitually fondles throughout the novel. Indeed, if strong selfhood is a secure house, then the manner of Septimus's death—"He had thrown himself from a window"—is a perfect sign for what it is he abjures. The "mangled"

Septimus literalizes the de-forming ebb of Clarissa's identity as a movement "out of doors, out of the window" in order to deliver himself up to those "voices of the dead" who represent, not only to him but to all the characters in the novel, the common life itself.

*M*rs. *Dalloway:*
Repetition as the Raising of the Dead

J. Hillis Miller

The shift from the late Victorian or early modern Thomas Hardy to a fully modernist writer like Virginia Woolf might be thought of as the transition to a new complexity and a new self-consciousnes in the use of devices of repetition in narrative. Critics commonly emphasize the newness of Virginia Woolf's art. They have discussed her use of the so-called stream-of-consciousness technique, her dissolution of traditional limits of plot and character, her attention to minutiae of the mind and to apparently insignificant details of the external world, her pulverization of experience into a multitude of fragmentary particles, each without apparent connection to the others, and the dissolution of the usual boundaries between mind and world. Such characteristics connect her work to that of other twentieth-century writers who have exploded the conventional forms of fiction, from Conrad and Joyce to French "new novelists" like Nathalie Sarraute. It might also be well to recognize, however, the strong connections of Woolf's work with the native traditions of English fiction. Far from constituting a break with these traditions, her novels are an extension of them. They explore further the implications of those conventions which Austen, Eliot, Trollope, and Thackeray exploited as the given conditions of their craft. Such conventions, it goes without saying, are elements of meaning. The most important themes of a given novel are likely to lie not in anything which is explictly affirmed, but in significances generated by

From *Fiction and Repetition: Seven English Novels.* © 1982 by J. Hillis Miller. Harvard University Press, 1982.

the way in which the story is told. Among the most important of those ways is Woolf's organizing of her novels around various forms of recurrence. Storytelling, for Woolf, is the repetition of the past in memory, both in the memory of the characters and in the memory of the narrator. *Mrs. Dalloway* (1925) is a brilliant exploration of the functioning of memory as a form of repetition.

The novel is especially fitted to investigate not so much the depths of individual minds as the nuances of relationship between mind and mind. If this is so, then a given novelist's assumptions about the way one mind can be related to others will be a generative principle lying behind the form his or her novels take. From this perspective the question of narrative voice can be seen as a special case of the problem of relations between minds. The narrator too is a mind projected by a way of speaking, a mind usually endowed with special access to other minds and with special powers for expressing what goes on there.

The manipulation of narrative voice in fiction is closely associated with that theme of human time or of human history which seems intrinsic to the form of the novel. In many novels the use of the past tense establishes the narrator as someone living after the events of the story have taken place, someone who knows all the past perfectly. The narrator tells the story in a present which moves forward toward the future by way of a recapitulation or repetition of the past. This retelling brings that past up to the present as a completed whole, or it moves toward such completion. This form of an incomplete circle, time moving toward a closure which will bring together past, present, and future as a perfected whole, is the temporal form of many novels.

Interpersonal relations as a theme, the use of an omniscient narrator who is a collective mind rising from the copresence of many individual minds, indirect discourse as the means by which that narrator dwells within the minds of individual characters and registers what goes on there, temporality as a determining principle of theme and technique—these are, I have argued elsewhere, among the most important elements of form in Victorian fiction, perhaps in fiction of any time, in one proportion or another. Just these elements are fundamental to Virginia Woolf's work too. It would be as true to say that she investigates implications of these traditional conventions of form as to say that she brings something new into fiction. This can be demonstrated especially well in *Mrs. Dalloway*. The novel depends on the presence of a narrator who remembers all and who has a power of resurrecting the past in her narration. In *Mrs. Dalloway* narration is repetition as the raising of the dead.

"Nothing exists outside us except a state of mind"—this seemingly casual and somewhat inscrutable statement is reported from the thoughts of the solitary traveler in Peter Walsh's dream as Peter sits snoring on a bench in Regent's Park. The sentence provides an initial clue to the mode of existence of the narrator of *Mrs. Dalloway*. The narrator is that state of mind which exists outside the characters and of which they can never be directly aware. Though they are not aware of it, it is aware of them. This "state of mind" surrounds them, encloses them, pervades them, knows them from within. It is present to them all at all the times and places of their lives. It gathers those times and places together in the moment. The narrator is that "something central which permeate[s]," the "something warm which [breaks] up surfaces," a power of union and penetration which Clarissa Dalloway lacks. Or, to vary the metaphor, the narrator possesses the irresistible and subtle energy of the bell of St. Margaret's striking half past eleven. Like that sound, the narrator "glides into the recesses of the heart and buries itself." It is "something alive which wants to confide itself, to disperse itself, to be, with a tremor of delight, at rest." Expanding to enter into the inmost recesses of each heart, the narrator encloses all in a reconciling embrace.

Though the characters are not aware of this narrating presence, they are at every moment possessed and known, in a sense violated, by an invisible mind, a mind more powerful than their own. This mind registers with infinite delicacy their every thought and steals their every secret. The indirect discourse of this registration, in which the narrator reports in the past tense thoughts which once occurred in the present moments of the characters' minds, is the basic form of narration in *Mrs. Dalloway*. This disquieting mode of ventriloquism may be found on any page of the novel. Its distinguishing mark is the conventional "he thought" or "she thought," which punctuates the narrative and reveals the presence of a strange one-way interpersonal relation. The extraordinary quality of this relation is hidden primarily because readers of fiction take it so much for granted. An example is the section of the novel describing Peter Walsh's walk from Clarissa's house toward Regent's Park: "Clarissa refused me, he thought"; "like Clarissa herself, thought Peter Walsh"; "It is Clarissa herself, he thought"; "Still the future of civilisation lies, he thought"; "The future lies in the hands of young men like that, he thought"—and so on, page after page. If the reader asks himself where he is placed as he reads any given page of *Mrs. Dalloway,* the answer, most often, is that he is plunged within an individual mind which is being understood from inside by an ubiquitous, all-knowing mind. This mind speaks from some indeterminate later point in time, a point always "after" anything the characters think or feel. The narrator's mind moves easily from one limited mind to another and knows them all at once. It speaks for them all. This form of language generates the local texture of *Mrs. Dalloway.* Its sequential structure is made of the juxtaposition of longer or shorter blocks of narrative in which the narrator dwells first within Clarissa's mind, then within Septimus Smith's, then Rezia Smith's, then Peter's, then Rezia's again, and so on.

The characters of *Mrs. Dalloway* are therefore in an odd way, though they do not know it, dependent on the narrator. The narrator has preserved their evanescent thoughts, sensations, mental images, and interior speech. She rescues these from time past and presents them again in language to the reader. Narration itself is repetition in *Mrs. Dalloway.* In another way, the narrator's mind is dependent on the characters' minds. It could not exist without them. *Mrs. Dalloway* is almost entirely without passages of meditation or description which are exclusively in the narrator's private voice. The reader is rarely given the narrator's own thoughts or shown the way the world looks not through the eyes of a character, but through the narrator's private eyes. The sermon against "Proportion" and her formidable sister "Conversion" is one of the rare cases where the narrator speaks for her own view, or even for Woolf's own view, rather than by way of the mind of one of the characters. Even here, the narrator catches herself up and attributes some of her own judgment of Sir William Bradshaw to Rezia: "This lady too [Conversion] (Rezia Warren Smith divined it) had her dwelling in Sir William's heart."

In *Mrs. Dalloway* nothing exists for the narrator which does not first exist in the mind of one of the characters, whether it be a thought or a thing. This is implied by those passages in which an external object—the mysterious royal motorcar in Bond Street, Peter Walsh's knife, the child who runs full tilt into Rezia Smith's legs, most elaborately the skywriting airplane—is used as a means of transition from the mind of one character to the mind of another. Such transitions seem to suggest that the solid existing things of the external world unify the minds of separate persons because though each person is trapped in his or her own mind and in his or her own private responses to external objects, nevertheless these disparate minds can all have responses, however different they may be, to the same event, for example to an airplane's skywriting. To this extent at least we all dwell in one world.

The deeper meaning of this motif in *Mrs. Dalloway* may be less a recognition of our common dependence on a solidly existing external world than a revelation that things exist for the narrator only when they exist for the characters. The narrator sometimes moves without transition out of the mind of one character and into the mind of another, as in the fourth paragraph of the novel, in which the reader suddenly finds himself transported from Clarissa's mind into the mind of Scrope Purvis, a character who never appears again in the novel and who seems put in only to give the reader a view of Clarissa from the outside and perhaps to provide an initial demonstration of the fact that the narrator is by no means bound to a single mind. Though she is bound to no single mind, she is dependent for her existence on the minds of the characters. She can think, feel, see only as they thought, felt, and saw. Things exist for her, she exists for herself, only because the others once existed. Like the omniscient narrators of *Vanity Fair*, *Middlemarch*, or *The Last Chronicle of Barset*, the omniscient narrator of *Mrs. Dalloway* is a general consciousness or social mind which rises into existence out of the collective mental experience of the individual human beings in the story. The cogito of the narrator of *Mrs. Dalloway* is, "They thought, therefore I am."

One implication of this relation between the narrator's mind and the characters' minds is that, though for the most part the characters do not know it, the universal mind is part of their own minds, or rather their minds are part of it. If one descends deeply enough into any individual mind one reaches ultimately the general mind, that is, the mind of the narrator. On the surface the relation between narrator and individual goes only one way. As in the case of those windows which may be seen through in a single direction, the character is transparent to the narrator, but the narrator is opaque to the character. In the depths of each individual mind, this one-way relationship becomes reciprocal. In the end it is no longer a relationship, but a union, an identity. Deep down the general mind and the individual mind become one. Both are on the same side of the glass, and the glass vanishes.

If this is true for all individual minds in relation to the universal mind, then all individual minds are joined to one another far below the surface separateness, as in Matthew Arnold's image of coral islands which seem divided, but are unified in the depths. The most important evidence for this in *Mrs. Dalloway* is the fact that the same images of unity, of reconciliation, of communion well up spontaneously from the deep levels of the minds of all the major characters. One of the most pervasive of these images is that of a great enshadowing tree which is personified, a great mother who binds all living things together in the manifold embrace of her leaves and branches. This image would justify the use of the feminine pronoun for the narrator, who is the spokeswoman for this mothering presence. No man or woman is limited to himself or herself, but each is joined to others by means of this tree, diffused like a mist among all the people and places he or she has encountered. Each man or woman possesses a kind of immortality, in spite of the abrupt finality of death: "did it not become consoling," muses Clarissa to herself as she walks toward Bond Street, "to believe that death ended absolutely? but that somehow in the streets of London, on the ebb and flow of things, here, there, she survived, Peter survived, lived in each other, she being part, she was positive, of the trees at home; of the house there, ugly, rambling all to bits and pieces as it was; part of people she had never met; being laid out like a mist between the people she knew best, who lifted her on their branches as she had seen the trees lift the mist, but it spread ever so far, her life, herself." "A marvellous discovery indeed—" thinks Septimus Smith as he watches the skywriting airplane, "that the human voice in certain atmospheric conditions (for one must be scientific, above all scientific) can quicken trees into life! . . . but they beckoned; leaves were alive; trees were alive. And the leaves being connected by millions of fibres with his own body, there on the seat, fanned it up and down; when the branch stretched he, too, made that statement." "But if he can conceive of her, then in some sort she exists," thinks the solitary traveler in Peter Walsh's dream, "and advancing down the path with his eyes upon sky and branches he rapidly endows them with womanhood; sees with amazement how grave they become; how majestically, as the breeze stirs them, they dispense with a dark flutter of the leaves charity, comprehension, absolution . . . let me walk straight on to this great figure, who will, with a toss of her head, mount me on her streamers and let me blow to nothingness with the rest." Even Lady Bruton, as she falls ponderously asleep after her luncheon meeting, feels "as if one's friends were attached to one's body, after lunching with them, by a thin thread."

This notion of a union of each mind in its depths with all the other minds and with a universal, impersonal mind for which the narrator speaks is confirmed by those notations in *A Writer's Diary* in which, while writing *Mrs. Dalloway,* Woolf speaks of her "great discovery," what she calls her "tunnelling process," that method whereby, as she says, "I dig out beautiful caves behind my characters: I think that gives exactly what I want; humanity, humour, depth. The idea is that the caves shall connect."

Deep below the surface, in some dark and remote cave of the spirit, each person's mind connects with all the other minds, in a vast cavern where all the tunnels end. Peter Walsh's version of the image of the maternal tree ends nevertheless on an ominous note. To reach the great figure is to be blown to nothingness with the rest. This happens because union with the general mind is incompatible with the distinctions, the limitations, the definite edges and outlines, one thing here, another thing there, of daylight consciousness. The realm of union is a region of dispersion, of darkness, of indistinction, sleep, and death. The fear or attraction of the annihilating fall into nothingness echoes through *Mrs. Dalloway*. The novel seems to be based on an irreconcilable opposition between individuality and universality. By reason of his or her existence as a conscious human being, each man or woman is alienated from the whole of which he or she is actually, though unwittingly or at best half-consciously, a part. That half-consciousness gives each person a sense of incompletion. Each person yearns to be joined in one way or another to the whole from which he or she is separated by the conditions of existence as an individual.

One way to achieve this wholeness might be to build up toward some completeness in the daylight world, rather than to sink down into the dark world of death. "What a lark! What a plunge!"—the beginning of the third paragraph of *Mrs. Dalloway* contains in miniature the two contrary movements of the novel. If the fall into death is one pole of the novel, fulfilled in Septimus Smith's suicidal plunge, the other pole is the rising motion of "building it up," of constructive action in the moment, fulfilled in Clarissa Dalloway's party. Turning away from the obscure depths within them, the characters, may, like Clarissa, embrace the moment with elation and attempt to gather everything together in a diamond point of brightness: "For Heaven only knows why one loves it so, how one sees its so, making it up, building it round one, tumbling it, creating it every moment afresh"; "what she loved was this, here, now, in front of her"; "Clarissa . . . plunged into the very heart of the moment, transfixed it, there—the moment of this June morning on which was the pressure of all the other mornings, . . . collecting the whole of her at one point." In the same way, Peter Walsh after his sleep on a park bench feels, "Life itself, every moment of it, every drop of it, here, this instant, now, in the sun, in Regent's Park, was enough." (This echoing from Clarissa to Peter, it is worth noting, is proof that Clarissa is right to think that they "live in each other.")

"The pressure of all the other mornings"—one way the characters in *Mrs. Dalloway* achieve continuity and wholeness is through the ease with which images from their pasts rise within them to overwhelm them with a sense of immediate presence. If the characters of the novel live according to an abrupt, discontinuous, nervous rhythm, rising one moment to heights of ecstasy only to be dropped again in sudden terror or despondency, nevertheless their experience is marked by profound continuities.

The remarkably immediate access the characters have to their pasts is one such continuity. The present, for them, is the perpetual repetition of the past. In one sense the moment is all that is real. Life in the present instant is a narrow plank reaching over the abyss of death between the nothingness of past and future. Near the end of the novel Clarissa thinks of "the terror; the overwhelming incapacity, one's parents giving it into one's hands, this life, to be lived to the end, to be walked with serenely; there was in the depths of her heart an awful fear." In another sense, the weight of all the past moments presses just beneath the surface of the present, ready in an instant to flow into consciousness, overwhelming it with the immediate presence of the past. Nothing could be less like the intermittencies and difficulties of memory in Wordsworth or in Proust than the spontaneity and ease of memory in *Mrs. Dalloway*. Repeatedly during the day of the novel's action the reader finds himself within the mind of a character who has been invaded and engulfed by a memory so vivid that it displaces the present of the novel and becomes the virtual present of the reader's experience. So fluid are the boundaries between past and present that the reader sometimes has great difficulty knowing whether he is encountering an image from the character's past or something part of the character's immediate experience.

An example of this occurs in the opening paragraphs of the novel. *Mrs. Dalloway* begins in the middle of things with the report of something Clarissa says just before she leaves her home in Westminster to walk to the florist on Bond Street: "Mrs. Dalloway said she would buy the flowers herself." A few sentences later, after a description of Clarissa's recognition that it is a fine day and just following the first instance of the motif of terror combined with ecstasy ("What a lark! What a plunge!"), the reader is "plunged" within the closeness of an experience which seems to be part of the present, for he is as yet ignorant of the place names in the novel or of their relation to the times of Clarissa's life. Actually, the experience is from Clarissa's adolescence: "For so it had always seemed to her, when, with a little squeak of the hinges, which she could hear now, she had burst open the French windows and plunged at Bourton into the open air."

The word "plunge," reiterated here, expresses a pregnant ambiguity. If a "lark" and a "plunge" seem at first almost the same thing, rising and falling versions of the same leap of ecstasy, and if Clarissa's plunge into the open air when she bursts open the windows at Bourton seems to confirm this identity, the reader may remember this opening page much later when Septimus leaps from a window to his death. Clarissa, hearing of his suicide at her party, confirms this connection by asking herself, "But this young man who had killed himself—had he plunged holding his treasure?" If *Mrs. Dalloway* is organized around the contrary penchants of rising and falling, these notions are not only opposites, but are also ambiguously similar. They change places bewilderingly, so that down and up, falling and rising, death and life, isolation and communication, are mirror images of one another rather than a confrontation of negative and positive orientations of the spirit. Clarissa's plunge at Bourton into the open air is an embrace of life in its richness, promise, and immediacy, but it is when the reader encounters it already an image from the dead past. Moreover, it anticipates Septimus's plunge into death. It is followed in Clarissa's memory of it by her memory that when she stood at the open window she felt "something awful about to happen." The reader is not surprised to find that in this novel which is made up of a stream of subtle variations on a few themes, one of the things Clarissa sees from the window at Bourton is "the rooks rising, falling."

The temporal placement of Clarissa's experiences at Bourton is equally ambiguous. The "now" of the sentence describing Clarissa's plunge ("with a little squeak of the hinges, which she could hear now"), is the narrator's memory of Clarissa's memory of her childhood home brought back so vividly into Clarissa's mind that it becomes the present of her experience and of the reader's experience. The sentence opens the door to a flood of memories which bring that faraway time back to her as a present with the complexity and fullness of immediate experience.

These memories are not simply present. The ambiguity of the temporal location of this past time derives from the narrator's use of the past tense conventional in fiction. This convention is one of the aspects of the novel which Woolf carries on unchanged from her eighteenth- and nineteenth-century predecessors. The first sentence of the novel ("Mrs. Dalloway said she would buy the flowers herself"), establishes a temporal distance between the narrator's present and the present of the characters. Everything that the characters do or think is placed firmly in an indefinite past as something which has always already happened when the reader encounters it. These events are resurrected from the past by the language of the narration, and placed before the present moment of the reader's experience as something bearing the ineradicable mark of their pastness. When the characters, within this general pastness of the narration, remember something from their own pasts, and when the narrator reports this in that indirect discourse which is another convention of *Mrs. Dalloway,* she has no other way to place it in the past than some version of the past tense which she has already been using for the "present" of the characters' experience: "How fresh, how calm, stiller than this of course, the air was in the early morning." That "was" is a past within a past, a double repetition.

The sentence before this one contains the "had" of the past perfect which places it in a past behind that past which is the "present" of the novel, the day of Clarissa's party. Still Clarissa can hear the squeak of hinges "now," and the reader is led to believe that she may be comparing an earlier time of opening the windows with a present repetition of that action. The following sentence is in the simple past ("the air was"), and yet it belongs not to the present of the narration, but to the past of Clarissa's girlhood. What has happened to justify this change is one of those subtle dislocations within the narration which are characteristic of indirect discourse as a mode of language. Indirect discourse is always a relationship between two distinguishable minds, but the nuances of this relationship may change, with corresponding changes in the way it is registered in words. "For so it had always seemed to her"—here the little word "had" establishes three identifiable times: the no-time or time-out-of-time-for-which-all-times-are-past of the narrator; the time of the single day of the novel's action; and the time of Clarissa's youth. The narrator distinguishes herself both temporally and, if one may say so, "spatially," from Clarissa and reports Clarissa's thoughts from the outside in a tense which she would not herself use in the "now" of her own experience. In the next sentence these distances between the narrator and Clarissa disappear. Though the text is still an indirect discourse in the sense that the narrator speaks for the character, the language used is much more nearly identical with what Clarissa might herself have said, and the tense is the one she would use: "How fresh, how calm, stiller than this of course, the air was in the early morning." The "was" here is the sign of a relative identity between the narrator's mind and the character's mind. From the point of view the narrator momentarily adopts, Clarissa's youth is at the same distance from the narrator as it is from Clarissa, and the reader is left with no linguistic clue, except the "stiller than this of course," permitting him to tell whether the "was" refers to the present of the narration or to its past. The "was" shimmers momentarily between the narrator's past and Clarissa's past. The subtly varying tense structure creates a pattern of double repetition in which three times keep moving together and then apart. Narration in indirect discourse, for Woolf, is repetition as distancing and merging at once.

Just as a cinematic image is always present, so that there is difficulty in presenting the pastness of the past on film (a "flashback" soon becomes experienced as present), so everything in a conventional novel is labeled "past." All that the narrator presents takes its place on the same plane of time as something which from the narrator's point of view and from the reader's is already part of the past. If there is no past in the cinema, there is no present in a novel, or only a specious, ghostly present which is generated by the narrator's ability to resurrect the past not as reality but as verbal image.

Woolf strategically manipulates in *Mrs. Dalloway* the ambiguities of this aspect of conventional storytelling to justify the power she ascribes to her characters of immediate access to their pasts. If the novel as a whole is recovered from the past in the mind of the narrator, the action of the novel proceeds through one day in the lives of its main characters in which one after another they have a present experience, often one of walking through the city, Clarissa's walk to buy flowers, Peter Walsh's walk through London after visiting Clarissa, Septimus and Rezia's walk to visit Sir William Bradshaw, and so on. As the characters make their ways through London the most important events of their pasts rise up within them, so that the day of *Mrs. Dalloway* may be described as a general day of recollection. The revivification of the past performed by the characters becomes in its turn another past revivified, brought back from the dead, by the narrator.

If the pressure of all the other moments lies on the present moment which Clarissa experiences so vividly, the whole day of the action of *Mrs. Dalloway* may be described as such a moment on a large scale. Just as Proust's *A la recherche du temps perdu,* a book much admired by Woolf, ends up with a party in which Marcel encounters figures from his past turned now into aged specters of themselves, so the "story" of *Mrs. Dalloway* (for there is a story, the story of Clarissa's refusal of Peter Walsh, of her love for Sally Seton, and of her decision to marry Richard Dalloway), is something which happened long before the single day in the novel's present. The details of this story are brought back bit by bit for the reader in the memories of the various characters as the day continues. At the same time the most important figures in Clarissa's past actually return during the day, Peter Walsh journeying from India and appearing suddenly at her door, then later coming to her party; Sally Seton, now married and the mother of five sons, also coming to her party.

The passage in *A Writer's Diary* about Woolf's "discovery," her "tunnelling process," takes on its full meaning when it is seen as a description of the way *Mrs. Dalloway* is a novel of the resurrection of the past into the present of the characters' lives. The tunnelling process, says Woolf, is one "by which I tell the past by instalments, as I have need of it." The "beautiful caves" behind each of the characters are caves into the past as well as caves down into the general mind for which the narrator speaks. If in one direction the "caves connect" in the depths of each character's mind, in the other direction "each [cave] comes to daylight at the present moment," the present moment of Clarissa's party when the important figures from her past are present in the flesh.

Woolf has unostentatiously, even secretly, buried within her novel a clue to the way the day of the action is to be seen as the occasion of a resurrection of ghosts from the past. There are three odd and apparently irrelevant pages in the novel which describe the song of an ancient ragged woman, her hand outstretched for coppers. Peter hears her song as he crosses Marylebone Road by the Regent's Park Tube Station. It seems to rise like "the voice of an ancient spring" spouting from some primeval swamp. It seems to have been going on as the same inarticulate moan for million of years and to be likely to persist for ten million years longer:

ee um fah um so
foo swee too eem oo.

The battered old woman, whose voice seems to come from before, after, or outside time, sings of how she once walked with her lover in May. Though it is possible to associate this with the theme of vanished love in the novel (Peter has just been thinking again of Clarissa and of her coldness, "as cold as an icicle"), still the connection seems strained, and the episode scarcely seems to justify the space it occupies unless the reader recognizes that Woolf has woven into the old woman's song, partly by paraphrase and variation, partly by direct quotation in an English translation, the words of a song by Richard Strauss, "Allerseelen," with words by Hermann von Gilm. The phrases quoted in English from the song do not correspond to any of the three English translations I have located, so Woolf either made her own or used another which I have not found. Here is a translation more literal than any of the three published ones I have seen and also more literal than Woolf's version:

Place on the table the perfuming heather,
Bring here the last red asters,
And let us speak again of love,
As once in May.

Give me your hand, that I may secretly press it,
And if someone sees, it's all the same to me;
Give me but one of your sweet glances,
As once in May.

It is blooming and breathing perfume today on every grave,
One day in the year is free to the dead,
Come to my heart that I may have you again,
As once in May.

Heather, red asters, the meeting with the lover once in May, these are echoed in the passage in *Mrs. Dalloway,* and several phrases are quoted directly: "look in my eyes with thy sweet eyes intently"; "give me your hand and let me press it gently"; "and if some one should see, what matter they?" The old woman, there can be no doubt, is singing Strauss's song. The parts of the song not directly echoed in *Mrs. Dalloway* identify it as a key to the structure of the novel. "One day in the year" is indeed "free to the dead," "Allerseelen," the day of a collective resurrection of spirits. On this day the bereaved lover can hope that the beloved will return from the grave. Like Strauss's song, *Mrs. Dalloway* has the form of an All Souls' Day in which Peter Walsh, Sally Seton, and the rest rise from the dead to come to Clarissa's party. As in the song the memory of a dead lover may on one day of the year become a direct confrontation of his or her risen spirit, so in *Mrs. Dalloway* the characters are obsessed all day by memories of the time when Clarissa refused Peter and chose to marry Richard Dalloway, and then the figures in those memories actually come back in a general congregation of persons from Clarissa's past. The power of narrative not just to repeat the past but to resurrect it in another form is figured dramatically in the action of the novel.

Continuity of each character with his own past, continuity in the shared past of all the important characters—these forms of communication are completed by the unusual degree of access the characters have in the present to one another's minds. Some novelists, Jane Austen or Jean-Paul Sartre, for example, assume that minds are opaque to one another. Another person is a strange apparition, perhaps friendly to me, perhaps a threat, but in any case difficult to understand. I have no immediate knowledge of what he is thinking or feeling. I must interpret what is going on within his subjectivity as best I can by way of often misleading signs—speech, gesture, and expression. In Woolf's work, as in Trollope's, one person often sees spontaneously into the mind of another and knows with the same sort of knowledge he has of his own subjectivity what is going on there. If the narrator enters silently and unobserved into the mind of each of the characters and understands it with perfect intimacy because it is in fact part of her own mind, the characters often, if not always, may have the same kind of intimate knowledge of one another. This may be partly because they share the same memories and so respond in the same way to the same cues, each knowing what the other must be thinking, but it seems also to be an unreflective openness of one mind to another, a kind of telepathic insight. The mutual understanding of Clarissa and Peter is the most striking example of this intimacy: "They went in and out of each other's minds without any effort," thinks Peter, remembering their talks at Bourton. Other characters have something of the same power of communication. Rezia and Septimus, for example, as he helps her make a hat in their brief moments of happiness before Dr. Holmes comes and Septimus throws himself out of the window: "Not for weeks had they laughed like this together, poking fun privately like married people." Or there is the intimacy of Clarissa and her servant Lucy: " 'Dear!' said Clarissa, and Lucy shared as she meant her to her disappointment (but not the pang); felt the concord between them."

In all these cases, there is some slight obstacle between the minds of the characters. Clarissa does after all decide not to marry Peter and is falling in love with Richard Dalloway in spite of the almost perfect communion she can achieve with Peter. The communion of Rezia and Septimus is intermittent, and she has little insight into what is going on in his mind during his periods of madness. Clarissa does not share with Lucy the pang of jealousy she feels toward Lady Bruton. The proper model for the relations among minds in *Mrs. Dalloway* is that of a perfect transparency of the minds of the characters to the mind of the narrator, but only a modified translucency, like glass frosted or fogged, between the mind of one character and the mind of another. Nevertheless, to the continuity between the present and the past within the mind of a given character there must be added a relative continuity from one mind to another in the present.

The characters in *Mrs. Dalloway* are endowed with a desire to take possession of these continuities, to actualize them in the present. The dynamic model for this urge is a movement which gathers together disparate elements, pieces them into a unity, and lifts them up into the daylight world in a gesture of ecstatic delight, sustaining the wholeness so created over the dark abyss of death. The phrase "building up" echoes through the novel as an emblem of this combination of spiritual and physical action. Thinking of life, Clarissa, the reader will remember, wonders "how one sees it so, making it up, building it round one." Peter Walsh follows a pretty girl from Trafalgar Square to Regent Street across Oxford Street and Great Portland Street until she disappears into her house, making up a personality for her, a new personality for himself, and an adventure for them both together: "it was half made up, as he knew very well; invented, this escapade with the girl; made up, as one makes up the better part of life, he thought— making oneself up; making her up." Rezia's power of putting one scrap with another to make a hat or of gathering the small girl who brings the evening paper into a warm circle of intimacy momentarily cures Septimus of his hallucinations and of his horrifying sense that he is condemned to a solitary death: "For so it always happened. First one thing, then another. So she built it up, first one thing and then another . . . she built it up, sewing." Even Lady Bruton's luncheon, to which she brings Richard Dalloway and Hugh Whitbread to help her write a letter to the *Times* about emigration, is a parody version of this theme of constructive action.

The most important example of the theme is Clarissa Dalloway's party, her attempt to "kindle and illuminate." Though people laugh at her for her parties, feel she too much enjoys imposing herself, nevertheless these parties are her offering to life. They are an offering devoted to the effort to bring together people from their separate lives and combine them into oneness: "Here was So-and-so in South Kensington; some one up in Bayswater; and somebody else, say, in Mayfair. And she felt quite continuously a sense of their existence; and she felt what a waste; and she felt what a pity; and she felt if only they could be brought together; so she did it. And it was an offering; to combine, to create." The party which forms the concluding scene of the novel does succeed in bringing people together, a great crowd from poor little Ellie Henderson all the way up to the Prime Minister, and including Sally Seton and Peter Walsh among the rest. Clarissa has the "gift still; to be; to exist; to sum it all up in the moment."

Clarissa's party transforms each guest from his usual self into a new social self, a self outside the self of participation in the general presence of others. The magic sign of this transformation is the moment when Ralph Lyon beats back the curtain and goes on talking, so caught up is he in the party. The gathering then becomes "something now, not nothing," and Clarissa meditates on the power a successful party has to destroy the usual personality and replace it with another self able to know people with special intimacy and able to speak more freely from the hidden depths of the spirit. These two selves are related to one another as real to unreal, but when one is aware of the contrast, as Clarissa is in the moment just before she loses her self-consciousness and is swept up into her own party, it is impossible to tell which is the real self, which the unreal: "Every time she gave a party she had this feeling of being something not herself, and that every one was unreal in one way; much more real in another . . . it was possible to say things you couldn't say anyhow else, things that needed an effort; possible to go much deeper."

An impulse to create a social situation which will bring into the open the usually hidden continuities of present with past, of person with person, of person with the depths of himself, is shared by all the principal characters of *Mrs. Dalloway*. This universal desire makes one vector of spiritual forces within the novel a general urge toward lifting up and bringing together.

This effort fails in all its examples, or seems in part to have failed. It seems so implicitly to the narrator and more overtly to some of the characters, including Clarissa. From this point of view, a perspective emphasizing the negative aspect of these characters and episodes, Peter Walsh's adventure with the unknown girl is a fantasy. Lady Bruton is a shallow, domineering busybody, a representative of that upper-class society which Woolf intends to expose in her novel. "I want to criticise the social system," she wrote while composing *Mrs. Dalloway,* "and to show it at work, at its most intense." Rezia's constructive power and womanly warmth does not prevent her husband from killing himself. And Clarissa? It could be a mistake to exaggerate the degree to which she and the social values she embodies are condemned in the novel. Woolf's attitudes toward upper-class English society of the nineteen-twenties are ambiguous, and to sum up the novel as no more than negative social satire is a distortion. Woolf feared while she was writing the novel that Clarissa would not seem attractive enough to her readers. "The doubtful point," she wrote in her diary a year before the novel was finished, "is, I think, the character of Mrs. Dalloway. It may be too stiff, too glittering and tinselly." There is in fact a negative side to Clarissa as Woolf presents her. She is a snob, too anxious for social success. Her party is seen in part as the perpetuation of a moribund society, with its hangers-on at court like Hugh Whitbread and a Prime Minister who is dull: "You might have stood him behind a counter and bought biscuits," thinks Ellie Henderson, "—poor chap, all rigged up in gold lace."

Even if this negative judgment is suspended and the characters are taken as worth our sympathy, it is still the case that, though Clarissa's party facilitates unusual communication among these people, their communion is only momentary. The party comes to an end; the warmth fades; people return to their normal selves. In retrospect there seems to have been something spurious about the sense of oneness with others the party created. Clarissa's power to bring people together seems paradoxically related to her reticence, her coldness, her preservation of an area of inviolable privacy in herself. Though she believes that each person is not limited to himself, but is spread out among other people like mist in the branches of a tree, with another part of her spirit she contracts into herself and resents intensely any invasion of her privacy. It almost seems as if her keeping of a secret private self is reciprocally related to her social power to gather people together and put them in relationship to one another. The motif of

Clarissa's frigidity, of her prudery, of her separateness runs all through *Mrs. Dalloway*. "The death of her soul," Peter Walsh calls it. Since her illness, she has slept alone, in a narrow bed in an attic room. She cannot "dispel a virginity preserved through childbirth which [clings] to her like a sheet." She has "through some contraction of this cold spirit" failed her husband again and again. She feels a stronger sexual attraction to other women than to men. A high point of her life was the moment when Sally Seton kissed her. Her decision not to marry Peter Walsh but to marry Richard Dalloway instead was a rejection of intimacy and a grasping at privacy. "For in marriage a little licence, a little independence there must be between people living together day in day out in the same house; which Richard gave her, and she him . . . But with Peter everything had to be shared; everything gone into. And it was intolerable." "And there is a dignity in people; a solitude; even between husband and wife a gulf," thinks Clarissa much later in the novel. Her hatred of her daughter's friend Miss Kilman, of Sir William Bradshaw, of all the representatives of domineering will, of the instinct to convert others, of "love and religion," is based on this respect for isolation and detachment: "Had she ever tried to convert any one herself? Did she not wish everybody merely to be themselves?" The old lady whom Clarissa sees so often going upstairs to her room in the neighboring house seems to stand chiefly for this highest value, "the privacy of the soul": "that's the miracle, that's the mystery; that old lady, she meant . . . And the supreme mystery . . . was simply this: here was one room; there another. Did religion solve that, or love?"

The climax of *Mrs. Dalloway* is not Clarissa's party but the moment when, having heard of the suicide of Septimus, Clarissa leaves her guests behind and goes alone into the little room where Lady Bruton has a few minutes earlier been talking to the Prime Minister about India. There she sees in the next house the old lady once more, this time going quietly to bed. She thinks about Septimus and recognizes how factitious all her attempt to assemble and to connect has been. Her withdrawal from her party suggests that she has even in the midst of her guests kept untouched the privacy of her soul, that still point from which one can recognize the hollowness of the social world and feel the attraction of the death everyone carries within him as his deepest reality. Death is the place of true communion. Clarissa has been attempting the impossible, to bring the values of death into the daylight world of life. Septimus chose the right way. By killing himself he preserved his integrity, "plunged holding his treasure," his link to the deep places where each man or woman is connected to every other man or woman. For did he not in his madness hear his dead comrade, Evans, speaking to him from that region where all the dead dwell together? "Communication is health; communication is happiness"—Septimus during his madness expresses what is the highest goal for all the characters, but his suicide constitutes a recognition that communication cannot be attained except evanescently in life. The only repetition of the past that successfully repossesses it is the act of suicide.

Clarissa's recognition of this truth, her moment of self-condemnation, is at the same time the moment of her greatest insight:

> She had once thrown a shilling into the Serpentine, never anything more. But he had flung it away. They went on living . . . They (all day she had been thinking of Bourton, of Peter, of Sally), they would grow old. A thing there was that mattered; a thing, wreathed about with chatter, defaced, obscured in her own life, let drop every day in corruption, lies, chatter. This he had preserved. Death was defiance. Death was an attempt to communicate; people feeling the impossibility of reaching the centre which, mystically, evaded them; closeness drew apart; rapture faded, one was alone. There was an embrace in death.

From the point of view of the "thing" at the center that matters most, all speech, all social action, all building it up, all forms of communication, are lies. The more one tries to reach this centre through such means the further away from it one goes. The ultimate lesson of *Mrs. Dalloway* is that by building it up, one destroys. Only by throwing it away can life be preserved. It is preserved by being laid to rest on that underlying reality which Woolf elsewhere describes as "a thing I see before me: something abstract; but residing in the downs or sky; beside which nothing matters; in which I shall rest and continue to exist. Reality I call it." "Nothing matters"—compared to this reality, which is only defaced, corrupted, covered over by all the everyday activities of life, everything else is emptiness and vanity: "there is nothing," wrote Woolf during one of her periods of depression, "—nothing for any of us. Work, reading, writing are all disguises; and relations with people."

Septimus Smith's suicide anticipates Virginia Woolf's own death. Both deaths are a defiance, an attempt to communicate, a recognition that self-annihilation is the only possible way to embrace that center which evades one as long as one is alive. Clarissa does not follow Septimus into death (though she has a bad heart, and the original plan, according to the preface Woolf wrote for the Modern Library edition of the novel, was to have her kill herself). Even so, the words of the dirge in *Cymbeline* have been echoing through her head all day: "Fear no more the heat o' th' sun / Nor the furious winter's rages." Clarissa's obsession with these lines indicates her half-conscious awareness that in spite of her love of life she will reach peace and escape from suffering only in death. The lines come into her mind for a last time just before she returns from her solitary meditation to fulfill her role as hostess. They come to signify her recognition of her kinship with Septimus, her kinship with death. For she is, as Woolf said in the Modern Library preface, the "double" of Septimus. In *Mrs. Dalloway,* Woolf said, "I want to give life and death, sanity and insanity." The novel was meant to be "a study of insanity and suicide; the world seen by the sane and the insane side by side." These poles are not so much opposite as reversed images of one another. Each has the same elemental design. The death by suicide Woolf originally planned for Clarissa is fulfilled by Septimus, who dies for her, so to speak, a substitute suicide. Clarissa and Septimus seek the same thing: communication, wholeness, the oneness of reality, but only Septimus takes the way sure to reach it. Clarissa's attempt to create unity in her party is the mirror image in the world of light and life of Septimus's vigorous appropriation of the dark embrace of death in his suicide: "Fear no more the heat of the sun. She must go back to them. But what an extraordinary night! She felt somehow very like him—the young man who had killed himself. She felt glad that he had done it; thrown it away." For Woolf, as for Conrad, the visible world of light and life is the mirror image or repetition in reverse of an invisible world of darkness and death. Only the former can be seen and described. Death is incompatible with language, but by talking about life, one can talk indirectly about death.

Mrs. Dalloway seems to end in a confrontation of life and death as looking-glass counterparts. Reality, authenticity, and completion are on the death side of the mirror, while life is at best the illusory, insubstantial and fragmentary image of that dark reality. There is, however, one more structural element in *Mrs. Dalloway,* one final twist which reverses the polarities once more, or rather which holds them poised in their irreconciliation. Investigation of this will permit a final identification of the way Woolf brings into the open latent implications of traditional modes of storytelling in English fiction.

I have said that *Mrs. Dalloway* has a double temporal form. During the day of the action the chief characters resurrect in memory by bits and pieces the central episode of their common past. All these characters then come together again at Clarissa's party. The narrator in her turn embraces both these times in the perspective of a single distance. She moves forward through her own time of narration toward the point when the two times of the characters come together in the completion of the final sentences of the novel, when Peter sees Clarissa returning to her party. Or should one say "almost come together," since the temporal gap still exists in the separation between "is" and "was"? "It is Clarissa, he said. For there she was."

In the life of the characters, this moment of completion passes. The party ends. Sally, Peter, Clarissa, and the rest move on toward death. The victory of the narrator is to rescue from death this moment and all the other moments of the novel in that All Souls' Day at a second power which is literature. Literature for Woolf is repetition as preservation, but preservation of things and persons in their antithetical poise. Time is rescued by this repetition. It is rescued in its perpetually reversing divisions. It is lifted into the region of death with which the mind of the narrator has from the first page been identified. This is a place of absence, where nothing exists but words. These words generate their own reality. Clarissa, Peter, and the rest can be encountered only in the pages of the novel. The reader enters this realm of language when he leaves his own solid world and begins to read *Mrs. Dalloway*. The novel is a double resurrection. The characters exist for themselves as alive in a present which is a resuscitation of their dead pasts. In the all-embracing mind of the narrator the characters exist as dead men and women whose continued existence depends on her words. When the circle of the narration is complete, past joining present, the apparently living characters reveal themselves to be already dwellers among the dead.

Clarissa's vitality, her ability "to be; to exist," is expressed in the present-tense statement made by Peter Walsh in the penultimate line of the novel: "It is Clarissa." This affirmation of her power to sum it all up in the moment echoes earlier descriptions of her "extraordinary gift, that woman's gift, of making a world of her own wherever she happened to be": "She came into a room; she stood, as he had often seen her, in a doorway with lots of people round her . . . she never

said anything specially clever; there she was, however; there she was";
"There she was, mending her dress." These earlier passages are in the
past tense, as is the last line of the novel: "For there she was." With
this sentence "is" becomes "was" in the indirect discourse of the
narrator. In that mode of language Clarissa along with all the other
characters recedes into an indefinitely distant past. Life becomes death
within the impersonal mind of the narrator and within her language,
which is the place of communion in death. There the fragmentary is
made whole. There all is assembled into one unit. All the connections
between one part of the novel and another are known only to the agile
and ubiquitous mind of the narrator. They exist only within the
embrace of that reconciling spirit and through the power of her words.

Nevertheless, to return once more to the other side of the irony,
the dirge in *Cymbeline* is sung over an Imogen who is only apparently
dead. The play is completed with the seemingly miraculous return to
life of the heroine. In the same way, Clarissa comes back from her
solitary confrontation with death during her party. She returns from her
recognition of her kinship with Septimus to bring "terror" and "ecstasy" to Peter when he sees her. She comes back also into the
language of the narration where, like Imogen raised from the dead, she
may be confronted by the reader in the enduring language of literature.

It is perhaps for this reason that Woolf changed her original plan
and introduced Septimus as Clarissa's surrogate in death. To have had
a single protagonist who was swallowed up in the darkness would have
falsified her conception. She needed two protagonists, one who
dies and another who dies with his death. Clarissa vividly lives through
Septimus's death as she meditates alone during her party. Then, having
died vicariously, she returns to life. She appears before her guests to
cause, in Peter Walsh at least, "extraordinary excitement." Not only
does Clarissa's vitality come from her proximity to death. The novel
needs for its structural completeness two opposite but similar movements, Septimus's plunge into death and Clarissa's resurrection from
the dead. *Mrs. Dalloway* is both of these at once: the entry into the
realm of communication in death and the revelation of that realm in
words which may be read by the living.

Though *Mrs. Dalloway* seems almost nihilistically to recommend
the embrace of death, and though its author did in fact finally take this
plunge, nevertheless, like the rest of Woolf's writing, it represents in
fact a contrary movement of the spirit. In a note in her diary of May
1933, Woolf records a moment of insight into what brings about a

"synthesis" of her being: "how only writing composes it; how nothing makes a whole unless I am writing." Or again: "Odd how the creative power at once brings the whole universe to order." Like Clarissa's party or like the other examples of building it up in *Mrs. Dalloway,* the novel is a constructive action which gathers unconnected elements into a solidly existing object. It is something which belongs to the everyday world of physical things. It is a book with cardboard covers and white pages covered with black marks. This made-up thing, unlike its symbol, Clarissa's party, belongs to both worlds. If it is in one sense no more than a manufactured physical object, it is in another sense made of words which designate not the material presence of the things named but their absence from the everyday world and their existence within the place out of place and time out of time which are the space and time of literature. Woolf's writing has as its aim bringing into the light of day this realm of communication in language. A novel, for Woolf, is the solace of death made visible. Writing is the only action which exists simultaneously on both sides of the mirror, within death and within life at once.

Though Woolf deals with extreme spiritual situations, her work would hardly give support to a scheme of literary history which sees twentieth-century literature as more negative, more "nihilistic," or more "ambiguous" than nineteenth-century literature. The "undecidability" of *Mrs. Dalloway* lies in the impossibility of knowing, from the text, whether the realm of union in death exists, for Woolf, only in the words, or whether the words represent an extralinguistic realm which is "really there" for the characters, for the narrator, and for Woolf herself. Nevertheless, the possibility that the realm of death, in real life as in fiction, really exists, is more seriously entertained by Woolf than it is, for example, by Eliot, by Thackeray, or by Hardy. The possibility that repetition in narrative is the representation of a transcendent spiritual realm of reconciliation and preservation, a realm of the perpetual resurrection of the dead, is more straightforwardly proposed by Virginia Woolf than by most of her predecessors in English fiction.

Narrative Structure(s) and Female Development: The Case of *Mrs. Dalloway*

Elizabeth Abel

> *I wish you were a Kangaroo and had a pouch for small Kangaroos to creep to.*
> VIRGINIA STEPHEN to Violet Dickinson (1903)

> *Our insight into this early, pre-Oedipus, phase comes to us as a surprise, like the discovery, in another field, of the Minoan-Mycenean civilization behind the civilization of Greece.*
> SIGMUND FREUD, "Female Sexuality" (1931)

We all know Virginia Woolf disliked the fixity of plot: "This appalling narrative business of the realist," she called it. Yet like all writers of fiction, she inevitably invoked narrative patterns in her work, if only to disrupt them or reveal their insignificance. In *Mrs. Dalloway,* a transitional work between the straightforward narrative of an early novel like *The Voyage Out* and the experimental structure of a late work like *The Waves,* Woolf superimposes the outlines of multiple, familiar yet altered plots that dispel the constraints of a unitary plan, diffuse the chronological framework of the single day in June, and enable an iconoclastic plot to weave its course covertly through the narrative grid. In this palimpsestic layering of plots, *Mrs. Dalloway* conforms to Gilbert and Gubar's characterization of the typically female text as one which both inscribes and hides its subversive impulses.

The story of female development in *Mrs. Dalloway,* a novel planned such that "every scene would build up the idea of C[larissa]'s charac-

From *The Voyage In: Fictions of Female Development,* edited by Elizabeth Able, Marianne Hirsch, and Elizabeth Langland. © 1983 by the Trustees of Dartmouth College. University Press of New England, 1983.

ter," is a clandestine story that remains almost untold, that resists direct narration and coherent narrative shape. Both intrinsically disjointed and textually dispersed and disguised, it is the novel's buried story. The fractured developmental plot reflects the encounter of gender with narrative form and adumbrates the psychoanalytic story of female development, a story Freud and Woolf devised concurrently and separately, and published simultaneously in 1925. The structure of Woolf's developmental story and its status in the novel illustrate distinctive features of female experience and female plots.

Woolf repeatedly acknowledged differences between male and female writing, detecting the influence of gender in fictional voice and plot. While insisting that the creative mind must be androgynous, incandescent, and unimpeded by personal grievance, she nevertheless affirmed that differences between male and female experience would naturally emerge in distinctive fictional shapes. She claims,

> No one will admit that he can possibly mistake a novel written by a man for a novel written by a woman. There is the obvious and enormous difference of experience in the first place. . . . And finally . . . there rises for consideration the very difficult question of the difference between the man's and the woman's view of what constitutes the importance of any subject. From this spring not only marked differences of plot and incident, but infinite differences in selection, method and style.
>
> (*A Writer's Diary*)

The experience that shapes the female plot skews the woman novelist's relationship to narrative tradition; this oblique relationship may further mold the female text. In a remarkable passage in *A Room of One's Own,* Woolf describes one way in which the difference in experience can affect the logic of the female text:

> And since a novel has this correspondence to real life, its values are to some extent those of real life. But it is obvious that the values of women differ very often from the values which have been made by the other sex; naturally, this is so. Yet it is the masculine values that prevail. . . . And these values are inevitably transferred from life to fiction. This is an important book, the critic assumes, because it deals with war. This is an insignificant book because it deals with the

> feelings of women in a drawing-room. A scene in a battle-
> field is more important than a scene in a shop—everywhere
> and much more subtly the difference of value persists. The
> whole structure, therefore, of the early nineteenth-century
> novel was raised, if one was a woman, by a mind which was
> slightly pulled from the straight, and made to alter its clear
> vision in deference to external authority. . . . the writer was
> meeting criticism. . . . She met that criticism as her temper-
> ament dictated, with docility and diffidence, or with anger
> and emphasis. It does not matter which it was; she was
> thinking of something other than the thing itself. . . . She
> had altered her values in deference to the opinions of others.

Woolf explicitly parallels the dominance of male over female values in
literature and life, while implying a different hierarchy that further
complicates the woman novelist's task. By contrasting the "values of
women" with those which "have been made by the other sex," Woolf
suggests the primacy of female values as products of nature rather than
culture, and of the named sex rather than the "other" one. No longer
the conventionally "second" sex, women here appear the source of
intrinsic and primary values. In the realm of culture, however, masculine values prevail and deflect the vision of the woman novelist, insert-
ing a duality into the female narrative, turned Janus-like toward the
responses of both self and other. This schizoid perspective can fracture
the female text. The space between emphasis and undertone, a space
that is apparent in Woolf's own text, may also be manifested in the gap
between a plot that is shaped to confirm expectations and a subplot at
odds with this accommodation. If the early nineteenth-century woman
novelist betrayed her discomfort with male evaluation by overt protes-
tation or compliance, the early twentieth-century woman novelist,
more aware of this dilemma, may encode as a subtext the stories she
wishes yet fears to tell.

Feminist literary criticism, Elaine Showalter states, presents us
with "a radical alteration of our vision, a demand that we see meaning
in what has previously been empty space. The orthodox plot recedes,
and another plot, hitherto submerged in the anonymity of the background, stands out in bold relief like a thumbprint." The excavation of
buried plots in women's texts has revealed an enduring, if recessive,
narrative concern with the story of mothers and daughters—with the
"lost tradition," as the title of one anthology names it, or, in psycho-

analytic terminology, with the "pre-Oedipal" relationship, the early symbiotic female bond that both predates and coexists with the hetero-sexual orientation toward the father and his substitutes. Frequently, the subtleties of mother-daughter alignments, for which few narrative conventions have been formulated, are relegated to the background of a dominant romantic or courtship plot. As women novelists increasingly exhaust or dismiss the possibilities of the romantic plot, however, they have tended to inscribe the maternal subplot more emphatically. In contemporary women's fiction, this subplot is often dominant; but in the fiction of the 1920s, a particularly fruitful decade for women and women's writing, the plot of female bonding began to vie repeatedly with the plot of heterosexual love. Woolf, Colette, and Cather high-lighted aspects of the mother-daughter narrative in works such as *My Mother's House* (1922), *To the Lighthouse* (1927), *Break of Day* (1928), *Sido* (1929), and *"Old Mrs. Harris"* (1932). In *Mrs. Dalloway,* written two years before *To the Lighthouse,* Woolf structures her heroine's development, the recessive narrative of her novel, as a story of pre-Oedipal attachment and loss.

In his essay, "Female Sexuality," Freud parallels the pre-Oedipal phase of female development to the allegedly matriarchal civilization lying behind that of classical Greece, presumably associated here with its most famous drama; his analogy offers a trope for the psychological and textual strata of *Mrs. Dalloway.* For Freud conflates, through the spatial and temporal meanings of the word "behind" (*hinter*), notions of evolution with those of static position. Clarissa Dalloway's recollected development proceeds from an emotionally pre-Oedipal female-centered natural world to the heterosexual male-dominated social world, a movement, Woolf implies, that recapitulates the broader sweep of history from matriarchal to patriarchal orientation. But the textual locus of this development, to revert to the archaeological implications of Freud's image, is buried *sub*text that endures throughout the do-mestic and romantic plots in the foreground: the metaphors of palimp-sest and cultural strata coincide here. The interconnections of female development, historical progress, and narrative structure are captured in Freud's image of a pre-Oedipal world underlying the individual and cultural origins we conventionally assign the names Oedipus and Athens.

Woolf embeds her radical developmental plot in a narrative matrix pervaded by gentler acts of revision; defining the place of this reces-sive plot requires some awareness of the larger structure. The narrative present, patterned as the sequence of a day, both recalls the structure of

Ulysses, which Woolf completed reading as she began *Mrs. Dalloway,* and offers a female counterpart to Joyce's adaptation of an epic form. *Mrs. Dalloway* inverts the hierarchy Woolf laments in *A Room of One's Own.* Her foregrounded domestic plot unfolds precisely in shops and drawing rooms rather than on battlefields, and substitutes for epic quest and conquest the traditionally feminine project of giving a party, of constructing social harmony through affiliation rather than conflict; the potentially epic plot of the soldier returned from war is demoted to the tragic subplot centering on Septimus Warren Smith. By echoing the structure of *Ulysses* in the narrative foreground of her text, Woolf revises a revision of the epic to accommodate the values and experience of women while cloaking the more subversive priorities explored in the covert developmental tale.

A romantic plot, which provides the dominant structure for the past in *Mrs. Dalloway,* also obscures the story of Clarissa's development. Here again, Woolf revises a traditional narrative pattern, the courtship plot perfected by Woolf's elected "foremother," Jane Austen. Woolf simultaneously invokes and dismisses Austen's narrative model through Clarissa's mistaken impression that her future husband is named Wickham. This slight, if self-conscious, clue to a precursor assumes greater import in light of Woolf's lifelong admiration for Austen and Woolf's efforts to reconstruct this "most perfect artist among women" in her literary daughter's image; these efforts structure Woolf's essay on Austen, written shortly after *Mrs. Dalloway.* Woolf's treatment of the romantic plot in *Mrs. Dalloway* reveals the temporal boundaries of Austen's narratives, which cover primarily the courtship period and inevitably culminate in happy marriages. Woolf condenses the expanded moment that constitutes an Austen novel and locates it in a remembered scene thirty years prior to the present of her narrative, decentering and unraveling Austen's plot. Marriage in *Mrs. Dalloway* provides impetus rather than closure to the courtship plot, dissolved into a retrospective oscillation between two alluring possibilities as Clarissa continues to replay the choice she made thirty years before. The courtship plot in this novel is both evoked through memories of the past and indefinitely suspended in the present, completed when the narrative begins and incomplete when the narrative ends, sustained as a narrative thread by Clarissa's enduring uncertainty. The novel provides no resolution to this internalized version of the plot; the final scene presents Clarissa through Peter Walsh's amorous eyes and allies Richard Dalloway with his daughter. The elongated courtship plot, the imperfectly resolved emotional triangle, becomes a screen for the developmental story that unfolds in fragments of memory, unexplained interstices between events, and narrative asides and interludes.

When Woolf discovered how to enrich her characterization by digging "beautiful caves" into her characters' pasts, her own geological image for the temporal strata of *Mrs. Dalloway,* she chose with precision the consciousness through which to reveal specific segments of the past. Although Clarissa vacillates emotionally between the allure of Peter and that of Richard, she remembers Peter's courtship only glancingly; the burden of that plot is carried by Peter, through whose memories Woolf relates the slow and tortured end of the relation with Clarissa. Clarissa's memories, by contrast, focus more exclusively on the general ambience of Bourton, her childhood home, and her love for Sally Seton. Significantly absent from these memories is Richard Dalloway, whose courtship of Clarissa is presented exclusively through Peter's painful recollections. Clarissa thinks of Richard only in the present, not at the peak of a romantic relationship. Through this narrative distribution, Woolf constructs two diversified poles structuring the flux of Clarissa's consciousness. Bourton is to Clarissa a pastoral female world spatially and temporally disjunct from marriage and the sociopolitical world of (Richard's) London. The fluid passage of consciousness between these poles conceals a radical schism.

Though the Bourton scenes Clarissa remembers span a period of several years, they are absorbed by a single emotional climate that creates a constant backdrop to the foregrounded day in June. Woolf excises all narrative connections between these contrasting extended moments. She provides no account of intervening events: Clarissa's marriage, childbirth, the move and adjustment to London. And she indicates the disjunction in Clarissa's experience by noting that the London hostess never returns to Bourton, which now significantly belongs to a male relative, and almost never sees Sally Seton, now the unfamiliar Lady Rosseter. Clarissa's life in London is devoid of intimate female bonds: she is excluded from lunch at Lady Bruton's and she vies with Miss Kilman for her own daughter's allegiance. Woolf structures Clarissa's development as a stark binary opposition between past and present, nature and culture, feminine and masculine dispensations—the split implicit in Woolf's later claim that "the values of women differ very often from the values which have been made by the other sex." Versions of this opposition reverberate throughout the novel in rhetorical and narrative juxtapositions. The developmental plot, which slides beneath the more familiar romantic plot through the gap between Peter's and Clarissa's memories, exists as two contrasting moments and the silence adjoining and dividing them.

Woolf endows these moments with symbolic resonance by a meticulous strategy of narrative exclusions that juxtaposes eras split by thirty years and omits Clarissa's childhood from the novel's temporal frame. There is no past in *Mrs. Dalloway* anterior to Clarissa's adolescence at Bourton. Within this selective scheme, the earliest remembered scenes become homologous to a conventional narrative point of departure: the description of formative childhood years. The emotional tenor of these scenes, moreover, suggests their representation of deferred childhood desire. Clarissa's earliest narrated memories focus on Sally's arrival at Bourton, an arrival that infuses the formal, repressive atmosphere with a vibrant female energy. The only picture of Clarissa's early childhood sketched in the novel suggests a tableau of female loss: a dead mother, a dead sister, a distant father, and a stern maiden aunt, the father's sister, whose hobby of pressing flowers beneath Littre's dictionary suggests to Peter Walsh the social oppression of women, an emblem of nature ossified by language/culture. In this barren atmosphere, Sally's uninhibited warmth and sensuality immediately spark love in the eighteen-year-old Clarissa. Sally replaces Clarissa's dead mother and sister, her name even echoing the sister's name, Sylvia. She nurtures Clarissa's passions and intellect, inspiring a love equal to Othello's in intensity and equivalent in absoluteness to a daughter's earliest bond with her mother, a bond too early ruptured for Clarissa as for Woolf, a bond which Woolf herself perpetually sought to recreate through intimate attachments to mother surrogates, such as Violet Dickinson: "I wish you were a Kangaroo and had a pouch for small Kangaroos to creep to." For Clarissa, kissing Sally creates the most exquisite moment of her life, a moment of unparalleled radiance and intensity: "The whole world might have turned upside down! The others disappeared; there she was alone with Sally. And she felt she had been given a present, wrapped up, and told just to keep it, not to look at it—a diamond, something infinitely precious, wrapped up, which, as they walked (up and down, up and down), she uncovered, or the radiance burnt through, the revelation, the religious feeling! —when old Joseph and Peter faced them." This kind of passionate attachment between women, orthodox psychoanalysts and feminists uncharacteristically agree, recaptures some aspect of the fractured mother-daughter bond. Within the sequence established by the novel, this adolescent love assumes the power of the early female bond excluded from the narrative.

The moment Woolf selects to represent Clarissa's past carries the full weight of the pre-Oedipal experience that Freud discovered with such a shock substantially predates and shapes the female version of the Oedipus complex, the traumatic turn from mother to father. As French psychoanalytic theory has clarified, the Oedipus complex is less a biologically ordained event than a symbolic moment of acculturation, the moment, in Freud's words, that "may be regarded as a victory of the race over the individual," that "initiates all the processes that are designed to make the individual find a place in the cultural community." For both women and men, this socialization exacts renunciation, but for women this is a process of poorly compensated loss, for the boy's rewards for renouncing his mother will include a woman like the mother and full paternal privileges, while the girl's renunciation of her mother will at best be requited with a future child, but no renewed access to the lost maternal body, the first love object for girls as well as boys, and no acquisition of paternal power. In *Mrs. Dalloway,* Woolf encapsulates an image of the brusque and painful turn that, whenever it occurs, abruptly terminates the earliest stage of female development and defines the moment of acculturation as a moment of obstruction.

Woolf organizes the developmental plot such that Clarissa's love for Sally precedes her allegiances to men; the two women "spoke of marriage always as a catastrophe." Clarissa perceives Peter in this period primarily as an irritating intruder. The scene that Clarissa most vividly remembers, the scene of Sally Seton's kiss, is rudely interrupted by Peter's appearance. Both the action and the language of this scene hint at psychological allegory. The moment of exclusive female connection is shattered by masculine intervention, a rupture signaled typographically by Woolf's characteristic dash. Clarissa's response to this intrusion images an absolute and arbitrary termination: "It was like running one's face against a granite wall in the darkness! It was shocking; it was horrible!" Clarissa's perception of Peter's motives—"she felt his hostility; his jealousy; his determination to break into their comradeship"—suggests an Oedipal configuration: the jealous male attempting to rupture the exclusive female bond, insisting on the transference of attachment to the man, demanding heterosexuality. For women this configuration institutes a break as decisive and unyielding as a granite wall. Clarissa's revenge is to refuse to marry Peter and to select instead the less demanding Richard Dalloway in order to guard a portion of her psyche for the memory of Sally. Woolf herself exacts poetic justice by subjecting Peter Walsh to a transposed, inverted replay of this crucial scene when Elizabeth, thirty years later, interrupts his emotional reunion with her mother by unexpectedly opening a door (in the granite wall?), asserting by her presence the primacy of female bonds. "Here is my Elizabeth," Clarissa announces to the disconcerted Peter, the possessive pronoun he finds so extraneous accentuating the intimacy of the mother-daughter tie.

Clarissa resists the wrenching, requisite shift from pre-Oedipal to Oedipal orientation, yet she submits in practice if not totally in feeling. The extent of the disjunction she undergoes is only apparent in the bifurcated settings of her history, the images reiterating radical divides, the gaps slyly inserted in the narrative. The most striking of these images and gaps concern Clarissa's sister Sylvia, a shadowy and seemingly gratuitous character, apparently created just to be destroyed. Her death, her only action in the novel, is recalled by Peter rather than by Clarissa and is related in two sentences. This offhand presentation both implants and conceals an exaggerated echo of Clarissa's split experience. A young woman "on the verge of life," Sylvia is abruptly killed by a falling tree that dramatically imposes a barrier to life in a gesture of destruction mysteriously associated with her father: "(all Justin Parry's fault—all his carelessness)." The shocking attribution of blame is only ostensibly discounted by parentheses: recall Woolf's parenthetical accounts of human tragedy in the "Time Passes" section of *To the Lighthouse*. The deliberate decision to indict the father contrasts with the earlier story, "Mrs. Dalloway in Bond Street," where Sylvia's death is depicted as a tranquil, vague event absorbed by nature's cyclical benevolence: "It used, thought, Clarissa, to be so simple . . . When Sylvia died, hundreds of years ago, the yew hedges looked so lovely with the diamond webs in the mist before early church." The violence of Sylvia's death in the novel and the very incongruity between the magnitude of the charge against her father and its parenthetical presentation suggest a story intentionally withheld, forcibly deprived of its legitimate proportions, deliberately excised from the narrative yet provocatively implied in it, written both into and out of the text. This self-consciously inscribed narrative gap echoes the gap in Clarissa's own narrative, as the dramatic severance of Sylvia's life at the moment of maturity echoes the split in her sister's development. The pastoral resonance of Sylvia's name also implies a larger female story of natural existence abruptly curtailed. A related narrative exclusion suggests a crucial untold tale about Clarissa's relation to her mother, remarkably unremembered and unmentioned in the novel except by a casual party guest whose brief comparison of Clarissa to her mother brings sudden tears to Clarissa's eyes. The story of the pain entailed in this loss is signaled by but placed outside the narrative in the double gesture of inclusion and exclusion that structures Woolf's narration of her heroine's development. By locating the clues to this discontinuous narrative in the marginal moments of her text, Woolf creates an inconspicuous subtext perceptible only to an altered vision.

Woolf's discrete suggestion of an intermittent plot is politically astute and aesthetically adept. Her insight into the trauma of female development does subvert the notion of organic, even growth culminating for women in marriage and motherhood, and she prudently conceals her implications of a violent adaptation. The narrative gaps also challenge the conventions of linear plot and suggest its distorted regimentation of experience, particularly the subjective experience of women. These gaps, moreover, are mimetically precise: juxtapositions represent sudden shifts, silence indicates absence and loss. Perhaps Woolf's most striking achievement, however, is her intuition of the "plot" Freud detected in female development. Despite Woolf's obvious familiarity with the popularized aspects of Freudian theory, and despite the close association of her Hogarth Press with Freudian oeuvre, there can be no question of influence here, for Freud first expounded his view of a distinctively female development the year of *Mrs. Dalloway*'s publication. Rather than influence, *Mrs. Dalloway* demonstrates the common literary prefiguration of psychoanalytic doctrine, which can retroactively articulate patterns implicit in the literary text. The similarities between these fictional and psychoanalytic narratives clarify the structure of Woolf's submerged developmental plot and the power of Freud's submerged demonstration of the loss implicit in female development.

Only late in life did Freud acknowledge the fundamentally different courses of male and female development. Prior to the 1925 essay entitled "Some Psychical Consequences of the Anatomical Distinction Between the Sexes," Freud clung, though with increasing reservations, to a view of sexual symmetry in which male and female versions of the Oedipal experience were fundamentally parallel. His growing appreciation of the pre-Oedipal stage in girls, however, finally toppled his view of parallel male and female tracks, inspiring a new formulation of the distinctively female developmental tasks. Female identity is acquired, according to this new theory, by a series of costly repressions from which the male child is exempt. The girl's developmental path is more arduous and bumpy than the boy's smoother linear route. For though the male child must repress his erotic attachment to his mother, he must undergo no change in orientation, since the mother will eventually be replaced by other women with whom he will achieve the status of the father; he suffers an arrest rather than a dislocation. The girl, in contrast, must reverse her course. Like the boy, she begins life erotically bonded with her mother in the symbiotic pre-Oedipal stage, but unlike him she must replace this orientation with a heterosexual attraction to her father. She must change the nature of her desire before renouncing it.

How, Freud repeatedly asks, does the girl accomplish this monumental shift from mother to father? Though the answers he proposes may be dubious, the persistent question indicates the magnitude of the event. The girl's entire sexuality is defined in this situation. She switches not only the object of her erotic interest, but also her erotic zone and mode, relinquishing the active, "masculine," clitoridal sexuality focused on her mother for the passive, receptive, "feminine," vaginal sexuality focused on her father. Freud goes so far as to call this change a "change in her own sex," for prior to this crucial shift, "the little girl is a little man." This comprehensive change in sexual object, organ, and attitude, the shift from pre-Oedipal to Oedipal orientation, inserts a profound discontinuity into female development, which contrasts with that of "the more fortunate man [who] has only to continue at the time of his sexual maturity the activity that he has previously carried out at the period of the early efflorescence of his sexuality." The psychosexual shift that occurs in early childhood, moreover, is often reenacted in early adulthood, for marriage typically reinstates a disruption in women's experience, confined until recently to a largely female sphere prior to the heterosexual contract of marriage.

The circuitous route to female identity, Freud acknowledged, is uniquely demanding and debilitating: "a comparison with what happens with boys tells us that the development of a little girl into a normal woman is more difficult and more complicated, since it includes two extra tasks [the change of sexual object and organ], to which there is nothing corresponding in the development of a man." No woman completes this difficult process unscathed. Freud outlines three developmental paths for women; all exact a substantial toll. If she follows the first, the girl negotiates the shift from mother to father by accepting the unwelcome "fact" of her castration, detected in comparisons between herself and little boys. Mortified by this discovery of inferiority, aware she can no longer compete for her mother with her better endowed brother, she renounces her active sexual orientation toward her mother, deprived like herself of the valued sexual organ, and accepts a passive orientation toward the superior father. Unfortunately, the girl's renunciation of active sexuality normally entails repressing "a good part of her sexual trends in general," and this route leads to sexual inhibition or neurosis, to "a general revulsion from sexuality." If she chooses the second path, the girl simply refuses this renunciation, clings to her "threatened masculinity," struggles to preserve her active orientation toward her mother, and develops what Freud calls a "masculinity complex," which often finds expression in homosexuality. Only the third "very circuitous" path leads to the "normal female attitude" in which the girl takes her father as the object of her passive eroticism and enters the female Oedipus complex. Curiously, however, Freud never describes this route, which turns out to be only a less damaging version of the first path toward inhibition and neurosis. To the extent that her sexuality survives her "catastrophic" repression of her "masculine" desire for her mother, the girl will be able to complete her turn to her father and seal her femininity by desiring his baby. "Normal" femininity is thus a fragile, tenuous proposition; no unique course is prescribed for its achievement. Freud's most optimistic prognosis assumes a doubly hypothetical, negative form: "If too much is not lost in the course of it [development] through repression, this femininity may turn out to be normal." The achievement of this femininity, moreover, is only the first stage, for the female Oedipus complex, like the male, must itself be overcome, and the hard-won desire for the father renounced and transferred to other men. Female development thus entails a double disappointment in contrast with the single renunciation required of men. No wonder Freud concludes the last of his essays on femininity by contrasting the youthful flexibility of a thirty-year-old male with the psychical rigidity of a woman the same age: "Her libido has taken up final positions and seems incapable of exchanging them for others. There are no paths open to further development; it is as though the whole process had already run its course and remains thenceforward insusceptible to influence—as though, indeed, the difficult development to femininity had exhausted the possibilities of the person concerned."

In *Mrs. Dalloway,* Woolf suggests the developmental turn that

Freud accentuates in his studies of femininity. The narratives they sketch share a radically foreshortened notion of development, condensed for Freud into a few childhood years, focused for Woolf in a single emotional shift. Both narratives eschew the developmental scope traditionally assumed by fiction and psychology, committed to detailing the unfolding of a life, and both stress the discontinuities specific to female development. Woolf, moreover, portrays the sexual and emotional calcification that Freud suggests is the toll of "normal" development. Clarissa is explicit about her unimpassioned response to men, a response she perceives as a failure and a lack, a guarding of virginity through motherhood and marriage. Her emotional and physical self-containment is represented by her narrow attic bed, where she reads Baron Marbot's memoirs of the retreat from Moscow, a victory achieved by icy withdrawal. The association of her bed with a grave—"Narrower and narrower would her bed be"—links her adult sexuality with death. Yet, in a passage of extraordinary erotic writing, Woolf contrasts the description of the narrow bed with Clarissa's passionate responses to women, implying through this juxtaposition the cost of the pivotal developmental choice:

> Yet she could not resist sometimes yielding to the charm of a woman, not a girl, of a woman confessing, as to her they often did, some scrape, some folly . . . she did undoubtedly then feel what men felt. Only for a moment; but it was enough. It was a sudden revelation, a tinge like a blush which one tried to check and then, as it spread, one yielded to its expansion, and rushed to the farthest verge and there quivered and felt the world come closer, swollen with some astonishing significance, some pressure of rapture, which split its thin skin and gushed and poured with an extraordinary alleviation over the cracks and sores! Then, for that moment, she had seen an illumination; a match burning in a crocus; an inner meaning almost expressed. But the close withdrew; the hard softened. It was over—the moment. Against such moments (with women too) there contrasted (as she laid her hat down) the bed and Baron Marbot and the candle half-burnt.

Woolf's language renders a passion that is actively directed toward women, and implicitly "masculine" in attitude and character, yet also receptive and "feminine," epitomized in the image of the match in the crocus, an emblem of active female desire that conflates Freud's sexual dichotomies. The power of the passage derives in part from the intermeshed male and female imagery, and the interwoven languages of sex and mysticism, a mélange that recurs in Clarissa's memory of Sally Seton's kiss. Fusion—of male and female, active and passive, sacred and profane—is at the heart of this erotic experience. Freud's opposition of active, "masculine," pre-Oedipal sexuality to the passive, "feminine," Oedipal norm denies the basis for this integration. Clarissa's momentary illumination is enabled only by the sexual orientation Freud devalues as (initially) immature and (subsequently) deviant. Woolf's passage suggests the potential completeness Freud denies the pre-Oedipal realm and calls into question the differential of normal from aberrant sexuality. The stark contrast between the passionate moment and the narrow bed, another juxtaposition that conceals a schism between two radically different sexual worlds, subverts the opposition normal/abnormal. Woolf here elevates Freud's second developmental path over the costly route toward "normal femininity," as she valorizes a spontaneous homosexual love over the inhibitions of imposed heterosexuality.

As the passage continues, the gap between the sexual options emblematized by the moment and the bed evolves into the familiar split between Sally Seton and Richard Dalloway, the split that structures the developmental plot. The allegorical image of the bed leads to a more concrete description of Clarissa's reaction to her husband's return: "if she raised her head she could just hear the click of the handle released as gently as possible by Richard, who slipped upstairs in his socks and then, as often as not, dropped his hot-water bottle and swore! How she laughed!" The contrast between the passionate moment with women and the narrow marital bed becomes a leap from the sublime to the (affectionately) ridiculous. Opening with the conjunction "But," the next paragraph signals a turn away from mundanity back to "this question of love . . . this falling in love with women," inaugurating Clarissa's lengthy and lyrical reminiscence of Sally Seton. The opposition between Clarissa's relationships with men and women modulates to the split between her present and her past, her orientation and emotional capacities on both sides of the Oedipal divide. Woolf, like Freud, reveals the cost of female development, but she inscribes a far more graphic image of the loss entailed, questions its necessity, and indicates the price of equating female development with acculturation through the rites of passage established by the Oedipus complex.

These are radical claims, and Woolf suggests them indirectly. In addition to her use of juxtaposition as a narrative and rhetorical strategy, Woolf encodes her development plot through characters who subtly reflect Clarissa's experience. Perhaps most interesting of these is the infrequently noticed Rezia Warren Smith, wife of Clarissa's acknowledged double who has drawn critical attention away from the mirroring function of his wife. Rezia's life, like her name, is abbreviated in the novel, yet the course of her "development" suggestively echoes that of the heroine. Like Clarissa, Rezia finds herself plucked by marriage from an Edenic female world with which she preserves no contact. Her memories highlight the exclusively female community of sisters collaboratively making hats in an Italian setting that is pastoral despite the surrounding urban context: "For you should see the Milan gardens!" she later exclaims, when confronted with London's "few ugly flowers stuck in pots!" The cultural shift from Italy to England, like the shift from Bourton to London, locates this idyllic female life in a distant, prelapsarian era—before the war, before industrialization, before marriage. Marriage and war explicitly coalesce for Rezia as agents of expulsion from this female paradise: Septimus comes to Milan as a British soldier and proposes to Rezia to alleviate his war-induced emotional anesthesia. Rezia's memories of Italy, a radiant temporal backdrop to her painful alienation in marriage and a foreign culture, provide a pointed parallel to Clarissa's memories of Bourton. And Rezia's final pastoral vision, inspired by the drug administered after Septimus's suicide, significantly begins with her sense of "opening long windows, stepping out into some garden," thus echoing Clarissa's first recollection of Bourton, where she had "burst open the French windows and plunged . . . into the open air." The death of her husband releases Rezia to return imaginatively to a past she implicitly shares with Clarissa: the female-centered world anterior to heterosexual bonds. After this moment of imaginative release and return, Rezia disappears from the novel, having accomplished the function of delicately echoing the bifurcated structure of the heroine's development.

The relation of Clarissa and Rezia exists only for the reader; the two women know nothing of each other. Woolf employs a different strategy for connecting Clarissa with Septimus, whose death severs the link between these female characters, releasing each to a new developmental stage, Rezia to return imaginatively to the past, Clarissa at last to transcend that past. Septimus's suicide enables Clarissa to resolve the developmental impasse that appears to be one cause of her weakened heart, her constricted vitality. Critics have amply explored Septimus's role as Clarissa's double. As important as this psychological doubling, however, is Woolf's revision of developmental plots, her decision to transfer to Septimus the death she originally imagined for Clarissa, to sacrifice male to female development, to preserve her heroine from fictional tradition by substituting a hero for a heroine in the plot of violently thwarted development, a plot that has claimed such heroines as Catharine Linton, Maggie Tulliver, Emma Bovary, Anna Karenina, Tess Durbeyfield, Edna Pontellier, Lily Bart, and Antoinette Cosway Rochester. By making Septimus the hero of a sacrificial plot that enables the heroine's development, Woolf reverses narrative tradition.

It is a critical commonplace that Clarissa receives from Septimus a cathartic, vicarious experience of death that releases her to experience life's pleasures more deeply. Woolf's terms, however, are more precise. The passage describing Clarissa's reaction to Septimus's suicide suggests that he plays a specific role in Clarissa's emotional development. Woolf composes this passage as a subtle but extended parallel to Clarissa's earlier reminiscence of her love for Sally and Bourton. The interplay between the language and structure of these two meditative interludes, the two major sites of the developmental plot, encodes Clarissa's exploration of a conflict more suppressed than resolved. By interpreting Septimus's suicide in her private language of passion and integrity, Clarissa uses the shock of death to probe her unresolved relation to her past. The suicide triggers Clarissa's recurrent preoccupation with this past, providing a perspective that enables her belatedly both to admit and to renounce its hold. On the day in June that encloses the action of *Mrs. Dalloway,* Clarissa completes the developmental turn initiated thirty years before.

Woolf prepares the parallels between the two passages by inaugurating both with Clarissa's withdrawal from her customary social milieu. The emotions prompting Clarissa's first meditation on Sally and the past are initially triggered by her exclusion from Lady Bruton's lunch. Woolf then describes Clarissa's noontime retreat to her solitary attic room as a metaphorical departure from a party: "She began to go slowly upstairs . . . as if she had left a party . . . had shut the door and gone out and stood alone, a single figure against the appalling night"; Clarissa is "like a nun withdrawing." Later that night, when Clarissa hears the news of Septimus's suicide, she does leave her party and retreats to an empty little room where "the party's splendor fell to the floor." The first passage concludes with her preparations for the party, the second with her deliberate return to that party. Within these enclosed narrative and domestic spaces, Clarissa relives through memory the passionate scene with Sally on the terrace at Bourton. The second passage replays in its bifurcated structure the male intervention that curtails the original scene. In this final version of the female/male juxtaposition, however, the emotional valences are reversed.

Clarissa's meditation on Septimus's death modulates, through her association of passion with death, to a meditation on her relation to her past. Woolf orchestrates the verbal echoes of this passage to evoke with increasing clarity the scene with Sally Seton. Septimus's choice of a violent, early death elicits in Clarissa the notion of a central self preserved: "A thing there was that mattered; a thing, wreathed about with chatter, defaced, obscured in her own life. . . . This he had preserved." The visual image of a vital, central "thing" initiates the link with the earlier description of passion as "something central which permeated." The echoes between these passages develop through their similar representations of passion's ebb: "closeness drew apart; rapture faded, one was alone"; "But the close withdrew; the hard softened. It was over—the moment." As Clarissa implies that only death preserves the fading moment of passion, she prepares for her repetition of the *Othello* line that has signified her love for Sally Seton: "If it were now to die, 'twere now to be most happy." The metaphor of treasure which precedes this explicit allusion to the scene with Sally further connects Clarissa's response to Septimus ("had he plunged holding his treasure?" she wonders) with her memory of Sally's kiss as "a present . . . a diamond, something infinitely precious." Septimus's death evokes in Clarissa the knowledge of what death saves and what she has lost; her grief is not for Septimus, but for herself. Woolf weaves the verbal web between the two passages to summon once again the crucial scene with Sally on the terrace at Bourton, to enable Clarissa to confront her loss. Clarissa's appreciation of this loss, at last fully present to her consciousness, crystallizes in the contrast that concludes this segment of the passage: "She had schemed; she had pilfered. She was never wholly admirable. . . . And once she had walked on the terrace at Bourton."

With this naming of the original scene, Woolf abruptly terminates Clarissa's recollection, replaying with a brilliant stroke Peter Walsh's interruption, the sudden imposition of the granite wall. The masculine intervention this time, though, is enacted not by Peter but by Richard, and not as external imposition but as choice. Clarissa's unexpected thought of Richard abruptly and definitely terminates the memory of Sally, pivoting the scene from past to present, the mood from grief to joy: "It was due to Richard; she had never been so happy." The dramatic and unexplained juxtaposition encapsulates the developmental plot and the dynamics of its central scenes. This final replay of the developmental turn, and final microcosm of Woolf's narrative method, however, represent the abrupt transition positively. The joy inspired by Clarissa's thought of Richard persists as she celebrates "this having done with the triumphs of youth." Woolf does not fill in the gap splitting past from present, grief from joy. We can only speculate that Septimus's sacrificial gift includes a demonstration of Clarissa's alternatives: to preserve the intensity of passion through death, or to accept the changing offerings of life. By recalling to Clarissa the power of her past *and* the only method of eternalizing it, he enables her fully to acknowledge and renounce its hold, to embrace the imperfect pleasures of adulthood more completely. Through Septimus, Woolf recasts the developmental impasse in the general terms of progression or death. In the final act of the developmental plot, she qualifies her challenge to the notion of linear, forward growth.

Woolf signals the shift in Clarissa's orientation by concluding the interlude with Clarissa's reaction to the old lady across the way, an unnamed character who only functions in the novel as an object of Clarissa's awareness. The earlier meditative passage concludes with Clarissa's reflection in the looking glass; this one with an analogous reflection of a future identity. After Clarissa's thoughts shift from Sally and the past to Richard and the present, Woolf turns the angle of vision one notch further to open a perspective on the future. The old lady solemnly prepares for bed, but this intimation of a final repose, recalling Clarissa's earlier ruminations on her narrowing bed, carries no onus for the heroine, excited by the unexpected animation of the sky, the news of Septimus's suicide, the noise from the party in the adjacent room. Release, anticipation, pleasure in change, regardless of its consequences—these are Clarissa's dominant emotions. Her identification with Septimus and pleasure in his suicide indicate her own relief in turning from her past. The gulf between Clarissa and the unknown lady discloses the female intimacy forfeited to growth, yet Clarissa's willingness to contemplate an emblem of age instead of savoring a memory of youth suggests a positive commitment to development— not to any particular course, but to the process of change itself. The vision of the old lady simultaneously concludes the developmental plot and the depiction of Clarissa's consciousness; the rest of the narrative turns to Peter and Sally. The developmental theme resides in the interplay between two interludes in the sequence of the day.

Freud's comparison of the pre-Oedipal stage in women to the Minoan-Mycenean civilization behind that of classical Greece provides a metaphor for the course and textual status of Clarissa's development. It also suggests a broader historical analogue to female development, though not an analogue Freud himself pursues. Freud's psychoanalytic version of ontogeny recapitulating philogeny assumes a genderless (that is, implicitly masculine) norm: personal development repeats the historical progression from "savage" to civilized races. In *Mrs. Dalloway*, Woolf intimates more specifically that *female* development condenses one strand of human history, the progression from matriarchal to patriarchal culture implicit in Freud's archaeological trope. Woolf's fascination during the years she was composing *Mrs. Dalloway* with the works of Jane Harrison and the *Oresteia*, which traces precisely the evolution from Mycenean to Athenian culture, may have fostered this concern with the relation of gender to cultural evolution. The developmental plot embedded in *Mrs. Dalloway* traces the outline of a larger historical plot, detached in the novel from its chronological roots and endowed with an uncustomary moral charge.

Woolf assigns the action of *Mrs. Dalloway* a precise date: 1923, shortly after the war that casts its shadow through the novel. Through the experience of Septimus Warren Smith and the descriptions of soldiers marching "as if one will worked legs and arms uniformly, and life, with its varieties, its irreticences, had been laid under a pavement of monuments and wreaths and drugged into a still yet staring corpse by discipline," she suggests that the military discipline intended both to manifest and cultivate manliness in fact instills rigor mortis in the living as well as the dead. For women, the masculine war is disruptive in a different way. Woolf's imagery and plot portray the world war as a vast historical counterpart to male intervention in female lives. In one pointed metaphor, the "fingers" of the European war are so "prying and insidious" that they smash a "plaster cast of Ceres," goddess of fertility and mother love, reminder of the force and fragility of the primary female bond. Rezia's female world is shattered by the conjunction of marriage and war. The symbolic association of war with the developmental turn from feminine to masculine orientation will be more clearly marked in *To the Lighthouse*, bisected by the joint ravages of nature and war in the divisive central section. By conflating Mrs. Ramsay's death with the violence of world war, Woolf splits the novel into disjunct portions presided over separately by the mother and the father.

In *Mrs. Dalloway,* Woolf more subtly indicates the masculine tenor of postwar society. The youngest generation in this novel is almost exclusively, and boastfully, male: Sally Seton repeatedly declares her pride in her "five great boys"; the Bradshaws have a son at Eton; "Everyone in the room has six sons at Eton," Peter Walsh observes at Clarissa's party; Rezia Warren Smith mourns the loss of closeness with her sisters but craves a son who would resemble his father. Elizabeth Dalloway is the sole daughter, and she identifies more closely with her father than her mother (the plaster cast of Ceres has been shattered in the war). Male authority, partially incarnate in the relentless chiming of Big Ben, is more ominously embodied in the Doctors Holmes and Bradshaw, the modern officers of coercion. Septimus is the dramatic victim of this authority, but Lady Bradshaw's feminine concession is equally significant: "Fifteen years ago she had gone under . . . there had been no scene, no snap; only the slow sinking, waterlogged, of her will into his. Sweet was her smile, swift her submission." The loose connections Woolf suggests between World War I and a bolstered male authority lack all historical validity, but within the mythology created by the novel the war assumes a symbolic function dividing a pervasively masculine present from a mythically female past.

Critics frequently note the elegiac tone permeating *Mrs. Dalloway,* a tone which allies the novel with the modernist preoccupation with the contrast between the present and the past. Nostalgia in *Mrs. Dalloway,* however, is for a specifically female presence and nurturance, drastically diminished in contemporary life. Woolf suggests this loss primarily in interludes that puncture the narrative, pointing to a loss inadequately recognized by the conventions of developmental tales. The most obvious of these interruptions, the solitary traveler's archehtypal vision, loosely attached to Peter Walsh's dream, but transcending through its generic formulation the limits of private consciousness, is not, as Reuben Brower asserts, a "beautiful passage . . . which could be detached with little loss," and which "does not increase or enrich our knowledge of Peter or of anyone else in the book." Through its vivid representation of a transpersonal longing for a cosmic female / maternal / natural presence that might "shower down

from her magnificent hands compassion, comprehension, absolution,"
the dream/vision names the absence that haunts *Mrs. Dalloway*. In the
mundane present of the novel, the ancient image of the Goddess,
source of life and death, dwindles to the elderly nurse sleeping next to
Peter Walsh, as in another self-contained narrative interlude, the mythic
figure of woman voicing nature's eternal, wordless rhythms contracts,
in urban London, to a battered old beggar woman singing for coppers.
The comprehensive, seductive, generative, female powers of the Goddess split, in the contemporary world, into the purely nurturant energy
of Sally Seton and the social graces of the unmaternal Clarissa, clad as a
hostess in a "silver-green mermaid's dress." The loss of female integration and power, another echo of the smashed cast of Ceres, is finally
suggested in the contrast between the sequence envisaged by the solitary traveler and the most intrusive narrative interlude, the lecture on
Proportion and Conversion, where Woolf appears to denounce in her
own voice the twin evils of contemporary civilization. Rather than a
sign of artistic failure, this interruption calls attention to itself as a
rhetorical as well as ideological antithesis to the solitary traveler's vision. Sir Bradshaw's goddesses of Proportion and Conversion, who
serve the ideals of imperialism and patriarchy, renouncing their status
as creative female powers, are the contemporary counterpart to the
ancient maternal deity, now accessible only in vision and dream. The
historical vista intermittently inserted in *Mrs. Dalloway* echoes the
developmental progress of the heroine from a nurturing, pastoral,
female world to an urban culture governed by men.

One last reverberation of the developmental plot takes as its
subject female development in the altered contemporary world. Through
the enigmatic figure of Elizabeth, Woolf examines the impact of the
new historical context on the course of women's development. Almost
the same age as her mother in the earliest recollected scenes at Bourton,
Elizabeth has always lived in London; the country to her is an occasional treat she associates specifically with her father. Elizabeth feels a
special closeness to her father, a noticeable alienation from her mother.
The transition so implicitly traumatic for Clarissa has already been
accomplished by her daughter. By structuring the adolescence of mother
and daughter as inverse emotional configurations, Woolf reveals the
shift that has occurred between these generations. As Clarissa vacillates
between two men, while tacitly guarding her special bond with Sally,
Elizabeth vacillates between two women, her mother and Miss Kilman,
while preserving her special connection with her father. Elizabeth's

presence at the final party manifests her independence from Miss Kilman; her impatience for the party to end reveals her differences from her mother. The last scene of the novel highlights Elizabeth's closeness with her father, whose sudden response to his daughter's beauty has drawn her instinctively to his side.

The opposing allegiances of daughter and mother reflect in part the kinds of female nurturance available to each. Elizabeth's relation with the grasping Miss Kilman is the modern counterpart to Clarissa's love for Sally Seton. Specific parallels mark the generational differences. Miss Kilman's possessive desire for Elizabeth parodies the lines that emblazon Clarissa's love for Sally: "If it were now to die, 'twere now to be most happy" becomes, for Elizabeth's hungry tutor, "If she could grasp her, if she could clasp her, if she could make her hers absolutely and forever and then die; that was all she wanted." Sally walks with Clarissa on the terrace at Bourton; Miss Kilman takes Elizabeth to the Army and Navy Stores, a commercial setting that exemplifies the web of social and military ties. Miss Kilman, as her name implies, provides no asylum from this framework. Losing the female sanctuary, however, brings proportionate compensations: Elizabeth assumes she will have a profession, will play some active role in masculine society. Woolf does not evaluate this new developmental course, does not tally losses and gains. If she surrounds the past with an aureole, she points to the future in silence. She offers little access to Elizabeth's consciousness, insisting instead on her status as enigma—her Chinese eyes, "blank, bright, with the staring incredible innocence of sculpture," her Oriental bearing, her "inscrutable mystery." Undecipherable, Elizabeth is "like a hyacinth, sheathed in glossy green, with buds just tinted, a hyacinth which has had no sun"; her unfolding is unknown, unknowable. Through the figure of Elizabeth as unopened bud, Woolf encloses in her text the unwritten text of the next developmental narrative.

The silences that punctuate *Mrs. Dalloway* reflect the interruptions and enigmas of female experience and ally the novel with a recent trend in feminist aesthetics. The paradoxical goal of representing women's absence from culture has fostered an emphasis on "blank pages, gaps, borders, spaces and silence, holes in discourse" as the distinctive features of a self-consciously female writing. Since narrative forms normally sanction the patterns of male experience, the woman novelist might signal her exclusion most succinctly by disrupting continuity, accentuating gaps between sequences. "Can the female self be expressed through plot or must it be conceived in resistance to plot? Must it lodge 'between the acts'?" asks Gillian Beer, the allusion to Woolf suggesting the persistence of this issue for a novelist concerned with the links of gender and genre. In her next novel Woolf expands her discrete silence to a gaping hole at the center of her narrative, a hole that divides the action dramatically between two disjunct days. *To the Lighthouse* makes explicit many of the issues latent in *Mrs. Dalloway*. The plot of female bonding, reshaped as the story of a woman's attempts to realize in art her love for an older woman, rises to the surface of the narrative; yet Lily's relationship with Mrs. Ramsay is unrepresented in the emblem Lily fashions for the novel, the painting that manifests a daughter's love for her surrogate mother as a portrait of the mother with her son. Absence is pervasive in *To the Lighthouse*. The gaps in *Mrs. Dalloway* are less conspicuous, yet they make vital and disturbing points about female experience and female plots. The fragmentary form of the developmental plot, where the patterns of experience and art intersect, conceals as insignificance a radical significance. The intervals between events, the stories untold, can remain invisible in *Mrs. Dalloway*—or they can emerge through a sudden shift of vision as the most absorbing features of Woolf's narrative.

The Unguarded Moment:
Mrs. Dalloway

Lucio Ruotolo

Seated in her drawing room, mending the dress she will wear that evening at her party, Clarissa Dalloway falls into the rhythm of sewing: "Quiet descended on her, calm, content, as her needle, drawing the silk smoothly to its gentle pause, collected the green folds together and attached them, very lightly, to the belt." The scene, culminating with the unexpected appearance of her former fiancé just returned from India, embodies Woolf's appreciation of artistic accomplishment and the accompanying temptation to enclose herself within the serenity of a thoroughly satisfying moment. Clarissa's motions, like those of some primordial weaver, are described as if reenacting the lives of all created beings rising and falling much as waves on a beach: "So on a summer's day waves collect, overbalance, and fall; collect and fall; and the whole world seems to be saying 'that is all.'" A sense of fulfillment builds in the passage to the antithetical shock of the doorbell ringing and Peter Walsh's crucial interruption.

What Woolf comes to see in the course of writing *Mrs. Dalloway* is how fully the creative impulse tends to isolate the signifier from the source of all rejuvenation, namely, his or her external world. Lulled into a wholeness free of imperfection, Clarissa seems to slip, with the narrator of "The Mark on the Wall," deeper and deeper away from the surface of modern life. In each instance Shakespeare supplies a modicum of control. His steadying influence occurs as she reads the lines

From *The Interrupted Moment: A View of Virginia Woolf's Novels.* © 1986 by the Board of Trustees of the Leland Stanford Junior University. Stanford University Press, 1986.

from *Cymbeline* displayed in a London book shop window: "Fear no more, says the heart. Fear no more, says the heart, committing its burden to some sea, which sighs collectively for all sorrows, and renews, begins, collects, lets fall."

Unlike Woolf's earlier narrator, however, and unlike her own earlier version of Clarissa, the heroine of *Mrs. Dalloway* responds to interruption in the very midst of indulging the most ecstatic vision of closure. Even as the movement of her arm sewing follows a Shakespearean cadence, her attention remains open and receptive to a radically disruptive rhythm:

> And the body alone listens to the passing bee; the wave breaking; the dog barking, far away barking and barking.
> "Heavens, the front-door bell!" exclaimed Clarissa, staying her needle. Roused, she listened.

In Virginia Woolf's first sketch for what was to become *Mrs. Dalloway,* Clarissa appears walking down Bond Street with the aristocratic assurance one might expect from a woman of her class. Thoroughly at home in a world of smart shops, well-groomed pedestrians, and the governing establishment—couriers are scurrying with messages between Fleet Street and the Admiralty—the proud Clarissa remains, on this June morning a few years after the end of the First World War, like young Jacob Flanders [of *Jacob's Room*] at Cambridge, fresh and "upright." A sense of wholeness pervades the scene; "for Mrs. Dalloway the moment was complete." The flag waving above Buckingham Palace (signaling the return of the king and queen), the policeman confidently directing traffic, Big Ben striking the time of day, inspire, moreover, a condescending ethnocentricity: "It was character she thought; something inborn in the race; what Indians respected."

Woolf's satiric intentions seem clear enough. If, as she puts it somewhat later [in *A Writer's Diary*], she wants "to criticize the social system and to show it at work," Mrs. Dalloway appears the vehicle of her reproof. And yet, in the course of this short story, she emerges as something more than a static object of satire. The crux of Woolf's sketch, unsettling Clarissa's classbound self-assurance, anticipates the revisions that will transform her from a stiff and tinselly society matron into her author's most famous heroine.

Having stepped into a glove shop (for here it is gloves rather than flowers that call her outdoors), Mrs. Dalloway of the sketch finds herself quite unexpectedly sympathizing with a shopgirl's less privileged life. "When we're in the country thought Clarissa. Or shooting.

She has a fortnight at Brighton. In some stuffy lodging." We can assume that the wife of a distinguished MP generally resists such speculations; crossing the boundaries of class invites impulsive, and potentially compromising, acts. Ironically, the fashionable shop has served in the past to allay disruptive emotions. If passion must exist in human life, let it be for gloves. And how better are we identified than by what we wear? "A lady is known by her gloves and her shoes, old Uncle William used to say." On this visit, however, the setting provides a different sort of connection. Probing the affairs of someone outside her world, Mrs. Dalloway discovers a new and wider basis for relationship, derived from an experience shared by all women. Yet even as she is imagining a working girl's discomfort (standing as she must all day behind the counter) on "the one day in the month" when the strain might prove particularly agonizing, something more fundamental than the barriers of class momentarily complicates—in terms of this study, interrupts—her inherited expectations. Clarissa's imaginative adventure results in contradictory responses: both a generous impulse to help and a no less powerful sense of reservation. "Dick had shown her the folly of giving impulsively."

In "The Russian Point of View," published in the same year as *Mrs. Dalloway,* Woolf praises writers such as Chekhov for confronting existential issues that prove elusive and inconclusive. English readers, she argues, are inclined to find such questions a threat to the very basis of their social and literary practice. She suggests further that English novelists, pressured to accept the hierarchical order of a class-structured culture, are "inclined to satire rather than to compassion, to scrutiny of society rather than understanding of individuals themselves." She may well be describing her own struggle with the earlier Mrs. Dalloway.

Once Clarissa questions her own favored status she invites what is to become with each revision an increasingly liberating form of discord. In the glove store a series of doubts arises to challenge the ground of her belief: faith in God ("one doesn't believe, thought Clarissa, any more in God"); life's smoothness ("It used, thought Clarissa, to be so simple"); and most centrally, social decorum itself ("Lady Bexborough, who opened the bazaar, they say, with the telegram in her hand—Roden, her favourite, killed—she would go on. But why, if one doesn't believe?").

Mrs. Dalloway falls back on noblesse oblige in answering these questions. One goes on for the sake of the underprivileged. The shopgirl, she would convince us and herself, "would be much more unhappy if she didn't believe." Bound by the limits of her class, Mrs. Dalloway in Bond Street gives up the adventure before it has begun.

While scholars differ over the nature of that "depth" Woolf sought to illuminate through her tunneling discovery, most agree that an altered sense of time past distinguishes her final revisions. *Mrs. Dalloway* is perhaps best described in this regard by J. Hillis Miller as "a novel of the resurrection of the past into the actual present of the characters' lives."

Mrs. Dalloway in Bond Street is revived by that sense of common history she shares with members of her class. In the final version, however, the past intrudes in the form of less hierarchical and more personal relationships to interrupt her experience of the present or at the very least to complicate it. What was previously exceptional in this novel becomes the norm. But it is more than the disruptive immediacy of suppressed or disregarded desires, past and present, that transforms Clarissa from an object of social satire to an existential heroine. The personal recollections disclosed by Woolf's tunneling process take on new significance when seen against the kaleidoscopic background of her more public world.

The dynamic of disjunction has a liberating effect. Loosening her hold on old supports, Clarissa finds herself with Septimus metaphorically at sea or, to employ a no less applicable cliché, up in the air. Called on to redefine the moment, she transcends, however tentatively, the constraints of gender, class, and hierarchy.

Instinct anchors Mrs. Dalloway in Bond Street to a world of unchanging roles: "There is this extraordinarily deep instinct, something inside one; you can't get over it; it's no use trying." From the opening pages of the novel, however, Clarissa's mind freely ranges over and through inherited assumptions, creating as she does "every moment afresh." If she is not serenely at home in the present, it is because, however timidly, she anticipates change with a mixture of dread and pleasure; even in recollection, as when in Bourton she recalls the solemnity and excitement of something unexpected "about to happen."

Though she remains loyally aristocratic, the reader is invited to other perspectives. Her gestures as well as her words take on a new transparency. So initially Woolf picks up the term "upright," which recurred frequently in the short story, and transforms the essentially static image into one of birdlike propensity for flight. On a street corner, "there she perched, . . . waiting to cross, very upright." This quality, observed by her neighbor, adds ambiguity as well as range to her thoughts, an ambiguity Clarissa prizes throughout the novel.

The opening pages develop Woolf's analysis of existential anxiety as an added aspect of Clarissa's willingness to question the given. The experience of emptiness and silence in the midst of London traffic—"a particular hush, or solemnity; an indescribable pause"—at once suspends and renews her sense of place and person. Where Mrs. Dalloway's advisers, the unnamed and impersonal "they," describe the experience as symptomatic of illness, Woolf quickly honors the effects of Clarissa's angst. When, in the next instant, clock time (Big Ben) begins again its heavy beat, so irrevocable and final, she seems more attuned to what Woolf, describing the ambience of Chaucer's *Canterbury Tales,* terms the "immense variety" of life. Clarissa's perceptions have in fact widened. She responds to the high and the low, the snobbish Hugh Whitbread, a fat lady passing in a cab, a dejected and destitute human being sitting on a doorstep. The events that typified Mrs. Dalloway in Bond Street's narrow, self-justifying response are no longer the source of aesthetic pleasure. Now she celebrates a largely classless pageant: "In people's eyes, in the swing, tramp, and trudge; in the bellow and the uproar; the carriages, motor cars, omnibuses, vans, sandwich men shuffling and swinging; brass bands; barrel organs; in the triumph and the jingle and the strange high singing of some aeroplane overhead was what she loved; life; London; this moment of June."

Unlike her predecessor, Clarissa derives neither assurance nor stability from her revelatory insights on the streets of London. Such moments—"What she loved was this, here, now, in front of her" —pass as quickly as they appear. Since the given remains perpetually inconclusive, existential encounters call for ever-renewed acts of re-creation. No less an aspect of time than the mind that creates them, words must never be allowed to sink into opaque singularity. Throughout Woolf's fictional world, language as well as personality resists the reifying intentions of a society bent on possession. It is in this light that she praises Sir John Paston, along with Chaucer, for having "the instincts of enjoyment rather than of acquisition." By contrast, the age's passion for "scientific" definition will appear as a symptom of collective social madness, an aberration that ironically overshadows Septimus's madness.

Toward the close of *A Room of One's Own,* Woolf discusses an instinct of something "real" that inspires her as a writer to look more deeply into her own convictions as well as the appearances of people and of things. The result is often unsettling. Great novelists—Hardy, Proust, Dostoevsky—by disrupting the reader's harmony with his world, in an important sense challenge the very conditions of sanity. Injuring our vanity by upsetting our order, such writers seldom tell us the "truth" we want to hear.

While Septimus and Clarissa represent two contrasting visions of truth, "Mrs. D. seeing the truth, Septimus seeing the insane truth," both reflect what will remain central aspects of Woolf's iconoclastic assumptions. The truths they witness and enact oppose the conforming aesthetics of what remains for her a parochially narrow culture.

With the publication of Woolf's diaries, it has become evident how spells of insanity or, more precisely, her recollections of those spells, helped form an aesthetic intention. The visual distortion that occurs when her mind's hold on things is threatened prompts her to revise the given. Septimus, reflecting as he does a central and traumatic part of the novelist's own personal history, sees the truth, however incoherently, in artistically prophetic terms. His tragedy is that he cannot finally affirm and communicate the explosive immediacy of such visions. He has received one shock too many.

To communicate depth in an age systematically incurious about its own social and personal motivations presupposes a disposition "to go down boldly and bring to light those hidden thoughts which are the most diseased." Woolf's essay on Montaigne, with its familiar plea, "Communication is health; communication is truth," informs the theme of *Mrs. Dalloway*. The confrontation with disease, however, does not lead her to affirm the ego's power to face and transcend infirmity. In an important sense, illness itself offers, as we have seen, a means of renewal. Whether such an assumption pertains to her personal life as well as to her art remains an open question.

"On Being Ill," we recall, suggests the advantage one may derive even from a slight case of influenza: "How tremendous the spiritual change that it brings, how astonishing, when the lights of health go down, the undiscovered countries that are then disclosed, what wastes and deserts of the soul, . . . what ancient and obdurate oaks are up-rooted in us by the act of sickness." The mind, as if on some imperialistic campaign "to cultivate the desert, educate the native," seeks in health to civilize the body, to maintain its sovereignty over the senses. "With the police off duty," the senses are free to roam. Seeing with the eyes of children, "we cease to be soldiers in the army of the upright."

If such excursions prove "unprofitable," they urge the mind from the elevating abstraction of pure thought to a less refined existence replete with sights and sounds and smells. D. H. Lawrence and even F. R. Leavis must surely approve Woolf's plea for a "reason rooted in the bowels of earth." The robust society she envisions will suspend its own "dominating" predilections in the expectation that "life is always and inevitably much richer than we who try to express it."

On the streets of London, in the grip of his hallucination, Septimus, like Clarissa, responds with childlike pleasure to phenomena that the crowd would reduce to objective clarity. The plane skywriting an advertisement urges a multitude of prospective customers to decipher the message. Eager to comply, they seek answers compulsively. "They were advertising toffee, a nursemaid told Rezia." Overhearing the woman spelling out the letters, "K . . . R . . . ," Septimus responds to a different rhythm: " 'Kay Arr' close to his ear, deeply, . . . like a grasshopper's, which rasped his spine deliciously and sent running up into his brain waves of sound which, concussing, broke." Her voice—it is his newest discovery—"can quicken trees into life." Septimus experiences the fullness of being and time as those around him cannot. Even the space between events strikes him as important.

Like some foreign visitor, Septimus the outsider sees familiar objects as if for the first time. At this point of the narrative, his only possibility of communication is with the omniscient reader, who, Woolf presumes, shares and relishes his insights; however disoriented and isolated, his world comes alive for us. We are reminded again of "On Being Ill" and its somewhat rash pronouncement that "the Chinese must know the sound of *Antony and Cleopatra* better than we do." The play is one that Septimus, with the ear of a common reader, earlier learned to love. But that was when he could still share his emotions; with Miss Pole he had discovered Shakespeare.

Septimus is not always open to external things. Whereas Clarissa allows the objects she perceives to grow in her mind, Septimus, fearing the collapse of meaning, often freezes the moment, chooses, in effect, to see and hear no more. To allow himself to tolerate the excitement of unmediated experience is to risk going mad. Moreover, his incongruous perceptions prove destructive because he appears unwilling to translate them into an idiom others can tolerate, much less appreciate. If we gain access to his richer vision, Rezia does not. His wife confesses she cannot even sit beside him once he has started to distort familiar objects; he makes "everything terrible," she complains, not without cause. Following the advice of the doctor, she urges her husband to take notice of "real things," of matters not so organically connected with his own feelings. This therapy of self-forgetfulness proves destructive of life as well as of art. As a growing indifference prevents relationship, his sense of alienation becomes all but intolerable: Septimus pictures himself as a half-drowned sailor alone on an ocean rock; his problem is that he feels not too much, but too little.

On the battlefront Septimus cultivated the same immovable and sustaining indifference that Mrs. Dalloway in Bond Street displayed before the "explosion" of a backfiring car. Trench warfare itself was a study in immobility. Between 1914 and 1918 the Allied lines on the Western Front, with few exceptions, remained essentially fixed, shifting only slightly, and no more than a few hundred yards from the Germans. Four years after the Armistice, the frozen reality of trench warfare still haunts the British imagination. A victim of this debilitating stasis, Septimus moves through the unreal streets of London like the characters of *The Waste Land,* without motivation or passion.

The first image of Septimus in the novel describes his sense of being blocked by the crowds, unable to pass since "everything had come to a standstill." We recall with irony Clarissa's closing thought in the sketch: "Thousands of young men had died that things might go on." The movement his wife Rezia urges on him—"Let us go on"—is denied him by a world in which movement and change appear aspects of sacrilege. Perception no less than bodily motion seems mesmerized by the ruling deities of state and business, anticipating the sister goddesses Proportion and Conversion who appear later. So the multitude cannot help looking at the prime minister's car (Rezia confesses as much) any more than it can resist the blandishments of advertising. When the car has passed, leaving "a slight ripple. . . . all heads were inclined the same way," toward a shop window promoting its wares.

Septimus remains the victim of shock as long as he resists his own chaotic insights, insights that both tempt and terrify him. Schooled in the values of his age long before he became a soldier, Septimus cannot be blamed for relying on its authority. (Ironically, his best chance for survival resides, as we shall see, in tolerating more eccentric visions of himself and others.) His prewar employer, Mr. Brewer, concerned in part by Septimus's health, counsels him in his fatherly way to more manly interests; in place of reading, "he advised football." The war completed Septimus's education. In the trenches he learned to be a man, winning the respect of his superiors ("he was promoted") and, more significantly, of his closest companion, Evans.

We may presume that on the front he had someone with whom to share his thoughts and at appropriate times, perhaps, even his feelings. The reader learns little of Evans, however. Rezia, having seen him once, describes him as quiet, strong, and "undemonstrative in the company of women." The two men "had gone through the whole show" together. The end of Evans, who is killed just before the Armistice, complementing the end of the war, leaves Septimus in fact with neither a sustaining environment nor an ongoing relationship. The battlefront had, after all, established with brutal simplicity the basis for human survival, the distinction between life and death and the nature of what must be done or, no less relevantly, what must not be done, if one is to go on living.

Thrown back on himself, Septimus discovers one evening, with panic, "that he could not feel." Not coincidentally it is the evening on which he has proposed marriage to Rezia. The loss of one refuge leads him rather quickly to seek another. Septimus marries, he makes it quite clear, not out of affection but out of the need for "safety." No less pertinent, the panic has hit him at a time of transition, although at this point what succeeding "show" can inspire the young man to renewed motion is not clear. Moreover, a particular time of day inspires unrest: "These sudden thunder-claps of fear" we hear, come "especially in the evening." Septimus fills the empty time by taking a wife. And what attracts him most in Rezia is her assured activity. Making hats with the other Italian girls—"It is the hat that matters most"—seems as divinely authorized as the deployment of armies. The sense that the girls are impelled by something other than feeling or thought for the moment quiets his deeper fear "that the world itself is without meaning."

Devoid of associative feeling, Septimus does not see, as he will later, that Rezia's vocation is in fact an expression of love. From the first description of her hands moving over each hat "like those of a painter," the beauty she experiences and urges Septimus to see is an aspect of the objects she creates. Not until he can begin to participate in her artistic creation does Septimus move toward health; the doctors, however, make short shrift of that.

Like some Lawrentian antihero, the early Septimus appears stirred by the idea people represent to him rather than by their presence. First Miss Pole serves to reinforce his expectations of literary success ("Was he not like Keats? she asked"). His government appears quick to utilize this romantic attachment to support a larger and more ominous abstraction. Septimus goes to war to make England safe for Miss Pole. Evans appears almost totally in abstract terms, his life no less theoretical in Septimus's mind than his death. Rezia represents the idea of sanctuary. In the course of the novel, Septimus is shaken, tragically, from his idea of her, and thereby finds both the beginning and the end of his life.

At those moments when Septimus overcomes fear and allows a vision of exquisite diversity to invade his being, his perceptions, while filtered through the author's consciousness, take on a creatively poetic form: the quivering of a leaf in the wind, flying swallows, flies rising and falling, the sound of a motor horn, "all of this, calm and reasonable as it was, made out of ordinary things as it was, was the truth now; beauty, that was the truth now. Beauty was everywhere." Keats has reemerged. But as in the poet's odes, the temptation is to freeze the moment and escape time's uncompromising slide through life toward death. Septimus, like Clarissa, "could not look upon the dead." The sayings he writes on the backs of envelopes acknowledging life and change seek also to create a shockproof world, permanent and self-sufficient, complete as the wholeness that Mrs. Dalloway in Bond Street expresses on her morning walk.

The very act of writing would appear an attempt, again like Jacob's, to fix the moment, to find coherence and sanity in wholeness and stasis. The world, however, continually interrupts his artistic and psychological effort to create a haven; Rezia in particular "was always interrupting," urging him to "look," urging him into a future he has chosen to avoid. It is no accident that Septimus breaks down completely as his wife makes plans for children of their own. Septimus shuns the future as he shuns death. Afraid of change, afraid to effect change, he capitulates as often as he resists: "Nothing could rouse him. Rezia put him to bed." The doctor she sends for initiates a therapy of self-control, which only reactivates his fear of life. The final diagnosis of Bradshaw (a specialist on war-inflicted trauma) is to insist on total separation from all sources of future shock, most notably from Rezia: "The people we are most fond of are not good for us when we are ill."

Between the acts of Bradshaw's intended scenario, before Septimus is to be placed in a rest home, he breaks through to the reality of Rezia's presence. Husband and wife wait in what appears to be a "pocket of still air," on "the edge" of some forest, where "warmth lingers, and the air buffets the cheek like the wing of a bird." In this suspended moment when, as with Clarissa in that interim before Big

Ben strikes, the processes of civilization are disengaged, Septimus comes to life.

Driven literally and metaphorically to the edge of history, he finally acts to deny those civilizing forces that would convert him to "reason." Before he jumps through the lodging-house window to his death, Septimus relaxes his will to remain sane. Lying on the sofa, he allows the very images of his madness, a bubbling variety of sights and sounds, to pour like water on him: "The sound of water was in the room and through the waves came the voices of birds singing. Every power poured its treasures on his head, and his hands lay there on the back of the sofa, as he had seen his hand lie when he was bathing, floating, on the top of the waves."

For the moment he surmounts his fears. With new courage he begins cautiously "to open his eyes, to see whether a gramophone was really there." Then, all but miraculously, as he accepts the chaotic reality of things in themselves, things that do not rely on his intellectual jurisdiction for their being in space, he begins to talk with Rezia, responds to her words and her work. The hat she is making for Mrs. Peters, he ventures, is too small: "an organ grinder's monkey's hat." Participating in her art, Septimus takes up the ribbons and beads and artificial flowers and creates a design, which Rezia happily sews into a hat. The action, if commonplace (and it is after all the smallest of events), signifies life at its fullest. For Woolf as well as Forster, connection is all.

The police, however, are not long inactive. Civilization returns with a vengeance to stamp its image on the faces of the weak. And Septimus will have none of it. His suicide is an act against those like Bradshaw who "make life intolerable." Clarissa's instinctive dislike of this overbearing man leads her finally to identify with Septimus. Both struggle to preserve a vague and ill-defined sense of goodness against those "doctors and wise men" who have long since decided about the nature of truth.

Despite her capacity for imaginative flight, Clarissa, like her counterpart, is tempted continually to crystallize the present, to make something more permanent of those unsettling moments that arise in the midst of daily routine. The temptation affects Woolf's notion of art as much as her character's notion of life. In either case, to poeticize the moment invites closure.

Clarissa, looking at the passing car at the same time as Septimus, renders the image into an "enduring symbol of the state," still the soul of her social identity. The sight of the seal the footman holds, "white, magical, circular," conveys a profound basis for the faith of all who watch—all but the dislocated Septimus. Mrs. Dalloway, standing outside the flower shop, "stiffened a little" at the thought of her own proximity to this source of majesty. That night she will preside at a grand party. The prime minister will be among the guests. Yet there, at her moment of crisis, when she must face the reality of Septimus's death alone, it will be the absence of patriarchal models, Peter and Richard as well as the prime minister, that leads to her recovery. Here on Oxford Street, as the many clocks strike eleven and as Septimus wanders in isolation through an unfamiliar world, bound to a sovereign he cannot see, the object of Clarissa's devotion remains reassuringly immanent. The religion she shares with the crowd of onlookers lifts her "beyond seeking and questing" into a world "all spirit, disembodied, ghostly," a world mirrored in the stillness of St. Paul's Cathedral, where the casual visitor may confront and glorify permanence. If there is no noise of traffic within, one may presume an extended metaphor; in the presence of authority everything outside, we recall, "had come to a standstill."

Clarissa's sense of belonging as she enters her house is drawn in no less clerical terms: she feels, we are told, like a nun returned from the lordly to a more private realm of worship, where death as well as life has lost its sting. "The hall of the house was cool as a vault." She feels cold and disembodied, her life shaped by the rhythm of a liturgy that would dull the mind to all but its own calming influence:

> Fear no more the heat o' the sun,
> Nor the furious winter's rages.

Even Shakespeare, reduced to opiate, entices the mind to rest. Surrounded once more by "familiar veils" and "old devotions"—the sounds of the Irish cook whistling from the kitchen, a member of the family typing—she feels at once "blessed and purified." She bends over the hall table, "bowed" as if in prayer, to give thanks to the powers who have allowed this special moment to flower "for her eyes only." If she does not believe in God, she knows to whom to give thanks: "above all to Richard her husband, who was the foundation of it." The table with its message pad, however, interrupts her liturgy: "The shock of Lady Bruton asking Richard to lunch without her made the moment in which she had stood shiver, as a plant on the river-bed feels the shock of a passing oar and shivers; so she rocked: so she shivered."

Like Septimus in madness, Clarissa's inclination is to withdraw from shock. Having read the note, she retreats to the privacy of an upstairs bedroom. We learn that she has been sick, and that her husband "insisted, after her illness that she must sleep undisturbed." Doctor and husband counsel separation as the remedy for disrupted feeling.

But as she is retiring Clarissa's mind, tunneling into past and present, widens the context of her world. In motion she is no longer one thing. If she is a "nun withdrawing," she is also "a child exploring." As on her walk, a variety of incidents arises to engage her attention. She pauses to indulge each new experience—a flash of green linoleum, the sound of a dripping faucet—and her sense of identity expands again to include that which is not herself. In loosening her hold on things, "seeing the glass, the dressing table, and all the bottles afresh," Clarissa finds she has all but forgotten her grievance against Lady Bruton.

Though her role as wife to Mr. Dalloway is by definition limiting (despite Richard's objection, what can she *do* short of giving parties?), Clarissa has the special talent "of making a world of her own wherever she happened to be." Whether, as Peter Walsh surmises, this is identifiably a "woman's gift," it anticipates the question of art's relationship to social function. Women, existing largely outside the world of power, can come in Woolf's view to acquire a more disinterested (as distinct from indifferent) respect for things in themselves. Clarissa's willingness continually to revise her relationship to the extended world of past and present challenges all who surround her to similar acts of re-creation. Her reconstituted moments challenge the presumptive formulations of an age that rarely questions itself. The safe alternative is parodied in that paragon of good taste, Hugh Whitbread, who, avoiding depth, spends his day placidly brushing surfaces.

In the attic room to which she has retired, Clarissa by contrast faces her own presuppositions, ranging from disappointment to envy, and the complexities these emotions bring to consciousness. If her husband has prompted isolation, a narrowing of exposure to others (reflected in the narrowness of her separate bed) as the basis for recuperation, she acknowledges a certain coldness of spirit with herself that tempts her from relationships; she prefers reading memoirs.

Her relationship with both men and women speaks of a lack of "something central which permeated; something warm which broke up surfaces and rippled the cold contact of man and woman, or of women together." More than sexual, the failure she confesses involves the inability to move out of herself into the existence of others, to leave the safe confines of her familiar past and present and risk the future. She lacks the "abandonment" of spirit that allows foreigners and only a few Englishwomen (she has in mind her friend Sally Seton) to say and do anything they please. And that, presumably, is why she married Richard rather than Peter in the first place. Or was there another motive?

As Clarissa tunnels into her past, we are struck by her willingness to raise those fundamental issues her society tends to avoid. She questions the meaning of "love," "life," and finally "death," struggling to face these realities as they confront her own existence. "This question of love" leads, in her attic room, to the insight that her feeling for Sally, unlike her feeling for a man, has been "completely disinterested." In contrast to detachment, disinterest presumes a passion for the thing in itself and the capability (Keats termed it a virtue of negation) of allowing what is other to remain so—to connect without imposing. Clarissa's objection to Peter's assertive egotism reflects Woolf's larger critique.

Had she married Peter she never would have known that dignity, the gulf between husband and wife, that underlies one of the author's fundamental convictions about human relationship. So particularly in marriage "a little independence there must be between people living together day in day out in the same house." This Richard has given her.

Rezia angers Septimus when, intruding on his serious thoughts, she exhorts him to take notice of other things or to share his insights with her; she was, we remember, "always interrupting." Clarissa, reflecting on her former life at Bourton, recalls how Peter intruded on "the most exquisite moment of her whole life," when Sally had kissed her. The shock of his insensitive comment—"Star-gazing?"—was understandably a source of grievance. "Oh this horror! she said to herself, as if she had known all along that something would interrupt, would embitter her moment of happiness." But even here a widening of thought takes place as Clarissa acknowledges: "Yet, after all, how much she owed to him later."

Peter, like Septimus, takes himself with guarded seriousness. Where fantasies invade the consciousness of either man, they remain largely self-sustaining romances, controlled and directed by the needs vanity prescribes. The important exception for Septimus is the one instance when he breaks through to Rezia. So Peter, pursuing an attractive woman in Trafalgar Square, remains omnisciently above the self-indulent scenario he envisions. His adventure leads him finally to stasis, to dream in Regent's Park of some spectral nurse, "champion of the rights of sleepers," who rules and protects him from the "fever of living." If move he must, "let me walk straight on to this great figure, who will, with a toss of her head, mount me on her streamers and let me blow to nothingness with the rest." In company with Jacob, Peter moves toward dissolution.

But Clarissa's disruptive presence, when Peter visits her home on this same June morning, will awaken him to a renewed desire for experience. Jarred into "idiosyncrasy," Peter finds himself appreciating an infinitely rich and changing environment as he walks through the London streets: "intangible things you couldn't lay your hands on— that shift in the whole pyramidal accumulation which in his youth had seemed immovable." Only when he arrives at the Dalloway party will he revert to old and guarded ways. But this is to come later, after he has intruded on Clarissa's privacy.

Clarissa's memories of Peter's continued assault on her defects— "How he scolded her"—similarly disturb her inclination to fall into thoroughly derivative and settled roles. Peter, undermining definition as he does, contributes to the healthy ambiguity Woolf develops in her protagonist. After thinking of her relationship with him, Clarissa "would not say of anyone in the world now that they were this or were that. . . . She would not say of Peter, she would not say of herself, I am this, I am that." So when he makes his unexpected entrance, interrupting her sewing, she resists the compulsion to reduce his being to the contours of a past grievance or, for that matter, to the reality of his own abrasive ideology.

Reacting to Peter rather than to her idea of him, Clarissa allows her impulses freedom to enlarge in the ensuing interview. While the moment is largely fictional—"It was as if the five acts of a play that had been very exciting and moving were now over and she had lived a lifetime in them and had run away, had lived with Peter, and it was now over"—her vision is only half made up. Free of grievance or judgment, she responds with enchantment to those substantial sounds and gestures that reveal her old friend. If Peter and Clarissa, separated as they are by time and circumstance, touch each other only tentatively—"as a bird touches a branch and rises and flutters away"—we are moved by their groping effort to reach one another.

What is to be loved or hated in another is often in Woolf a composite based on the most fragmentary of details: Clarissa's recollection, for example, of Peter's half-opening a penknife. Typically for Woolf, human intercourse occurs on the boundary of the mind's knowledge, some obscure communion deeper than ideology and more fundamental than sex. The experience tends to point beyond language itself and, insofar as it remains susceptible to description, urges her toward a special rendering of the novel as a vehicle for communication. In this regard, *Mrs. Dalloway* anticipates *The Waves*. Along with her heroine, Woolf considers the English language rich and flexible enough to convey radically disparate notions of human authenticity. Clarissa's "offering"—the sense, however vague, of her party-giving— seeks a more spontaneous basis for talk as well as for other forms of social relationship. Inspired to bring people together for no reason whatsoever, Mrs. Dalloway could imagine neither Peter nor her husband acting with such unpremeditated abandon.

The disposition of the party in *Mrs. Dalloway* and Clarissa's role as hostess have led many readers to emphasize its author's satirical intention. If Woolf and her Bloomsbury friends had a preference for parties, and of course they did, only Clive Bell (many of whose personal qualities can be seen in Peter Walsh) had a taste for high society. Can one imagine any character present at the Dalloway party comfortably included at a Bloomsbury Thursday evening? Even so, Clarissa's motives in giving parties, the reality she seeks to create and share, reflect a number of important Bloomsbury assumptions. With G. E. Moore, Clarissa would call her guests to celebrate "the pleasures of human intercourse and the enjoyment of beautiful objects," which is to say the value of things in themslves (*Principia Ethica*). No less crucial, art remains for her an intrinsic good rather than the means of an end. Through her revised protagonist, the novelist struggled to formulate the proper role for the artist, a task that led directly to her representation of Lily Briscoe in *To the Lighthouse* and beyond that to her most experimental novel, *The Waves*.

The problem of making a successful party, like the problem of making a good book, is to create the conditions that will inspire mutuality. The good hostess, like the good writer, while technically in charge, remains unnoticed. Things start to move at the Dalloway party when Clarissa, standing at the top of the stairs, steps back and allows the random talk of people to move at its own course. But first her intention to control events must be thwarted; once again the catalyst is

Peter Walsh. The thought of his criticism throws her into confusion: "It was extraordinary how Peter put her into these states just by coming and standing in a corner. He made her see herself." Peter's wandering away just when Clarissa would speak to him increases her frustration. At the same time she realizes a failure in her role: everything about the party is "going wrong . . . falling flat." The guests appear walking about aimlessly, bunched in corners and, worst of all, like "Ellie Henderson, not even caring to hold themselves upright." The familiar word signals Clarissa's retreat. Ellie in her "weaponless state," deprived of self-assurance, has cause for poor posture. It is Richard who moves to talk with her as Clarissa, under the spell of grievance, remains stationary.

At this point the narrative directs us to a yellow curtain, designed with exotic birds, that is blowing out gently from an open window. In her earlier meeting with Peter, the first recollection of the past they share is "how the blinds used to flap at Bourton." Now, mysteriously, as if the space outside somehow affects the moment, the party suddenly comes to life. What seems to motivate this change is merely the image of one undistinguished guest, Ralph Lyon, beating back the curtain as he goes on talking. The gesture is as unpremeditated as Lily Briscoe's impulsive act of drawing a line across the center of her canvas at the end of *To the Lighthouse*. Clarissa's sense—"It had begun. It had started"—is accompanied by a new impulse that holds her back: "She must stand there for the present."

At Bourton, Peter predicted "she would marry a Prime Minister and stand at the top of a staircase." The image fulfilled in his mind her role as "the perfect hostess." So he sees her at this moment (although Richard Dalloway, not even in the cabinet, has fallen far short of such expectations). But he misreads Clarissa's impulse. Far from some majestic desire to oversee the party, she is affected by the demand to let things be. She has created the festivity; now her task is to allow the party to develop a life of its own.

Descending to her guests, this time in the guise of anonymity, Clarissa celebrates the movement that surrounds her; "one felt them going on, going on." No longer stiffly self-conscious, she moves with less severity; "her prudery, her woodenness were all warmed through now." Woolf emphasizes Clarissa's unbridled motion as she glides, or more precisely "floats," from one group to the next. Like a mermaid, "lolloping on the waves and braiding her tresses she seemed, having that gift still; to be; to exist

. . . all with the most perfect ease and air of a creature floating in its element."

If Clarissa finds it difficult to define the meaning of "this thing she called life," she has, with Septimus, broken through to the reality of "something not herself." At the close of the novel, she can imagine his suicide as "an attempt to communicate," because she extends, as Mrs. Dalloway in Bond Street could not, the narrow limits of her social role. Unlike the young guests at her party, Clarissa will not solidify. Having relinquished command, she entertains a world of motion and change.

Mrs. Dalloway and the Social System

Alex Zwerdling

"I want to criticise the social system, & to show it at work, at its most intense." Woolf's provocative statement [in *A Writer's Diary*] about her intentions in writing *Mrs. Dalloway* has regularly been ignored. It denies the traditional view of her work as apolitical and indifferent to social issues, the view that allowed Forster to say with confidence that "improving the world she would not consider" or Jean Guiguet to insist that "the mechanical relations between individuals, such as are imposed by the social structure, dominated by concepts of class and wealth . . . are not her problem." *Mrs. Dalloway* reveals that such generalizations do not hold up under scrutiny. The novel is in large measure an examination of a single class and its control over English society—the "governing class," as Peter Walsh calls it. Woolf's picture of Clarissa Dalloway's world is sharply critical, but as we will see it cannot be called an indictment, because it deliberately looks at its object from the inside.

Woolf examines the governing class of England at a particular moment in history. Unlike *The Waves, Mrs. Dalloway* has a precise historical setting, which it is important to understand. It takes place on a day in June 1923, five years after the end of the First World War. Peter Walsh, who has been out of England since the war, notes the transformation of society in that period: "Those five years—1918 to 1923—had been, he suspected, somehow very important. People looked

From *Virginia Woolf and the Real World.* © 1986 by the Regents of the University of California. University of California Press, 1986.

different. Newspapers seemed different," and morals and manners had changed. There are a number of other topical references in the novel that its first readers would certainly have understood. The early 1920s brought to an end the Conservative-Liberal coalition in British politics; the elections of 1922 and 1923 marked the eclipse of the Liberals and the rise of Labour. For the first time the Labour Party became the official government opposition. It was only a matter of time before this "socialist" power, with its putative threat to the governing class examined in the novel, would be in office. Indeed, Conservative MP's like Richard Dalloway are already making plans for that event. He will write a history of Lady Bruton's family when he is out of Parliament, and she assures him that the documents are ready for him at her estate "whenever the time came; the Labour Government, she meant." The Conservative prime minister who appears at Clarissa's party at the end of the book remained in office only until January 1924, when he was succeeded by the first Labour prime minister, Ramsay MacDonald. And though the new government lasted less than a year, the Labour Party has remained the ruling or opposition party ever since. *Mrs. Dalloway* was published in 1925; Woolf's first readers would certainly have been aware of these crucial events.

The historical references suggest that the class under examination in the novel is living on borrowed time. Its values—"the public-spirited, British Empire, tariff-reform, governing-class spirit," in Peter's words—were very much under attack. Characters like Lady Bruton, Miss Parry, and Peter himself are identified with Britain's imperial mission, but the empire was crumbling fast. In 1922 the Irish Free State was proclaimed and the last English troops left Dublin. When Lady Bruton cries in dismay, "Ah, the news from India!" she probably has in mind the beginnings of the agitation for independence in that country. The *Times* in June 1923 was full of "news from India" sure to disturb someone with her values: imperial police "overwhelmed and brutally tortured by the villagers" (June 2); "Extremists Fomenting Trouble" (June 23); "Punjab Discontent" (June 29). Peter Walsh goes to Clarissa's party not only to see her again but also "to ask Richard what they were doing in India—the conservative duffers."

As a class and as a force, then, the world to which the Dalloways belong is decadent rather than crescent. The party at the end of the novel, for all its brilliance, is a kind of wake. It reveals the form of power without its substance. When the prime minister finally arrives, he is described as looking "so ordinary. You might have stood him behind a counter and bought biscuits—poor chap, all rigged up in gold lace." And the imagery of the last section suggests rigidity, calcification, the exhumation of relics: "Doors were being opened for ladies wrapped like mummies in shawls with bright flowers on them." Clarissa's ancient aunt, whom Peter had mistakenly thought dead, appears at the party: "For Miss Helena Parry was not dead: Miss Parry was alive. She was past eighty. She ascended staircases slowly with a stick. She was placed in a chair. . . . People who had known Burma in the 'seventies were always led up to her." Even the young people of the class, in Clarissa's words, "could not talk. . . . The enormous resources of the English language, the power it bestows, after all, of communicating feelings . . . was not for them. They would solidify young."

Solidity, rigidity, stasis, the inability to communicate feelings—these are central concepts in *Mrs. Dalloway*. As they apply to the governing class in the novel, they point to something inflexible, unresponsive, or evasive in their nature that makes them incapable of reacting appropriately to the critical events of their time or of their own lives. The great contemporary event of European history had of course been the First World War, and it is no exaggeration to say with one critic [Bernard Blackstone] that "deferred war-shock" is the major theme of *Mrs. Dalloway*. Though the war had transformed the lives of millions of people, only one character in the novel—Septimus Smith—seems to have counted its cost, both to the victims of the slaughter and to the survivors. He does not, of course, belong to the governing class, whose way of responding to the war is crucially different. Woolf suggests that they are engaged in a conspiracy to deny its pain or its significance. Their ideal is stoicism, even if the price they pay is petrifaction. Clarissa consistently idealizes the behavior of Lady Bexborough, "who opened a bazaar, they said, with the telegram in her hand, John, her favourite, killed." The sentence comes from one of several passages in which the war is mentioned, a section in which Clarissa complacently muses, "For it was the middle of June. The War was over . . . thank Heaven—over. It was June. The King and Queen were at the palace." The easy assumption that the war is a thing of the past and need no longer be a subject of concern is also voiced in Richard Dalloway's momentary thought for the "thousands of poor chaps, with all their lives before them, shovelled together, already half forgotten," and in the words of "little Mr. Bowley, who had rooms in the Albany and was sealed with wax over the deeper sources of life": "poor women, nice little children, orphans, widows, the War—tut-tut."

Neither Virginia Woolf nor any of her Bloomsbury associates could have brought themselves to say "the War—tut-tut." "Curse this war; God damn this war!" the man in her story "The Mark on the Wall" cries out. For all of them, the war was an unmitigated catastrophe that forced them to examine their consciences and make major ethical decisions—whether to declare themselves conscientious objectors, whether to participate in any form. If the war had any justification, it could be only as a liberating force likely to transform society and human relations. Perhaps the brave new world it might help to bring to birth could make one believe in its necessity. In *The Years,* this hope for the regeneration of humanity is expressed in the crucial air raid scene that takes place in 1917. Eleanor asks, with the ardor and desperation of a character in Chekhov, "When will this new world come? When shall we be free? When shall we live adventurously, wholly, not like cripples in a cave?" But in *The Years,* as in *Mrs. Dalloway,* the hopes for a new society are betrayed by the return of the old. The sacrifice has been meaningless. As Clarissa Dalloway says in the short story out of which the novel grew, "Thousands of young men had died that things might go on."

The sense of living in the past, of being unable to take in or respond to the transformations of the present, makes the governing class in *Mrs. Dalloway* seem hopelessly out of step with its time. Peter turns Miss Parry's glass eye into a symbol: "It seemed so fitting—one of nature's masterpieces—that old Miss Parry should turn to glass. She would die like some bird in a frost gripping her perch. She belonged to a different age." Woolf gives us a picture of a class impervious to change in a society that desperately needs or demands it, a class that worships tradition and settled order but cannot accommodate the new and disturbing. Lady Bradshaw is described, in an extraordinary phrase, as feeling "wedged on a calm ocean." But the calm is only on the surface; there is turbulence beneath. The class, in fact, uses its influence to exclude and sequester alien or threatening forces—the Septimus Smiths, the Doris Kilmans—and to protect itself from any sort of intense feeling. It may well be this calculated emotional obtuseness that has kept it in power, since Woolf makes it clear (in the sky-writing scene) that many others in the society long for a restoration of the status quo ante. The political activities of the novel—Richard's committees, Lady Bruton's emigration project, Hugh Whitbread's letters to the *Times,* the ritual appearance of the prime minister—are all essentially routine in nature and suggest that it is only by ignoring the more devastating facts and deep scars of recent history that the "social system" has managed to keep functioning. Perhaps Woolf saw a necessary connection in unstable times between traditional political power and the absence of empathy and moral imagination.

Certainly the governing class in the novel demonstrates these qualities. It worships Proportion, by which it really means atrophy of the heart, repression of instinct and emotion. A. D. Moody [in *Virginia Woolf*] has pointed to the impulse in the class "to turn away from the disturbing depths of feeling, and towards a conventional pleasantness or sentimentality or frivolousness." Richard Dalloway, for example, finds it impossible to tell his wife that he loves her or even, for that matter, to say the word "I": "The time comes when it can't be said; one's too shy to say it. . . . Here he was walking across London to say to Clarissa in so many words that he loved her. Which one never does say, he thought. Partly one's lazy; partly one's shy." When the desperate Septimus stammers "I—I—" in Dr. Bradshaw's consulting room, Sir William cautions, "Try to think as little about yourself as possible." That this repression of feeling is very much the product of upper-class training is suggested not only in *Mrs. Dalloway* but in a crystallizing minor incident in *The Years:* "Here a footman's white-gloved hand removing dishes knocked over a glass of wine. A red splash trickled onto the lady's dress. But she did not move a muscle; she went on talking. Then she straightened the clean napkin that had been brought her, nonchalantly, over the stain."

Such unruffled self-control has everything to do with the ability to retain power and to stay sane. The characters in *Mrs. Dalloway* who cannot learn to restrain their intense emotions (Septimus, Miss Kilman, even Peter Walsh) are all in serious trouble. They are the outsiders in a society dedicated to covering up the stains and ignoring the major and minor tremors that threaten its existence. When such people become too distressing, they are dealt with by the "authorities," agents of the governing class like the psychiatrist Sir William Bradshaw who act to make sure that "these unsocial impulses . . . [are] held in control." For the anesthesia of the governing class must not be permitted to wear off. And so Sir William "made England prosper, secluded her lunatics, forbade childbirth, penalised despair, made it impossible for the unfit to propagate their views." This whole section of the novel makes us realize that the complacency of the governing class is not a natural state but must be constantly defended by the strenuous activity of people like Sir William. There is a conspiracy to keep any kind of vividness, any intense life, at a safe distance. The doctor's gray car is furnished in monotone, with gray furs and silver gray rugs "to match its sober suavity."

This sense of living in a cocoon that protects the class from disturbing facts and feelings is reiterated in the treatment of its relations with its servants. Lady Bruton, for example, floats gently on "the grey tide of service which washed round [her] day in, day out, collecting, intercepting, enveloping her in a fine tissue which broke concussions, mitigated interruptions, and spread round the house in Brook Street a fine net where things lodged and were picked out accurately, instantly." Service is assumed to be part of the natural order by the governing class, dependable in its regular rhythms, creating an environment of basic security by maintaining a predictable daily routine. The fact that the entire system is based on the power and wealth of one class and the drudgery of another is ignored by master and servant alike in an unending ritual of deception and self-deception, as Woolf sarcastically suggests:

> And so there began a soundless and exquisite passing to and fro through swing doors of aproned, white-capped maids, handmaidens not of necessity, but adepts in a mystery or grand deception practised by hostesses in Mayfair from one-thirty to two, when, with a wave of the hand, the traffic ceases, and there rises instead this profound illusion in the first place about the food—how it is not paid for; and then that the table spreads itself voluntarily with glass and silver, little mats, saucers of red fruit; films of brown cream mark turbot; in casseroles severed chickens swim; coloured, undomestic, the fire burns; and with the wine and the coffee (not paid for) rise jocund visions before musing eyes; gently speculative eyes; eyes to whom life appears musical, mysterious.

It is a way of life that seems part of some eternal order, functioning without apparent friction or even choice. But Woolf makes us see the connection between the elegance and composure of the governing class and the ceaseless activity of the lower. Clarissa Dalloway, in a little hymn of praise to her servants, mentally thanks them "for helping her to be . . . gentle, generous-hearted." She sends her "love" to the cook, Mrs. Walker, in the middle of one of her parties; but we are given a vivid glimpse of the pandemonium below stairs not visible to the guests pleasantly floating on "the grey tide of service":

> Did it matter, did it matter in the least, one Prime Minister more or less? It made no difference at this hour of the night to Mrs. Walker among the plates, saucepans, cullenders, frying-pans, chicken in aspic, ice-cream freezers, pared crusts of bread, lemons, soup tureens, and pudding basins which, however hard they washed up in the scullery, seemed to be all on top of her, on the kitchen table, on chairs, while the fire blared and roared, the electric lights glared, and still supper had to be laid.

The relationship between master and servant in *Mrs. Dalloway* is typical of the gulf between all classes in the novel. Clarissa's party is strictly class-demarcated. No Septimus, no Rezia, no Doris Kilman could conceivably set foot in it. Miss Kilman, indeed, bitterly notes that "people don't ask me to parties." Even impoverished gentlefolk, like Clarissa's cousin Ellie Henderson, are invited only under pressure and out of habit. Clarissa defends her parties as an expression of her ideal of unity, the wish to bring together "so-and-so in South Kensington; some one up in Bayswater; and somebody else, say, in Mayfair," and critics have often stressed her ability to merge different worlds and create a feeling of integration. But the London neighborhoods she mentions are upper-middle-class preserves, the residential areas where the members of the Dalloway set are likely to live (though Bayswater might require an amusing explanation). Clarissa's integration is horizontal, not vertical.

The Dalloways shut out not only the Septimus Smiths and the Doris Kilmans but the artists as well. The novel makes it clear that their world is consistently and uneasily philistine. Though a token poet makes an appearance at Clarissa's party, her set has a deep distrust of writers, precisely because they might disturb its complacency. Richard opines that "no decent man ought to read Shakespeare's sonnets because it was like listening at keyholes (besides, the relationship was not one that he approved)." Sally says of Hugh Whitbread that "he's read nothing, thought nothing, felt nothing"; Dr. Bradshaw "never had time for reading"; and Lady Bruton, though Lovelace or Herrick once frequented her family estate, "never read a word of poetry herself." This indifference or hostility to literature is symptomatic of the class's

lack of curiosity about life outside its precincts. In the novel an obsession with Shakespeare (as in the thoughts of Septimus and Clarissa) is a
kind of shorthand indication that the soul has survived, that some kind
of sympathetic imagination is still functioning.

Clarissa's instant empathy with Septimus when his suicide is mentioned at her party is in marked contrast to the way her set usually
deals with outsiders. His death shatters her composure and touches her
in a profoundly personal way. This is not at all the manner in which
the rest of the governing class treats the threatening presences by
which it is surrounded. Their method is rather to turn the individual
into a "case," as Bradshaw does in mentioning Septimus in the first
place: "They were talking about this Bill. Some case Sir William was
mentioning, lowering his voice. It had its bearing upon what he was
saying about the deferred effects of shell shock. There must be some
provision in the Bill." In this way of treating alien experience, the
living Septimus becomes a category, his life an "it" to be considered
by government committees drafting legislation. The ability to translate
individual human beings into manageable social categories is one of the
marks of the governing-class mentality Woolf examines in the novel.
They have learned to think and talk in officialese. Richard "champi-
oned the downtrodden . . . in the House of Commons." A young
woman he passes in the park ("impudent, loose-lipped, humorous")
immediately becomes an example of "the female vagrant" in a passage
that perfectly suggests his need to keep people at a distance: "Bearing
his flowers like a weapon, Richard Dalloway approached her; intent he
passed her; still there was time for a spark between them—she laughed
at the sight of him, he smiled good-humouredly, considering the
problem of the female vagrant; not that they would ever speak." Lady
Bruton's emigration project is designed for "young people of both
sexes born of respectable parents." Sir William sees Septimus as merely
another of "these prophetic Christs and Christesses." These examples
suggest that the governing class has remained unruffled by viewing all
social problems as involving distinct categories of people different
from themselves. Like all good administrators, they compartmentalize
in order to control and make things manageable.

These managerial skills are used to keep the society stable and to
retain power. Emigration is a way of handling the massive unemploy-
ment of the period; benefits in cases of delayed shell shock will separate the lunatics who insist on flaunting their rage or guilt about the
war from those who are trying to forget it; Richard's work on com-

mittees for "his Armenians, his Albanians" might defuse another explosive international situation. All the governing-class types in the
novel think of themselves as progressive reformers, even the unctuous
Hugh Whitbread, whose "name at the end of letters to the *Times,*
asking for funds, appealing to the public to protect, to preserve, to
clear up litter, to abate smoke, and stamp out immorality in parks,
commanded respect." But behind the public concern and tradition of
social service is the need to dominate, the habit of power. It is here that
one can see the social system "at work, at its most intense." Its symbol
is the figure of Dr. Bradshaw, preaching Proportion but worshiping
Conversion, a goddess who "feasts on the wills of the weakly, loving
to impress, to impose, adoring her own features stamped on the face of
the populace," a deity at work not only in Sir William's consulting
room but also "in the heat and sands of India, the mud and swamp of
Africa, the purlieus of London, wherever, in short, the climate or the
devil tempts men to fall from the true belief which is her own." The
passage clearly connects the "case" of Septimus Smith with British
imperialism and social repression and reveals the iron hand in a velvet
glove. It is entirely appropriate that this psychiatrist-policeman and the
Prime Minister should be invited to the same party.

The passages concerning Dr. Bradshaw are markedly different in
tone from the rest of the book, but this is not simply because Woolf is
writing out of her own painful experience of how mental derangement
is handled by some professional therapists. Such "treatment" is itself a
symptom of a disease in the social system—the easy assumption of the
habit of command. It connects with Woolf's angry criticism of the
patriarchy in *A Room of One's Own* and *Three Guineas* as well as with
her satiric picture of the imperial policeman in *Between the Acts,* her
symbol of Victorian England, who tells the audience:

> *Go to Church on Sunday; on Monday, nine sharp, catch the City*
> *Bus. On Tuesday it may be, attend a meeting at the Mansion*
> *House for the redemption of the sinner; at dinner on Wednesday*
> *attend another—turtle soup. Some bother it may be in Ireland;*
> *Famine. Fenians. What not. On Thursday it's the natives of Peru*
> *require protection and corruption; we give 'em what's due. But*
> *mark you, our rule don't end there. It's a Christian country,*
> *our Empire; under the White Queen Victoria. Over thought*
> *and religion; drink; dress; manners; marriage too, I wield my*
> *truncheon.*

In *Mrs. Dalloway* too the representatives of power wield their trun-
cheons. "What right has Bradshaw to say 'must' to me?" Septimus
demands. Behind philanthropy and reform, industriousness, morality,
and religion there is the same impulse—telling others how to live,
"forcing your soul," as Clarissa puts it. In a diary entry about Victorian
philanthropists, Woolf reveals how repugnant the easy assumption of
power in this class was to her: "More & more I come to loathe any
dominion of one over another; any leadership, any imposition of the
will."

The fundamental conflict in *Mrs. Dalloway* is between those who
identify with Establishment "dominion" and "leadership" and those
who resist or are repelled by it. The characters in the novel can be seen
as ranged on a sort of continuum with Bradshaw at one end and
Septimus at the other. Thus far I have concentrated on the characters at
the Establishment end of the scale: Sir William, Hugh Whitbread, Lady
Bruton, Miss Parry, and Richard Dalloway. Among the rebels (present
or former) we must count Septimus Smith, Doris Kilman, Sally Seton,
and Peter Walsh, though there are important distinctions among them.
And in the center of this conflict—its pivot, so to speak—stands
Clarissa Dalloway.

Septimus Smith is instantly seen as a threat to governing-class
values not only because he insists on remembering the war when
everyone else is trying to forget it but also because his feverish intensity of feeling is an implicit criticism of the ideal of stoic impassivity.
In Woolf's preliminary notes for the novel, she treats this as the essence
of Septimus's character: "He must somehow see through human nature—
see its hypocrisy, & insincerity, its power to recover from every
wound, incapable of taking any final impression. His sense that this is
not worth having." Septimus comes through the war unscathed—"The
last shells missed him"—but afterward discovers a psychic wound
from which he has no wish to recover because it is a badge of honor in
a society that identifies composure with mental health. The mark of his
sensibility is perpetual turbulence, as in this passage: "The excitement
of the elm trees rising and falling, rising and falling with all their leaves
alight and the colour thinning and thickening from blue to the green of
a hollow wave. . . . Leaves were alive; trees were alive." It is as if
Septimus were a repository for the suppressed feelings of the rigidly
controlled people around him, those like Mr. Bowley "sealed with
wax over the deeper sources of life." Far from being sealed, Septimus
is a seething cauldron of emotions constantly threatening to overflow,

a sacrificial victim or scapegoat who takes upon himself the sins of omission rather than commission. Woolf planned that he "should pass through all extremes of feeling." Like Leontes in *The Winter's Tale,* Septimus is "a feather for each wind that blows," but his emotional instability is a compensation for his society's repression and can be understood and judged only in relation to it.

For Septimus has not always been a rebel. He begins, indeed, like the classic ambitious working-class boy entering the Establishment: moving to the city from the provinces, "improving himself" by taking evening classes, impressing his superiors at work and in the army by his ability and detachment. He volunteers early in the war, and when his friend Evans is killed, he congratulates himself "upon feeling very little and very reasonably. The War had taught him. It was sublime. He had gone through the whole show, friendship, European War, death, had won promotion, was still under thirty and was bound to survive." But this mood of self-congratulation is suddenly displaced by the "appalling fear . . . that he could not feel." His stoic fortitude in the face of slaughter sends him into a panic incomprehensible to a society that idealizes Proportion. For his fear of emotional aridity is finally greater than his dread of insanity. And so he surrenders to the force of feeling in all its variety and intensity—guilt, ecstasy, loathing, rage, bliss. His emotions are chaotic because they are entirely self-generated and self-sustained; he becomes a pariah. That Septimus should have no contact with the Dalloway set is absolutely essential to Woolf's design, though it has often been criticized as a structural flaw of the novel. And among the people in his own world, Rezia has no idea what goes on in his mind; Dr. Holmes recommends bromides, golf, and the music hall; Sir William orders seclusion and bed rest. His only companion is the dead Evans, whom he must resurrect in fantasy. He is alone.

It is no wonder that the resultant vision of the world is as distorted as the governing-class view. Where Richard complacently sees his times as "a great age in which to have lived," Septimus is conscious only of "the brute with the red nostrils" all around him. In Shakespeare, in Dante, in Aeschylus, he can find only one message: "loathing, hatred, despair." His wife's innocent wish for a child is seen as an example of the "filth" of copulation, and the ordinary run of humanity at his office is "leering, sneering, obscene . . . oozing thick drops of vice." All this is an obvious projection of his own guilt, which he feels simultaneously: "He had not cared when Evans was killed; that was worst; . . . and was so pocked and marked with vice that women shuddered when they saw him in the street." These black feelings are unendurable and consistently alternate with their opposites, with pastoral visions of a world of eternal beauty and harmony. In his fantasy, Evans is brought back to life and the sparrows sing "how there is no crime . . . how there is no death." Though Septimus is intended to serve as an antithesis to the governing-class spirit, he is in no sense a preferable alternative to it. And he, too, is finally forced to pretend that the war's cost was not real, that death is an illusion. He is a victim not only of the war but of the peace, with its insistence that all could be forgotten and the old order reestablished. The pressure to do so is eventually too much for him, and he succumbs.

Like Septimus, Doris Kilman is a war victim. Dismissed from her teaching position because "she would not pretend that the Germans were all villains," she must earn her living by occasional tutorial instruction. The degrading poverty and isolation her dismissal brings about embitters her profoundly, making her despise herself and her society in alternate flashes of emotion. Like Septimus, she cannot control "the hot and turbulent feelings which boiled and surged in her." And also like him, she finds release in a quasi-mystical experience that momentarily assuages her distress. But her religious calm is temporary; her passionate nature continues to vent itself in unpredictable and uncontrollable surges—her murderous hatred of Mrs. Dalloway; her agonized love for Elizabeth: "If she could grasp her, if she could clasp her, if she could make her hers absolutely and for ever and then die; that was all she wanted." But what hope is there that the discreditable feelings Doris Kilman harbors—her lesbian attachment to Elizabeth, her class rage, her contempt for British jingoism during the war—could ever see the light of day? The lid of convention is heavily and firmly in place in the world around her, and so her intense emotional life must be lived entirely in her own mind, where it takes on a nightmare quality comparable to that of Septimus. She, too, is alone.

Between the extremes of Dr. Bradshaw and Hugh Whitbread on the one hand and Septimus and Doris Kilman on the other, Woolf invents three characters who cannot be placed so easily: Sally Seton, Peter Walsh, and Clarissa. Though all belong to the upper middle class, all have gone through a passionate rebellious phase, rejecting what their world stood for—the worship of convention, the inevitability of the class structure, the repression of feeling. As young women,

Sally and Clarissa planned "to found a society to abolish private property"; they read the utopian socialists and talked about "how they were to reform the world." Sally once radiated "a sort of abandonment, as if she could say anything, do anything," that made Clarissa fall passionately in love with her. The girlhood attachment was as intense as Miss Kilman's feeling for Elizabeth. Clarissa too had longed for a *Liebestod:* " 'If it were now to die 'twere now to be most happy.' That was her feeling—Othello's feeling, and she felt it, she was convinced, as strongly as Shakespeare meant Othello to feel it, all because she was coming down to dinner in a white frock to meet Sally Seton!" Sally's unconventional behavior and readiness to take risks strike Clarissa as wonderful and dangerous, bound "to end in some awful tragedy; her death; her martyrdom." The extravagant terms suggest Septimus's fate, but Sally's future course is anything but tragic: she marries "a bald man with a large buttonhole who owned, it was said, cotton mills at Manchester" and surfaces at Clarissa's party as the prosperous Lady Rosseter, the mother of five boys, her voice "wrung of its old ravishing richness." Her rebellion is merely a youthful stage in the process that transforms "the wild, the daring, the romantic Sally" into a marginally acceptable adult member of her class.

Peter's rebellion is longer lived but no more dependable. He too revolts against convention in youth, becomes a socialist, defines himself as an outsider:

> He was not old, or set, or dried in the least. As for caring what they said of him—the Dalloways, the Whitbreads, and their set, he cared not a straw—not a straw (though it was true he would have, some time or other, to see whether Richard couldn't help him to some job). Striding, staring, he glared at the statue of the Duke of Cambridge. He had been sent down from Oxford—true. He had been a Socialist, in some sense a failure—true. Still the future of civilization lies, he thought, in the hands of young men like that; of young men such as he was, thirty years ago; with their love of abstract principles; getting books sent out to them all the way from London to a peak in the Himalayas; reading science; reading philosophy. The future lies in the hands of young men like that, he thought.

The passage is a good example of Woolf's satiric exposure of her character's illusions. We come to know Peter better than he knows himself, can see through his heroic posturing ("striding, staring"), his rhetoric ("the future of civilization"), his verbal formulas and clichés ("he cared not a straw"). His whole personality in middle age is a flimsy construct designed to reassure himself that the passion and radicalism of his youth are not dead. At various moments in the novel he fantasizes himself a romantic buccaneer, a solitary traveler, and "as young as ever." He continues to patronize the conservatism of people like Richard Dalloway and the social conventions crystallized in Clarissa's role of hostess.

Nevertheless, he is as firmly a part of the Establishment by this time as Lady Rosseter. Though no great success, he is not a failure either, has "done just respectably, filled the usual posts adequately" as a colonial administrator, and expects to use the influence of the people he patronizes—Richard's, Hugh's—to find a position in England. The old school tie is fully exploited. The class conditioning he rejects so violently in youth returns in middle age almost against his will, makes him feel "moments of pride in England; in butlers; chow dogs; girls in their security" and see the ambulance coming for Septimus as a symbol of British efficiency, "one of the triumphs of civilisation." This compromised rebellion or permanently inhibited aggression is epitomized in the pocket knife Peter carries and is forever opening and closing, a weapon that becomes a toy in his hands.

Yet a part of his youth has survived intact—his passion for Clarissa; the emotional anesthesia of his set has not managed to kill off the deepest attachment he has ever felt. He recalls every incident of their painful courtship in precise detail and can summon up the intense emotions of that time in all their power: "He had spoken for hours, it seemed, with the tears running down his cheeks." His susceptibility to sudden gusts of feeling "had been his undoing in Anglo-Indian society," Peter thinks, and it is true that he is in some sense an emotional exhibitionist. But in a world that penalizes despair and idealizes Lady Bexborough's ramrod bearing, the passions have no legitimate channel and will flow unpredictably. Peter's tears and moments of joy are paler variants of Septimus's rages and rapturous visions. What one sees throughout *Mrs. Dalloway* is a single disease that takes different forms. Peter's or Septimus's or Doris Kilman's emotional compulsiveness and display, their gaudiness or profligacy, are the antithesis of the denial of feeling in the governing class. But both are failures to maintain a natural flow of response commensurate with the occasion or situation, a failure that expresses itself variously as the inhibition or exhibition of emotion. Perhaps Woolf's complex attitude is paradoxically also rooted in an ideal of Proportion, though in a form very different from the goddess Dr. Bradshaw worships. In *Macbeth* Macduff breaks down on hearing that his wife and children have been brutally murdered. When he is encouraged to "dispute it like a man," he replies, with great dignity, "I shall do so; / But I must also feel it as a man" (4.4.219–20). It is precisely this dual commitment to self-control and to emotional expression that the characters in *Mrs. Dalloway* lack.

In the Establishment rebels the failure is related to the passage of time. Peter notes that the "governing-class spirit" had grown on Clarissa, "as it tends to do," but the same could be said about Sally or about Peter himself. Woolf was interested in the process through which an independent, responsive, emotionally supple young man or woman is gradually transformed into a conventional member of his or her class. Her interest in this change of human beings through time underlay what she called "my prime discovery so far" in writing *Mrs. Dalloway:* "my tunnelling process, by which I tell the past by instalments, as I have need of it." As J. Hillis Miller has shown, *Mrs. Dalloway* "is a novel of the resurrection of the past into the actual present of the characters' lives" (though for some of these characters the past can no longer be resuscitated: Lady Bradshaw, for example, had "gone under" fifteen years before). Even Septimus is out of touch with his former self; his youthful passions for Shakespeare, for England, for Miss Isabel Pole are now utterly alien to him, dismissed by the narrator as "such a fire as burns only once in a lifetime."

In Sally, Peter, and Clarissa, Woolf traces the process of socialization from the extended moment in which each was intensely alive—young, brash, open, taking emotional risks—to the stage of conventionality. The class to which these characters belong, it is made clear, is not at all hospitable to such intense feelings. Gradually it blunts, denies, trivializes, or absorbs them, transforming the young rebels into wooden creatures whose public lives no longer express their buried selves. The result is a failure of imaginative sympathy and emotional resonance, an absence of "something central which permeated," as Clarissa puts it in a highly critical summary of her own failings, "something warm which broke up surfaces and rippled the cold contact of man and woman, or of women together."

But Clarissa is harder on herself than her creator is. For *Mrs. Dalloway* finally presents a sympathetic picture of someone who has surrendered to the force of conventional life and permitted her emotions to go underground. Woolf's decision to record Clarissa's thoughts and feelings as well as her words and actions is crucial and represents a deliberate change in her own attitude toward such people. The Dalloways had made an extended appearance in her first novel, *The Voyage Out* (1915), where they were treated with unremitting satiric contempt and where their inner lives were kept dark. We can trace Woolf's conception of Clarissa Dalloway through several stages, from her first appearance in *The Voyage Out,* to her resurrection in the short story "Mrs. Dalloway in Bond Street" (1923), to her flowering in the novel that grew out of that story. In *The Voyage Out* the Dalloways are simply caricatures of their class—worldly, jingoistic, snobbish, smug, philistine, and utterly devoid of inwardness. They exist in a self-contained satiric pocket of the novel and make no connection with the characters the author takes seriously. When Woolf decided to write about them again in the next decade, she must have felt that she had done them an injustice. But even in "Mrs. Dalloway in Bond Street," in which something approximating stream of consciousness is first used to reveal Clarissa's inner life, the character who emerges remains a satiric object. She is utterly loyal to her country, her class, and its leaders. As she passes Buckingham Palace, she treats the monarch's ceremonial functions as an example of British "character": "something inborn in the race; what Indians respected. The Queen went to hospitals, opened bazaars—the Queen of England, thought Clarissa, looking at the Palace."

In the course of revising "Mrs. Dalloway in Bond Street" to make it into the first section of the novel, Woolf modifies most of the cruder manifestations of Clarissa's snobbishness and complacency. For example, in the story she thinks, "It would be intolerable if dowdy women came to her party! Would one have liked Keats if he had worn red socks?" But in the novel a dowdy woman (Ellie Henderson) is invited to her party, though reluctantly, and the young poet Jim Hutton appears wearing red socks, "his black being at the laundry." In the course of the book Clarissa becomes less a typical member of her class and more an individual. This impression is reinforced by some of the titles Woolf apparently considered using—"The Life of a Lady," "A Lady of Fashion"—before she settled on *Mrs. Dalloway.* She was convinced that the book would be an advance on her previous work because "the human soul will be treated more seriously." Clarissa Dalloway became the first character in Woolf's fiction whose inner life is completely known to us.

Clarissa has troubled readers from the first. Woolf noted in her diary that Lytton Strachey complained of "some discrepancy in Clarissa herself; he thinks she is disagreeable & limited, but that I alternately laugh at her, & cover her, very remarkably, with myself." And she recalls nearly abandoning the novel because she found the main character "in some way tinselly. Then I invented her memories. But I think some distaste for her persisted." This ambiguity of response is reflected in nearly all subsequent commentary on the novel, the attacks on or defenses of Clarissa determined in part by the critic's attitude toward convention and governing-class values. In one of the most interesting treatments of the novel, A. D. Moody insists that Clarissa is not an individualized character at all but merely an embodiment of society's code, an "animated mirror" of the shallow world she reflects. But other commentators have stressed Clarissa's progress to "the freedom of full maturity" (Isabel Gamble) or her determination "never to bow to the laws of limitation set up in society, but instead to carry a sense of freedom and love into her world" (Alice van Buren Kelley).

What seems to me to account for such discrepancies is that Clarissa's is essentially a laminated personality, made up of distinct layers that do not interpenetrate. Like Peter and Sally she has both a conformist and a rebellious side, a public and a private self. But though it is true that the governing-class spirit has increasingly come to dominate her life, the stream of her thoughts and feelings shows us that the various strata of her personality are all intact and that the movement from rebellion to conformity is not necessarily inexorable or irreversible. Certainly convention dominates her words and actions. She has indeed become "the perfect hostess," as Peter predicted she would, with all the suppression of self that this ideal demands. She is proud that she is descended from courtiers and sees herself continuing a great tradition: "She, too, was going that very night to kindle and illuminate; to give her party." And like the other Establishment characters in the novel, she worships the stoical ideal and connects it with the war: "This late age of the world's experience had bred in them all, all men and women, a well of tears. Tears and sorrows; courage and endurance; a perfectly upright and stoical bearing. Think, for example, of the woman she admired most, Lady Bexborough, opening the bazaar." The passage suggests an apparently inevitable sequence in Clarissa's mind from misery to endurance to rigidity. This ideal of conduct is manifested in her original decision to reject Peter Walsh, with all his emotional violence, and marry the stolid and reliable Richard Dalloway. When she tells Peter their affair is over, he recalls "She was like iron, like flint, rigid up the backbone."

But though the decision to give up Peter and Sally and identify herself with the governing-class spirit is never reversed, it is also never final, because Clarissa continually goes over the reasons for her choice thirty years later. This accounts for her obsession with the past, for her continued attraction to Peter and vulnerability to his criticism, decades after the issue was supposedly settled. At one point Peter thought he could write her obituary: "It was her manner that annoyed him; timid; hard; arrogant; prudish. 'The death of the soul.' He had said that instinctively, ticketing the moment as he used to do—the death of her soul." But Clarissa's soul is not dead; it has only gone underground. She has moments in which she feels herself "invisible; unseen; unknown," a mood she connects with her married state and public identity, "this being Mrs. Dalloway; not even Clarissa any more; this being Mrs. Richard Dalloway." In her world the soul has no public function and can only survive in solitude. But even her marriage to Richard is not really a betrayal of self so much as a compact between two people to live together yet allow the soul a little breathing space: "And there is a dignity in people; a solitude; even between husband and wife a gulf; and that one must respect, thought Clarissa . . . for one would not part with it oneself, or take it, against his will, from one's husband, without losing one's independence, one's self-respect— something, after all, priceless."

In feeling this need for solitude, Clarissa is expressing one of Woolf's own cherished beliefs. In her essay on E. M. Forster she describes a technique of his fiction that applies equally to her own: "He is always constrained to build the cage—society in all its intricacy and triviality—before he can free the prisoner." Even Mrs. Ramsay in *To the Lighthouse,* one of Woolf's most social characters, can allow herself to think: "To be silent; to be alone. All the being and the doing, expansive, glittering, vocal, evaporated; and one shrunk, with a sense of solemnity, to being oneself, a wedge-shaped core of darkness, something invisible to others." In her essay on Elizabethan drama Woolf suggests that a modern audience has an absolute need for some exploration of the private as against the public self. Immersed as we are in the "extravagant laughter, poetry, and splendour" of an Elizabethan play, we gradually become aware that there is something we are being denied: "It is solitude. There is no privacy here. Always the door opens and someone comes in. . . . Meanwhile, as if tired with company, the mind steals off to muse in solitude; to think, not to act; to comment, not to share; to explore its own darkness, not the bright-lit-up surfaces of others."

There is an exact parallel here to Clarissa's withdrawal from the party at the climax of *Mrs. Dalloway* in order to reflect on Septimus's suicide. The little room is a solitary retreat where "the party's splendour fell to the floor, so strange it was to come in alone in her finery." And in this solitude Clarissa allows herself to think about Septimus's death with full imaginative sympathy, understanding his feelings and situation instinctively with some part of her self that scarcely functions in the public world she normally inhabits. She realizes that Septimus had managed to rescue in death an inner freedom that her own life is constantly forcing her to barter away: "A thing there was that mattered; a thing, wreathed about with chatter, defaced, obscured in her own life, let drop every day in corruption, lies, chatter. This he had preserved." Septimus is Clarissa's conscience, is indeed the conscience of the governing class, though only she is willing to acknowledge him. In doing so, she sees her acceptance of the governing-class code in a highly critical light: "She had schemed; she had pilfered. She was never wholly admirable. She had wanted success, Lady Bexborough and the rest of it. And once she had walked on the terrace at Bourton." This juxtaposition of present and past stresses the loss of the intense feeling of her youth, for it was on the terrace at Bourton that she had known "the most exquisite moment of her whole life," when Sally kissed her on the lips and released the torrent of Clarissa's first romantic passion.

In feeling a sense of kinship with Septimus, Clarissa is crossing class lines in her imagination, for certainly he is beyond the pale of her set. Woolf moves in this passage from the traditional social satire of the English novelist of manners to what she called "The Russian Point of View" in one of her essays. Unlike the class-obsessed English writer, Dostoevsky is indifferent to class barriers and social identity: "It is all the same to him whether you are noble or simple, a tramp or a great lady. Whoever you are, you are the vessel of this perplexed liquid, this cloudy, yeasty, precious stuff, the soul." Though they have never exchanged a word, on the deepest level Septimus and Clarissa are kin. And so, for all their mutual hatred, are Clarissa and Miss Kilman. Just before she withdraws to the little room, Clarissa has a moment of contempt for her social triumphs, which she feels "had a hollowness; at arm's length they were, not in the heart." At the same instant she recalls "Kilman her enemy. That was satisfying; that was real. Ah, how she hated her—hot, hypocritical, corrupt; with all that power;

Elizabeth's seducer. . . . She hated her: she loved her. It was enemies one wanted, not friends." These reactions to Septimus and Doris Kilman (with their characteristic mixture of exalted and base feelings) together suggest that Clarissa's soul is far from dead, that she can resurrect the intense emotions of youth despite the pressure of a society determined to deny them quarter.

In such passages Woolf gives Clarissa her pivotal role, balancing the anesthesia of the governing class against the fervor of a Septimus Smith or a Doris Kilman. At the same time, Peter Walsh is asking himself, "What is this terror? what is this ecstasy? . . . What is it that fills me with extraordinary excitement?" And replying, "It is Clarissa." These ardent feelings will probably never be translated into action, or even speech. It seems improbable that the outer life of Peter or Clarissa will change, for "the social system" Woolf describes in *Mrs. Dalloway* is not likely to be transformed soon enough to allow either of them to build their lives on the flow as well as the containment of emotion, especially since both must also be regarded as accomplices to if not agents of repression. Woolf was too convinced of the fundamental inertia in human nature and institutions to imagine a rapid transformation of either. But she as conscious of change, too, in both societal and individual values, even if it sometimes appeared to be taking place in geological rather than human time. *Mrs. Dalloway* captures a moment in which the domination of the ideal of rigid self-control began to seem oppressive rather than admirable. In illuminating the price the characters in her novel have had to pay to live under the sway of this ideal, Woolf is not only fulfilling her ambition "to criticise the social system, and to show it at work, at its most intense," but also contributing indirectly to its replacement by one less hostile to the buried life of feeling in every human being. She knew that even the most fundamental institutions and forms of behavior could be altered. . . . Her sense of continual transformation also affected her vision of what looked like mankind's most enduring social arrangement—the family.

Chronology

1882	Adeline Virginia Stephen born in London on January 25 to Leslie Stephen, statesman and man of letters, and Julia Duckworth Stephen. Her father had one (insane) daughter from a previous marriage, her mother three children from an earlier marriage; together they had four more children: Vanessa, Julian Thoby, Virginia, and Adrian. Virginia educated at home by her parents.
1895	Julia Stephen dies; Leslie Stephen goes into deep mourning; Virginia has a severe mental breakdown. Household run by Julia's daughter Stella Duckworth, who postpones her marriage until Vanessa is old enough to take over.
1897	Stella Duckworth marries, becomes pregnant, and dies.
1902	Leslie Stephen knighted.
1904–5	Death of Sir Leslie Stephen in 1904. Virginia has a second mental breakdown and tries to commit suicide by jumping out of a window. Vanessa, Thoby, Virginia, and Adrian move to Bloomsbury. Virginia publishes first essays; soon becomes a regular book reviewer for the *Times Literary Supplement*. She also teaches at an evening college for working men and women.
1906	The four Stephens travel to Greece, where Vanessa and Thoby become ill; Thoby dies of typhoid fever at the age of 26.
1907	Vanessa Stephen marries artist Clive Bell; Virginia and Adrian room together near the Bells.
1910	First post-Impressionist Exhibition, engineered by Virginia's friend, critic Roger Fry. She later wrote that "in or about December, 1910, human character changed." Gradual gathering of "Bloomsbury Group," comprising such

	people as Lytton Strachey, Roger Fry, Duncan Grant, Desmond MacCarthy, John Maynard Keynes, and E. M. Forster.

1912–15   Virginia Stephen marries Leonard Woolf on August 10, 1912. She has third mental breakdown, which lasts for three years. During this time she completes novel, *The Voyage Out* (originally titled *Melymbrosia*), but its publication is delayed by breakdown, and the war which is declared on August 4, 1914. Finally published in 1915 by her half-brother, Gerald Duckworth. Woolf begins diary.

1917   The Woolfs buy a secondhand printing press and set up the Hogarth Press in their basement. Later, the Press will publish Forster, Dostoevsky, T. S. Eliot, Katherine Mansfield, Freud, and Gorki.

1918   The war ends, November 11.

1919   Publishes novel, *Night and Day,* with Gerald Duckworth; and collections of short stories with Hogarth Press.

1921   Publishes *Monday or Tuesday,* short fiction, with Hogarth Press. From this time, all her books will be published by the Press.

1922   Publishes *Jacob's Room.*

1925   Publishes *Mrs. Dalloway* and *The Common Reader,* a collection of essays. The Hogarth Press moves from the Woolfs' basement in Richmond to London.

1927   Publishes *To the Lighthouse.*

1928   Publishes *Orlando,* a fictional "biography" of Woolf's friend and, possibly, lover, Vita Sackville-West.

1929   Publishes book-length, feminist essay, *A Room of One's Own.*

1931   Publishes *The Waves.*

1932   Publishes *The Common Reader: Second Series.*

1933   Publishes *Flush,* a "biography" of Elizabeth Barrett Browning's spaniel.

1935   Produces *Freshwater, A Comedy in Three Acts* for her friends.

1937   Publishes *The Years.* Nephew Julian Bell killed in the Spanish Civil War.

1938   Publishes pacifist, feminist essay, *Three Guineas.*

1939   War declared on September 3; the Woolfs prepare to commit suicide if England invaded.

1940   Publishes *Roger Fry: A Biography.* Completes draft of

Between the Acts. During Battle of Britain, London home destroyed by bombs.

1941   At the onset of another mental breakdown, which she fears will be permanent, Virginia Woolf fills her pockets with stones and drowns herself in the River Ouse on March 28, leaving suicide notes for her husband and sister. In subsequent years, her husband Leonard publishes various essays, short stories, letters, and diaries of hers, as well as several autobiographies which detail their life together.

1969   Leonard Woolf dies.

Contributors

HAROLD BLOOM, Sterling Professor of the Humanities at Yale University, is the author of *The Anxiety of Influence, Poetry and Repression,* and many other volumes of literary criticism. His forthcoming study, *Freud: Transference and Authority,* attempts a full-scale reading of all of Freud's major writings. A MacArthur Prize Fellow, he is general editor of five series of literary criticism published by Chelsea House. During 1987–88, he served as Charles Eliot Norton Professor of Poetry at Harvard University.

ALLEN MCLAURIN has published *Virginia Woolf: The Echoes Enslaved* and, with Robin Majumdar, has edited *Virginia Woolf: The Critical Heritage.*

HERMIONE LEE is Lecturer in English and Related Literature at the University of York. She is the author of studies of Woolf, Philip Roth, and Elizabeth Bowen.

MARIA DIBATTISTA is Associate Professor of English at Princeton University. She is the author of *Virginia Woolf's Major Novels: The Fables of Anon.*

PERRY MEISEL is Associate Professor of English at New York University. Besides *The Absent Father,* his study of Woolf and Walter Pater, he is the author of a critical work on Hardy.

J. HILLIS MILLER is Professor of English at the University of California, Irvine. His many works include studies of Dickens and Hardy, as well as *The Disappearance of God* and *Fiction and Repetition: Seven English Novels.*

ELIZABETH ABEL, Assistant Professor of English at the University of California, Berkeley, is the author of studies of Jean Rhys, Doris

Lessing, and Virginia Woolf, as well as editor of *Writing and Sexual Difference*.

LUCIO RUOTOLO is Professor of English at Stanford University. His books include *Six Existential Heroes* and *The Interrupted Moment: A View of Virginia Woolf's Novels*.

ALEX ZWERDLING is Associate Professor of English at the University of California, Berkeley. He is the author of *Virginia Woolf and the Real World*.

Bibliography

Albright, Daniel. "Virginia Woolf." In *Personality and Impersonality: Lawrence, Woolf, and Mann*, 96–197. Chicago: University of Chicago Press, 1978.

Alexander, Jean. *"Mrs. Dalloway* and *To the Lighthouse."* In *The Venture of Form in the Novels of Virginia Woolf*, 85–104. Port Washington, N.Y.: Kennikat, 1974.

Apter, T. E. "Perception and Imagination: *Mrs. Dalloway* and Her Party." In *Virginia Woolf: A Study of Her Novels*, 50–72. New York: New York University Press, 1979.

Bazin, Nancy Topping. *"Jacob's Room* and *Mrs. Dalloway."* In *Virginia Woolf and the Androgynous Vision*, 102–23. New Brunswick, N.J.: Rutgers University Press, 1973.

Bell, Quentin. *Virginia Woolf: A Biography*. 2 vols. New York: Harcourt Brace Jovanovich, 1972.

Bennet, Joan. *Virginia Woolf: Her Art as a Novelist*. 2d ed., enlarged. Cambridge: Cambridge University Press, 1964.

Brower, Reuben. "Something Central Which Permeated: *Mrs. Dalloway."* In *The Fields of Light: An Experiment in Critical Reading*, 123–37. Oxford: Oxford University Press, 1951.

Donahue, Delia. *"Mrs. Dalloway."* In *The Novels of Virginia Woolf*, 95–105. Rome: Bulzoni Editore, 1977.

Dowling, David. *"Mrs. Dalloway."* In *Bloomsbury Aesthetics and the Novels of Forster and Woolf*, 136–48. London: Macmillan, 1985.

Ebert, Teresa L. "Metaphor, Metonymy and Ideology: Language and Perception in *Mrs. Dalloway." Language and Style* 18 (1985): 152–64.

Frazer, June M. *"Mrs. Dalloway:* Virginia Woolf's Greek Novel." *Research Studies* 47 (1979): 221–28.

Fromm, Harold. "Virginia Woolf: Art and Sexuality." *Virginia Quarterly Review* 55 (1979): 441–59.

Frye, Joanne S. *"Mrs. Dalloway* as Lyrical Paradox." *Ball State University Forum* 23 (1982): 42–56.

Gorsky, Susan Rubinow. *Virginia Woolf*. Boston: Twayne, 1978.

Haring-Smith, Tori. "Private and Public Consciousness in *Mrs. Dalloway* and *To the Lighthouse."* In *Virginia Woolf: Centennial Essays*, edited by Elaine K. Ginsberg and Laura Moss Gottlieb, 143–62. Troy, N.Y.: Whitston, 1983.

Harper, Howard. *"Mrs. Dalloway."* In *Between Language and Silence: The Novels of*

Virginia Woolf, 109–34. Baton Rouge: Louisiana State University Press, 1982.

Hasler, Jörg. "Virginia Woolf and the Chimes of Big Ben." *English Studies* 63 (1982): 142–58.

Henke, Suzette A. *"Mrs. Dalloway:* The Communion of Saints." In *New Feminist Essays on Virginia Woolf,* edited by Jane Marcus, 125–47. Lincoln: University of Nebraska Press, 1981.

———. " 'The Prime Minister': A Key to *Mrs. Dalloway.*" In *Virginia Woolf: Centennial Essays,* edited by Elaine K. Ginsberg and Laura Moss Gottlieb, 127–41. Troy, N.Y.: Whitston, 1983.

Hessler, John G. "Moral Accountability in *Mrs. Dalloway.*" *Renascence* 30 (1978): 126–36.

Hochman, Baruch. "Virginia Woolf: The Self in Spite of Itself." In *The Test of Character: From the Victorian Novel to the Modern,* 157–76. Rutherford, N.J.: Fairleigh Dickinson University Press, 1983.

Jensen, Emily. "Clarissa Dalloway's Respectable Suicide." In *Virginia Woolf: A Feminist Slant,* edited by Jane Marcus, 162–79. Lincoln: University of Nebraska Press, 1983.

Kelley, Alice van Buren. *"Mrs. Dalloway."* In *The Novels of Virginia Woolf: Fact and Vision,* 88–113. Chicago: University of Chicago Press, 1973.

Kenney, Susan M., and Edward J. Kenney, Jr. "Virginia Woolf and the Art of Madness." *The Massachusetts Review* 23 (1982): 161–85.

Leaska, Mitchell. *"Mrs. Dalloway."* In *The Novels of Virginia Woolf: From Beginning to End,* 85–117. New York: John Jay, 1977.

Love, Jean O. *Virginia Woolf: Sources of Madness and Art.* Berkeley: University of California Press, 1977.

Majumdar, Robin. *Virginia Woolf: An Annotated Bibliography.* New York: Garland, 1976.

Majumdar, Robin, and Allen McLaurin, eds. *Virginia Woolf: The Critical Heritage.* London: Routledge & Kegan Paul, 1975.

Moody, A. D. *Virginia Woolf.* Edinburgh: Oliver & Boyd, 1963.

———. "The Unmasking of Clarissa Dalloway." *Review of English Literature* 3 (1962): 67–79.

Naremore, James. *"Mrs. Dalloway."* In *The World without a Self: Virginia Woolf and the Novel,* 77–111. New Haven: Yale University Press, 1973.

Poole, Roger. *The Unknown Virginia Woolf.* Atlantic Highlands, N.J.: Humanities Press, 1982.

Rahv, Philip. "Mrs. Woolf and Mrs. Brown." In *Literature and The Sixth Sense.* Boston: Houghton Mifflin, 1969.

Richter, Harvena. *Virginia Woolf: The Inward Voyage.* Princeton: Princeton University Press, 1970.

Rigney, Barbara Hill. " 'The Sane and the Insane': Psychosis and Mysticism in *Mrs. Dalloway.*" In *Madness and Sexual Politics in the Feminist Novel: Studies in Brontë, Woolf, Lessing and Atwood,* 39–64. Madison: University of Wisconsin Press, 1978.

Rosenberg, Stuart. "The Match in the Crocus: Obtrusive Art in Virginia Woolf's *Mrs. Dalloway.*" *Modern Fiction Studies* 13 (1967): 211–20.

Rosenman, Ellen Bayuk. *"Mrs. Dalloway."* In *The Invisible Presence: Virginia Woolf and the Mother-Daughter Relationship,* 75–92. Baton Rouge: Louisiana State University Press, 1986.

Rosenthal, Michael. *"Mrs. Dalloway."* In *Virginia Woolf,* 87–102. London: Routledge & Kegan Paul, 1979.

Ruotolo, Lucio, "Clarissa Dalloway." In *Virginia Woolf: Revaluation and Continuity,* edited by Ralph Freedman, 38–55. Berkeley: University of California Press, 1980.

Schlack, Beverly Ann. *"Mrs. Dalloway."* In *Continuing Presences: Virginia Woolf's Use of Literary Allusion,* 51–76. University Park: The Pennsylvania State University Press, 1979.

Spilka, Mark. "On Mrs. Dalloway's Absent Grief: A Psycho-Literary Speculation." *Criticism* 21 (1979): 1–33.

Squier, Susan M. "The Carnival and Funeral of *Mrs. Dalloway*'s London." In *Virginia Woolf and London: The Sexual Politics of the City,* 91–121. Chapel Hill: University of North Carolina Press, 1985.

Steward, Jack F. "Impressionism in the Early Novels of Virginia Woolf." *Journal of Modern Literature* 9 (1982): 237–66.

Trombley, Stephen. *All That Summer She Was Mad: Virginia Woolf: Female Victim of Male Medicine.* New York: Continuum, 1982.

Virginia Woolf Miscellany, 1973–.

Virginia Woolf Quarterly, 1972–.

Wyatt, Jean M. "*Mrs. Dalloway*: Literary Allusion as Structural Metaphor." *PMLA* 88 (1973): 440–51.

Acknowledgments

"The Symbolic Keyboard: *Mrs. Dalloway*" by Allen McLaurin from *Virginia Woolf: The Echoes Enslaved* by Allen McLaurin, © 1973 by Cambridge University Press. Reprinted by permission of Cambridge University Press.

"*Mrs. Dalloway*" by Hermione Lee from *The Novels of Virginia Woolf* by Hermione Lee, © 1977 by Hermione Lee. Reprinted by permission of Methuen & Co. Ltd.

"Mrs. Dalloway: Virginia Woolf's Memento Mori" by Maria DiBattista from *Virginia Woolf's Major Novels: The Fables of Anon* by Maria DiBattista, © 1980 by Yale University. Reprinted by permission of Yale University Press.

"Virginia Woolf and Walter Pater: Selfhood and the Common Life" (originally entitled "The Common Life") by Perry Meisel from *The Absent Father: Virginia Woolf and Walter Pater* by Perry Meisel, © 1980 by Yale University. Reprinted by permission of Yale University Press.

"*Mrs. Dalloway*: Repetition as the Raising of the Dead" by J. Hillis Miller from *Fiction and Repetition: Seven English Novels* by J. Hillis Miller, © 1982 by J. Hillis Miller. Reprinted by permission of the publisher, Harvard University Press, Cambridge, Massachusetts.

"Narrative Structure(s) and Female Development: The Case of *Mrs. Dalloway*" by Elizabeth Abel from *The Voyage In: Fictions of Female Development*, edited by Elizabeth Abel, Marianne Hirsch, and Elizabeth Langland, © 1983 by the Trustees of Dartmouth College. Reprinted by permission of University Press of New England.

"The Unguarded Moment: *Mrs. Dalloway*" by Lucio Ruotolo from *The Interrupted Moment: A View of Virginia Woolf's Novels* by Lucio Ruotolo, © 1986 by the Board of Trustees of the Leland Stanford Junior University. Reprinted by permission of the publisher, Stanford University Press.

"*Mrs. Dalloway* and the Social System" by Alex Zwerdling from *Virginia Woolf and the Real World* by Alex Zwerdling, © 1986 by the Regents of the University of California. Reprinted by permission of the University of California Press.

Index